I0822390

HELLO

praise for david carpenter

"Carpenter's stories are beautifully honed acts of generosity. Reading each one is like happening upon an unexpected gift. We return from Carpenter country with a new appreciation for the people and creatures of our own everyday countries, especially the ones we have all too often forgotten."

Warren Cariou

"David Carpenter is my favourite Saskatchewan writer. The Steinbeck of the Stubble Jumpers is wry, darkly comic, lyrical, realistic, and clever. Most important, he has artistic integrity."

Patricia Robertson, *Toronto Star*

"Perhaps Carpenter's greatest skill is his ability to balance and combine the comic and the pathetic, which is the hardest of all to manage. He does manage it and is able to combine all his separate effects and swirl them deftly into great dramatic climaxes that mark him as a master story-teller."

Joan Givner

HELLO

New short fiction

SHADOWPAW PRESS

DAVID CARPENTER

HELLO
By David Carpenter

Shadowpaw Press
Regina, Saskatchewan, Canada
www.shadowpawpress.com

Edited by Dave Margoshes

Hardcover ISBN: 978-1-998273-27-0
Ebook ISBN: 978-1-998273-28-7

Shadowpaw Press is grateful for
the financial support of Creative Saskatchewan.

contents

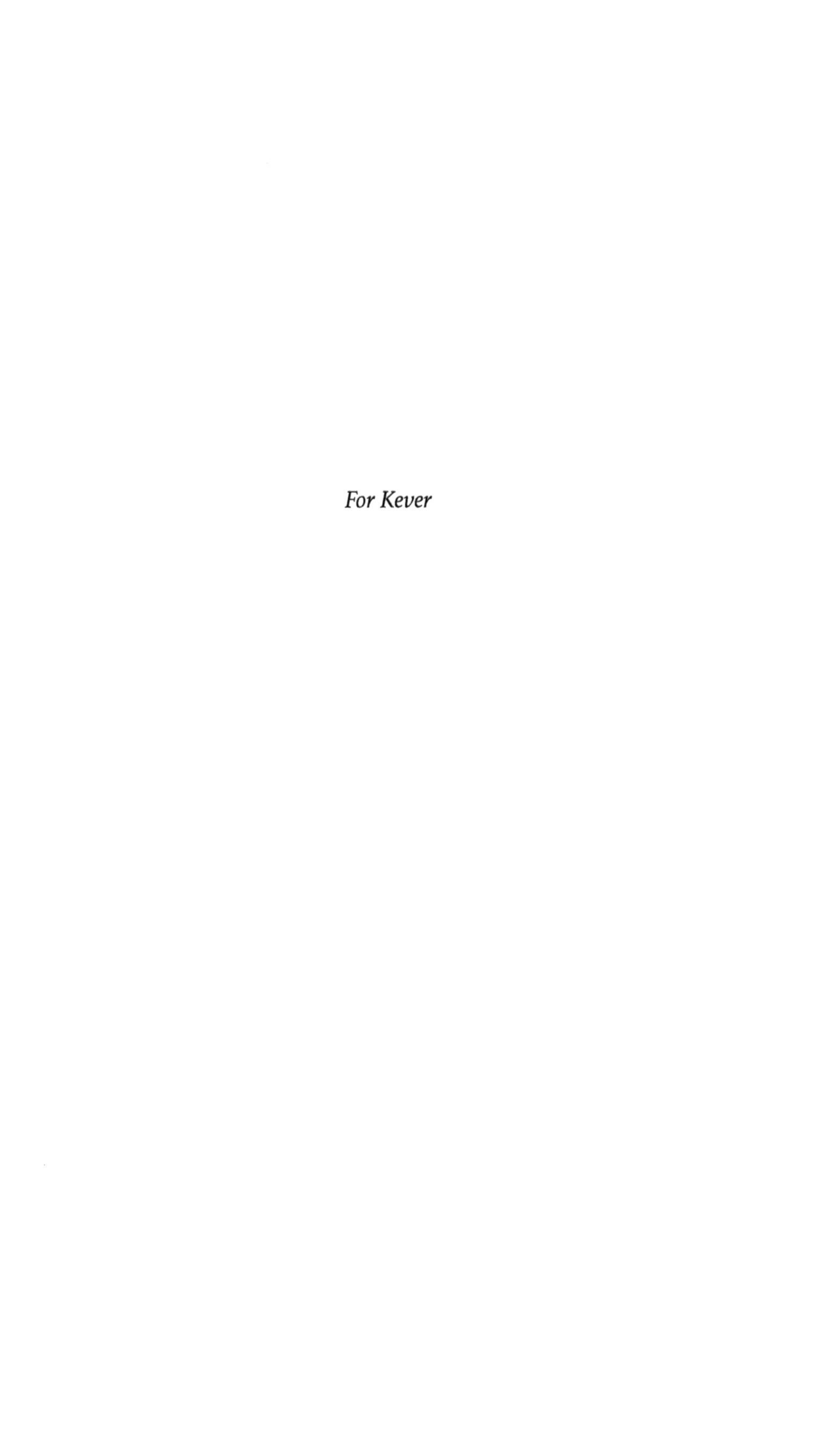

For Kever

the ethel suite

I

1983, early September

HE RAISES his head from a deep slump in roughly the shape of a question mark. Dozing in a chair after lunch can't be good for the neck. He blinks out at the bleary sky and glances at the phone because it's almost time. He'll wait another twenty minutes before he dials. By then, she should be home from the airport. Funny word, dial, a persistent word. The new phones have musical buttons, but you still dial people up. These days, your phone number becomes your song. In the grand scheme of things, this call will rank as one of a billion in the mundane lives of people with nothing better to do. Nevertheless, there is an urgency to this call. For him, these days, the phone, the annoying black impersonal square-buttoned jangly phone, is a lifeline.

Again, he gazes at the sky, a brownish-grey drift from horizon to horizon. When the sun appears, it glows vivid crimson. Smoke from the forest fires. The elm trees across the street are blurry today. He hasn't fully recovered from cataract surgery, so his eyes conspire to intensify the smoky effect. This atmosphere is ideal for gloomy thoughts and bothersome questions, like the one pursuing him all week: Who is he now? Or better still: Who might he try to become?

Now that he's sold the jewellery store, the question gains some gravity. Faithful husband, now widower? Retiree? A senior citizen, decrepit for seventy-four? An old Jew with nothing to do? Labels shift around in the shuffling deck of his brain, presenting themselves like tarot cards for his approval. Nothing fits. He doesn't feel quite as Jewish as he thinks he should, whatever that means. He's a retired businessman and a widower, but these hardly serve to define him. He's never been a womanizer, but does he qualify as an eternally faithful husband? Probably not.

Today, perhaps, he is just Elliot. Elliot, son of Izzy. He was the older of the two Schuman brothers, prevailed upon by his parents to set a good example for his younger brother by taking on his obligations at an early age. Elliot was as compliant toward these expectations as he was burdened by them. Every Saturday, Elliot went to Talmud Torah for Jewish lessons (his father's term), and afterwards, his father would whisk him downtown to learn the business. The Schumans were just barely observant, celebrating only the big holidays and keeping a minimally kosher home. A synagogue is where you meet your life's partner, Izzy liked to say, because that's where he met Ida.

Elliot's father did his watchmaker's apprenticeship at the turn of the century in France and Germany, and when the family immigrated to Canada, he made his start repairing jewellery, clocks, and watches in Montreal. Ever the cautious entrepreneur, Izzy moved into selling half-dollar watches on the side. He cajoled his two younger brothers into the business to handle the sales and do the books, and together, they managed to buy a small shop. A worker more than a talker, Izzy was better behind the bench than he was with the customers. He did quality work, and they kept returning.

Young Elliot was Izzy's designated protégé in the back of the shop, and very soon, he showed a knack for repairing chains, sizing rings, and working the metal for his father, hammering silver and scrap gold out of salvaged pieces, working the steel from soft to hard. In the years after the Great War, the spare parts for their watches were hard to come by. From time to time, the Schumans had to improvise, and with his father's guidance, Elliot rose to the challenge of making these parts. The tools fascinated him, like the tweezers and the tiny pliers he would use for the repair of mesh purses. He liked filing metals and polishing trinkets. He thought of them as individual treasures, works of art. He loved anything made of gold. Someday, Izzy intimated, he might let Elliot have a go at the clocks.

His two uncles gave Elliot much of their attention. He loved the idle gabbing and the shop talk between them and his father. Elliot was their quiet observer in the corner, their biggest fan.

When Elliot's younger brother, Danny, came of age, he too went down to the shop on Saturdays after Hebrew lessons and fumbled his way through the mysteries of bench work. He was a reluctant learner, slouching around the back room like an old man. In the Schuman family, there was a tacit understanding that the boys would join their father and their bachelor uncles to work together and someday manage their own stores under the banner of Schuman Brothers. Izzy had big hopes for his boys, Elliot the repairman, Danny the work in progress.

Danny had a great smile and a winning personality, but he had little patience for fiddling with tiny tools and clasps and no desire at all to grope around the guts of a watch. So, in the second year of his apprenticeship, Danny took over the deliveries. This he could handle on his bicycle. He went from deliveries to the front counter and evolved into the family's youngest salesman, the charmer of all charmers, a handsome boy whose greatest yearnings (career in Vaudeville, radio show, impresario like Ziegfeld, clarinet virtuoso, maybe all of the above) kept him at some distance from the room at the back of the shop.

Elliot was glad enough to be the boy at the bench in the back room that smelled of lubricating oils, tools, glues, and the cigarettes and the bodies of the three older men. Straining and squinting with his magnifying headband, his mouth full of buck teeth set in a permanent grimace that looked like a failed smile, he tweezed, hammered, filed, and polished away. When the relatives sorted through the Schuman family lore, young Elliot was usually identified as the one who was born grown up. And he always seemed to tolerate brother Danny, who would tap-dance at a funeral if you dared him.

Elliot's uncles, Eli and Marvin, decided to take Schuman Brothers west, and in 1927, they found a good location in Edmonton: a floundering business downtown, just off Jasper Avenue, owned by a fellow who had been more of a jewellery traveller than a jeweller or a watch repairman. He had neglected the repair side of things and lost his contract to repair the CNR watches. He had built up an inventory of expensive baubles and gotten over-extended, so the uncles bought him out and moved into his spacious building downtown. When the boys grew older, Eli and Marvin began making overtures to Izzy and Ida about letting the boys come west to work at their new establishment.

Over my dead body, said Ida to her husband. *The boys are only sixteen and eighteen, Izzy. Here is where you need them.* After some intense bargaining at home, Izzy offered a compromise. *Danny, you can have,* he said. *Summers only. But Elliot, he stays.* The reply from Edmonton was, *No thanks.* It was Elliot the uncles wanted for their repair shop, so both of the boys stayed put.

At this time, Elliot had been granted free rein to repair watches. At first, he had a go at the inexpensive ones, the Gruens, Elgins, and Hamilton watches from the States. Within a year of Elliot's entry into this enticing world, his father led him to the even more intricate realm of forty-dollar watches. These had tiny round jewels in their innards, synthetic rubies that were cemented into forks, and they had to lie at a certain angle and protrude a certain distance. At school, Elliot had been good at mathematics, and this came in handy when he had to figure out gem placement, gear teeth, gear ratios, and wheel sizes for the watches. All these workings he beheld through his right eye, from which protruded his lens, a four-power loupe that went everywhere with him like a prosthetic limb. Cowboys wore their six guns, sheriffs wore their badges, firemen had their neat hats, Elliot had his loupe. A little Spinoza, he was, calculating, grimacing, squinting with his right eye, scanning the top of his table with his left eye in search of the tweezers, rejoicing in his newfound coordination between eye and tool. Once he had worked his way from five-dollar to forty-dollar watches, he was granted access to the European watches, which cost more money than Elliot could earn in a year. As he passed his hours on the bench, the clocks and the watches would tick as though they were all trying to talk to him.

By the time he had turned twenty-one and his father had hired an additional repairman, the uncles called again for Elliot to work at the repair bench. He told his father he was ready. More than likely, it would be only a couple of months. Danny and the new employee could hold the fort until Elliot came back. Izzy wrote his two brothers and said, *My eldest is yours, but he's not* all *yours. Elliot is a loan. Send him back wiser in the fall.* But they all realized, the uncles first, Elliot next, and Ida and Izzy last of all, that he would never return to the shop in Montreal.

So here he was, fifty-three years later, a rich man in a sumptuous condo, an Edmontonian, scarcely connected anymore to the remnants of his family in Montreal, somewhat distanced from the Edmonton Jewish community, but never mistaken for a Gentile. *Elliot has done very well for himself,* people would say, *but he's never around. Maisy organized his social life, and now that she's gone, he's like a hermit.* More than once, Elliot has overheard this take on his life. But he isn't a hermit to Rennie. Rennie the entrepreneur! He has become Rennie's unofficial uncle, his investment counsellor, his Solomon on worldly matters. And he sure as hell isn't a hermit to Rennie's mother.

Her name is Ethel. At sixty-eight years, she is still fuelled with nervous energy, lean and watchful like a wary rodent. A bit anti-social but a great snuggler, and in spite of her hard life, still attractive to Elly. Still focused on the minutiae of Rennie's life. Never satisfied with her lot. She was the only woman ever to side-track him, however briefly, from his marriage. Every week, he phones her.

He checks his watch again. It runs on batteries, and it doesn't tick. Who would have conceived of such a gadget when Elliot was a young man of twenty-one at the back of the store? He'll give Ethel ten minutes, and then he will push the buttons and play her song. *Three four five six seven five three. Do re me fa so me do. "When I Grow Too Old to Dream.*" He sings it out loud like Ezio Pinza in a rich baritone.

On the mantel above the gas fireplace, young Maisy from the early 1930s observes him from her picture frame with a trace of skepticism. But Elly remembers the night and the party when he was a callow dreamer in his early twenties, a virgin yet. She stood before him, looking up into his eyes as though she were about to take his pulse.

"For God's sake, Elly, ask me to dance."

"Good point," he said, and they began to shuffle slowly in a circle. How many human bodies in his twenty-plus years had he brushed up against in street cars and stores and such? Hundreds? Thousands? But when he and Maisy came together for their first dance, and he held her hand and rested his other hand on her shoulder blade, his heart pounded with a terrifying hope—as though someone had granted him a wish, a truly improbable wish. A nudge from the world, the push of circumstance, it was pushing him toward his destiny and away from his parents in Montreal, away from his brother Danny, perhaps even away from the backroom in his uncles' store. And in the fall of 1931, he and Maisy were married. They had less than twenty-five years together before the cigarettes shut down her lungs and took her away.

Carpe Diem. Carpe Diem.

He reaches for the phone and dials the number of Ethel Mudge, the love of his later life. It rings three, four, five times.

"Come on, Ethel. Up and at 'em."

2

Ethel's father was a fine raconteur who had read the complete works of Sir Walter Scott. He had tried and failed to pass on to his daughter his love of literature, outdoor recreation, witty repartee, horse racing, and fast-money schemes. Her devout mother, however, had succeeded nicely in implanting life lessons that may well have begun before little Ethel could speak. These lessons took the shape of cautionary tales about dreamers who were inclined toward book reading, outdoor recreation, witty repartee, horse racing, and fast-money schemes.

How Hardy Mudge had managed to slip past the bastion of these motherly warnings, God only knew. But somehow, he had managed it; young Ethel had swallowed the bait, and there would be hell to pay.

Hardy had been selling encyclopedias, Bibles, cleaning implements, and women's garments door-to-door, depending on which company he was travelling with. He was always good at the sales pitch but not much good at minding the shop. He rose enthusiastically to the challenge of soft-soaping his customers and delighted in recounting his weekly conquests (not all of them strictly commercial) to his colleagues wherever they met to compare notes. But after a weekend of good fellowship in a hotel bar, as often as not, he would find himself steaming down the CN line to the next town with a hangover and an empty wallet, moaning *never again.* He had regular fits of self-recrimination that would last at least as long as his next paycheque, and then he'd return to the pleasures and the challenges of the road.

In the summer of 1937, Hardy had fallen into one of the longest periods of self-recrimination he had ever experienced, and a stretch of sobriety had ensued that was so steadfast and profound that it threatened to drag him into the shackles of respectability. One Friday afternoon, he was knocking on doors in a nicely treed neighbourhood near the South Saskatchewan River in the town of Saskatoon. He knocked on the door of a large boarding house, and a pretty young lady answered. She had a half-awake look about her as though she were bored with her life and looking for some adventure. A single line of sweat meandered from her temple to her chin.

Before Ethel had entirely opened the door, a tall man was already talking at her at a fearful clip. He stopped briefly to gawk.

"Miss, I hope you're havin' a better day than I am."

"Oh," she said, "this should be real straightforward." Ethel opened the door a little further. "Did you bring your own ladder?"

"Sweetheart, in my trade, we only use ladders for a quick ex-cape. Ha ha ha."

The man handed her a catalogue entitled *The Lady of the House.*

"What's this?"

"This, my dear, will be your guide to a vast array of products, everything for the ladies from dish soap to *dessous.*"

"De soo?"

"Yes, Miss. Our line includes gals' knickers, maternity frocks, corsets, and such. It's all here. *Dessous* for every filly for every stage of her life. I take it you are living at home and that your mother might be in the vicinity?"

Ethel glared at him. All morning, Lord help us, she had been waiting for a tradesman to replace some shingles on their leaking roof.

"Cat gotcher tongue, Miss?"

"She's upstairs."

The man unfastened his sample case and took out a package of pink soap. "This is a free sample of Vinolia, my dear, a guarantee to you and your mother of day-long fragrant daintiness for your skin."

"We were waiting for the repairman," Ethel said, gliding past Hardy as swift as a bird. She pointed to a hand-lettered sign on the front door. "Did you see that?"

"Young lady," he said, "there is great legions of fellers livin' off relief out there, men I know personally, fellers who have lost all hope, just passin' the jug around in a state of despair. Not this gent. Hardy comes to work each day with a smile on his face and pounds the pavement from dawn till dusk. And Hardy doesn't just sell items from a case—"

"Hardy?"

"Hardy Mudge, at your service, Miss. He sells undergarments, he sells the Good Book, he sells cleaning implements, but he also sells hope. What is your name, young lady?"

"Ethel Ringrose," she said.

"I sell hope and I sell success because in times like these, Ethel, a feller can ill afford to sit around and mope."

The man could not seem to stop yakking. As her mother might say, *These times are sent to try us.*

The young lady's eyelids were drooping. Maybe she sported this look to show Hardy how unimpressed she was with his patter. Or maybe the girl just couldn't help it. A pretty girl like that should not have her eyelids at half-mast. It was unbecoming. He went away from her door, down the sidewalk, carrying before him an image of her face. That look, stuck in neutral. Something in her sullen eyelids summoned Hardy's predatory instincts, that and her comely figure. He expected, however, that her face would fade as all women's faces tended to do after a brief encounter, but all the way down the CN line from city to town, her face seemed to float before him.

Two months later, he returned to Saskatoon. Instead of staying at the King George, where his fellow travellers bunked, he threw himself on the mercy of Ethel and her mother and asked to rent a room at their boarding house on Temperance Street. This would allow him to ply his trade from one end of Saskatoon to the other and to pursue his amorous mission during off hours.

A room was available, and Hardy moved in. The street was lined with two-and-a-half-storey frame houses, but the Ringrose house was bulkier. It was shaped square and jaunty like a wedding cake, and it had three full storeys crowned by a widow's peak. No drink or women allowed. The gentlemen stayed on the second and third floors in small rooms with a shared bath at the end of each corridor. Hardy had little quarrel with this chaste and sober regime. He soon discovered that Ethel's room was on the northwest corner of the ground floor, and for the first few nights after supper, he would go for a smoke and a stroll past her bedroom window and gaze soulfully at the sunset. There, she might glimpse him, a thoughtful man with a song of sadness and yearning in his heart.

Thus began the courtship of Ethel Ringrose and her parents. Mrs. Ringrose and her daughter handled the cleaning and the meal duties, and Mr. Ringrose took to his pipe after dessert and coffee and entertained Mudge and the other gentlemen with his tales of the sporting life and other such manly pursuits.

During the first few days at the Ringrose house, Hardy gathered in several assumptions: that the family was a cohesive unit, that young Ethel was their only living heir, that the big rooming house with the newly repaired roof was paid for, that old Ringrose was in full control of his finances, and that the boarding house might well be the headquarters of a larger empire. On several occasions, Hardy had seen rough-looking men with bags of merchandise chatting softly with Ethel's father. Were they traders, these rugged fellows? Were they not entirely legit? None of them stayed at the boarding house.

Old Ringrose seemed scarcely the type to preside over a gang of thieves. But any man of dubious employment in the depths of the Depression who could afford to hire a tradesman to fix his roof was surely a man of means. Mudge persisted in these assumptions as he pursued his trade up and down the CN line. He returned each month to his room in the boarding house with gifts of bonbons and flowers for Ethel and her mother.

Young Ethel seemed joylessly committed to hard work. When Mudge commented on her devotion to the drudgery of cleaning house, she answered him with one of her mother's mottoes.

"To work is to pray."

The men were chatting at the other end of the breakfast table: a new manager for the gas plant, a young man with an amputated arm, two school teachers, a meat salesman. One of the men stood and glanced at his watch. Another gulped down the last of his coffee and stood as well.

"An admirable sentiment, Ethel. May I call you Ethel?"

She lifted her despondent eyelids and shot him a suspicious glance. Her eyes were light brown.

"If those fellows on the breadlines would work harder and frolic less," she continued, "this Depression would disappear overnight. If I was running for the Premier, that's what I would tell them."

The men were filing out from the breakfast table, and soon Hardy and Ethel were alone in the dining room. He remained in his chair as she stacked plates and carried them into the kitchen.

"Laziness," said Mudge. "You would stamp it out, Ethel? Just like that?"

"I would, Mr. Mudge. Laziness is a sin."

He watched her as she finished clearing the breakfast table. At another time, in another place, he would mock this piety of hers, haul out his flask and set her straight on the facts of life, but her mother was hovering in the kitchen. It was Monday morning, and he was caught up in the resentment that she radiated. This little outburst, he decided, should go into the books as a meeting of the minds.

"Speakin' of hard labour, my dear, it's time I did my share." He flashed her a brilliant smile, grabbed his sample case and strode from the room.

It was a melancholy courtship. Whenever he stayed through the weekend at the Ringrose house, he would accompany Ethel and her mother to church and sing hymns by her side. Ethel liked choir music, and she sang with a high, sweet tremolo that reminded Hardy of songbirds. He had a fine tenor voice that was suited equally to churches and bar-rooms.

They risked their first kisses in the backyard of the boarding house on chilly October nights when the wind stirred a skeletal rattle among the leafless cottonwoods. To all of Hardy's frivolous ways, Ethel acted as a corrective force, and when at last she decided that he was, at worst, a prattler who meant well, she agreed to consider his proposal.

It was a long engagement, during which Hardy was much on the road and trying his best not to get too far off the rails. If he had occasional lapses with old girlfriends and drinking buddies, he was quick to mend his ways and re-assume his newly acquired resistance to temptation. For Hardy Mudge, to work was never to pray, never to succumb to the call of duty and its accompanying yoke; it was to sell himself, over and over again, so as to prove that he was a success and a splendid fellow, a generous man to all of his pals and to all his female customers, even the ones disinclined to share their beds with him. If asked what the challenge of his work was, he'd say it was just to stay positive. He did this by talking, day after day, talking without cease, without inhibition, without even listening, telling people about the virtues of his stock, explaining why they were second to none, telling jokes and flattering customers, spreading optimism—

That was it. Spreading optimism throughout the neighbourhoods by talking, if necessary, until he was hoarse.

Mr. Mudge seemed to like his work. He always paid the rent on time. Ethel and her mother at last concluded that, possibly, he could be headed for success.

"You could do worse," her mother said one night as she washed and Ethel dried. "You'd be free of this mess."

Ethel thought she was referring to the daily round of egg- and gravy-stained dishes in the kitchen. "I don't mind," she said.

"He said he'd tell you. Did he tell you?"

"Mother, what are you talking about?"

"Your father. He's lost the house. He's talking to Mr. Massey to seek, you know, to seek an—"

"Dad has lost the house?"

"A few months and we'll be out on the street. That's my prediction. I'm glad your sister got out while the getting was good."

"But where did the money go?"

"Where? It went to his *friends.* Lord help us. They bring him some samples, they all say the same thing. So and so's found a rich vein up at Great Slave, or over in B.C., or Timbuktu for all I know. Your father grubstakes the man, the man heads for the train station, and he never sees him again."

"Those fellows who phone Dad at night, the ones who come to the house?"

"Prospectors, they call themselves. Confidence men is what I call them. Your father can't get enough of them. He borrows money on the house to pay them. I married a fool for a quick dollar, and don't you do the same."

Ethel fidgeted with her dish towel and stared at the floor.

"I have no time for that nonsense," her mother said.

"Hardy told me he had to work his way up from a water boy to a labourer and worse. He has to hustle pretty hard to keep this job."

Ethel's mother looked up from her sink. "Well, then. You keep him on the straight and narrow, he might work out all right."

"I guess so."

"One more thing, my dear. Don't you go telling Hardy that your father is flat broke. Now would be the wrong time for that."

In the late spring of 1939, a few months before the war broke out, Ethel and Hardy were married. Hardy had relocated to Edmonton, where he reckoned his prospects would be better. The newlyweds rented a little basement flat a few blocks north of Jasper Avenue, not far from downtown and not far from where Ethel's married sister, Margaret, lived. In the first year of her marriage, Ethel went from falling in love with Hardy to loving him in spite of himself, to feeling sorry for him, to being more than occasionally exasperated with him, to enduring his uncertain moods, his drunken advances, his hang-overs, his idle schemes for making money, and finally, to resenting him. Six months of married life seemed to be his limit, and he enlisted with the field battery in Edmonton. By the late fall of 1939, Hardy was on board the troop train from Camp Wainwright to Petawawa to join the other artillery units. As the train chuffed its way east, Ethel said a silent *good riddance*. Her eyelids resumed their vigil at half-mast, and she went looking for a job.

To prepare herself, she applied for a secretarial course at the downtown business college. Margaret and her husband helped Ethel with the rent for the duration of her training. When her sister asked about this new turn of events in her life, she replied that she was lucky to be in training for a job.

But don't you get lonely?

For what?

For a man, silly.

I have no time for that nonsense.

Later on, when people asked Hardy about the sudden turns in *his* life (England, separation, the war), he had to admit that he'd had an okay go of it. By the time his unit was heading for the bloody Italian campaign, he was recovering in a British military hospital from a hip fracture he had sustained while chasing a cat up a tree in Aldershot at three in the morning. He took his time recovering in England and lingered there doing paperwork for the army before he went home to Ethel.

When, at last, he returned to Canada, Ethel suggested that he sleep on the chesterfield until he'd "worked things out." She had moved to a new place in their old neighbourhood, a small townhouse flat with an upstairs bedroom. At least it was bigger than their old basement apartment, it had a telephone, and the rent was affordable.

"Work what things out?" he said.

"You know. What you're going to do. "

That was an easy one. He was going to sit down and smell the flowers. Get the lay of the land. Check out his situation.

"Your situation?" she said.

Ethel was looking at him funny like he spoke in a foreign language or something. She reminded Hardy of a movie star, that little gal who did the nasty roles. Betty something. Hutton or Grable.

"You mean work-wise?"

"Hardy, you've had more than five years to think about it. What did you come up with?"

She was giving him the third degree, that's what she was doing. He shrugged at her and patted down his tunic for cigarettes. *Bette Davis, that's the one.*

"Are you going back on the road?" she said.

"I don't know. I haven't thought about it much."

"I was afraid of that."

"What do you mean? I'm scarcely home, I'm not even unpacked, you haven't even offered me a drink, we're just gettin'—"

"That's another thing," she said.

"What do you mean?"

"You know what I mean," she said. "You used to drink a lot. Is that still part of the plan?"

"That's a helluva way to greet your husband after five and a half—"

"Let's put it this way, Hardy." She crossed her arms and planted herself before him like a street cop. "You're welcome to my home. You can sleep down here, I'll give you a place to hang your hat, but no drinking. Period. You have to choose. You have to choose between me and the bottle. And you have to get work."

He stood up from the chesterfield, perhaps a bit too suddenly, and wavered for a moment, glaring at Ethel, who stood calmly before him. "Never," he said, perhaps a bit too loud, "never make a man choose between his wife and the bottle."

She smiled a little sadly. "Where in God's name did you learn that one?"

Hardy stewed over the new regime for a few days. After a week of sober reflection, in which he wandered around the block every day, eyes on the sidewalk, and read the paper and did a lot of smoking, he received a letter that felt like the hand of Providence. Hardy announced to Ethel that a friend from his outfit named Mumford, who lived on the West Coast, had written to him that there was lots of work opening up on the fishing boats. He had already bought his train ticket.

"I'll be back in the spring," he said with a note of hope in his voice. "And that's a promise."

Ethel had managed without Hardy during the war and she continued to manage in his new period of absence. For a few months, she and her sister ran the tuck shop at the Armouries. By this time, Ethel had completed her training course at the business college. She had learned to type and to do elementary shorthand, and she had picked her way into the mysteries of accounting. Buoyed by the recommendations of her instructors, she gained employment at a jewellery store.

Her new employer was Mr. Schuman, a homely man with a warm, buck-toothed smile. If Hardy Mudge struck her, in retrospect, as all flash and no substance, her new boss struck her as the opposite. He was a Jewish fellow who read a lot of books. Not frivolous books like her father read, but important-sounding books about history and economics and things like that. He told her during the interview that he could only hire her for a few months on spec because he had no idea whether the business would thrive in these times. But his wife needed a break from working at the store.

"So," he concluded.

"I understand."

"Reporters, politicians," he said, "they keep telling us on the news that the Great Depression is history and that things are looking up in the postwar." Mr. Schuman had a way of gazing at the ceiling or the walls when he talked to her. "But I don't know. I get suspicious when politicians start to sound optimistic. And around here, downtown, you don't find a bunch of spendthrifts crowding my counters. But if the business picks up in the new year, maybe I can give you more work."

He glanced back at her, swallowed, and looked away.

Ethel did triple duty as store clerk, bookkeeper, and cleaner. No time for cigarettes or a coffee break. Sometimes when Ethel reviewed books and inventory with Mr. Schuman, he would shake his head and sigh and wonder out loud how they could possibly make it through the winter. If they did not do better in the coming quarter, he would have to let her go. He never quite said this to her, but the implication was there all the same.

Hardy phoned her long-distance one night from his friend's place in Esquimalt and told her he was making good money on the fishing boats and that he'd be out on the Coast a little longer than he had planned. She let Hardy know she was okey-dokey with that arrangement, all the best, don't forget to write. What she couldn't figure out was why he bothered to phone her, why he kept promising that he would return to Edmonton. The writing was plainly on the wall, so why couldn't the man just read it?

Ethel had begun to feel yearnings for a man in her life. She would never admit this to her sister or anyone else because she was not sure she approved of such doings. Marriage. Intimacy. Getting herself lost in some ooze of desire and emotions. She had no time for that nonsense. It was too perilous, right? Too unpredictable. She was over that silliness. Men noticed her; she knew that for sure. At the business college, in the store, at the odd gathering Margaret and her husband would throw. These intimations from fellows included her own boss. Mr. Schuman was happily married, so he was out of the question. But occasionally, he gave her that yearny look, or else he dwelt too long on a conversation that had nothing to do with work. Or sometimes he would laugh at something she said, something that, in her opinion, wasn't all that funny, and with his laughter came the blushing. He had a shy, restrained way about him and a warmth to his horsey smile that always made her feel welcome. It did not seem to matter to Mr. Schuman that the girl he smiled at so frequently was the same girl who cleaned the toilet a half hour before the store opened.

Ethel loved the inventory in Mr. Schuman's store, which he had inherited, along with the store, after his uncles had passed away. This line of jewellery seemed absurdly pricey for the times: a selection of turn-of-the-century brooches made of tourmalines and amethysts; several chokers from the same era fashioned from turquoise, rubies, and pearls set in serpentine links of gold; a lovely twin-emerald pendant necklace referred to sardonically by Mr. Schuman as *The Chain;* several platinum bracelets composed of alternating jade pieces and diamond clusters; unsellable diamond engagement rings from the roaring twenties; European-made pocket watches attached to ornate gold fobs; and Mr. Schuman's own recent creations, mostly bracelets and necklaces that he had fashioned out of a miscellany of stones from older jewellery. *To keep up with the times,* he said. And there they had languished under glass, the baubles purchased with the store in the late twenties by Mr. Schuman's uncles, an inventory as unattainable as the good life in Edmonton in 1946.

Leduc changed everything. Imagine that. It was too much for Ethel to take in. A bunch of oil wells gushing all over the place. Suddenly, dirt-poor farmers with mineral rights were selling out and buying brand-new cars. Some of them bought small airplanes. They bought new tractors, new trucks, and farm implements straight from the store. Oilmen from Texas and Oklahoma moved to Alberta, brought their families with them, rented houses. Suddenly, farm machinery dealers had money, and they expanded their offerings to the farmers. Small prairie towns began to crawl out of the dust. Small businesses were popping up all over Edmonton, and their jingles flooded the radio stations.

One day, Ethel was helping Mr. Schuman bring out some necklaces and rings from the safe. Mr. Schuman retired to the back room to do watch repairs. A smartly dressed mother and recently married daughter entered the store. As they looked around, Mr. Schuman trotted back to the watch repair room, leaving Ethel alone behind the counter. The elder of the two ladies went straight for an item that had caught her eye.

"My-my," she said to her daughter, "will you look at that."

Ethel came over to the largest of the display counters, and the daughter smiled at her. Her mother was admiring a necklace—the Chain. Ethel's heart seemed to do a little flip and she almost called Mr. Schuman out of the backroom.

"You all have not succumbed," said the mother to Ethel, with a trace of Texas gentility in her voice, "to the new fashions." She cast a meaningful glance at her daughter. "And I applaud you."

"Oh, Mother, you need some serious modernizin'."

"Young lady," the mother said to Ethel, pointing to the velvet-lined tray, "might I try on that piece?"

Ethel handed it to the daughter, who, in turn, fixed the clasp at the back of her mother's neck. Ethel passed the lady a hand mirror, and she beamed, and her daughter sighed approvingly.

The mother was the first to speak. "Like my daddy might have said, 'Ah'm a-gonna git me this thing afore she does.' "

They all laughed, and the grand lady seemed to glow. In a matter of minutes she had purchased the Chain for herself and a pendant for her daughter that sported a one-karat white diamond encircled by small sapphires.

"I need to get rid of this stuff," said the mother, rooting through her purse, "before I get on the plane." She came up with a large wad of Canadian currency.

When mother and daughter had left, Mr. Schuman emerged from the workshop, squinting around his loupe. For such a homely man, he was oddly attractive; he had a way of slipping past Ethel's guard.

"What was that all about?"

Ethel didn't say a word. She pointed to the empty tray and then to the cash register. Something seemed to dawn in Mr. Schuman's eyes, and for a wonderful moment, Ethel and Mr. Schuman could not stop smiling at each other.

"That lady," he said. And then he mouthed the words, *The full price?*

She nodded.

"Well," said Mr. Schuman, "I might just have a future in the jewellery business. And you, young lady, I'd say you've got a job for the next good while."

The sale of the Chain was the first olive out of the jar, and Mr. Schuman's business continued to pick up. He and his wife Maisy went on their first big holiday, a summer visit to Montreal. Mr. Schuman hired another girl to work with Ethel, but even then, they were sometimes run off their feet. Finally, he brought in his brother from Montreal to buttress the sales department.

Schuman's watch repair business, his jewellery business, and his clock trade had all intensified, so Brother Danny's arrival was timely. Danny was a whiz with the customers. Mr. Schuman hired yet another girl and made his brother head of the sales department. Danny was quite a lad with the women. He flirted with the customers, with the new girl, and with Ethel, and he even flirted with Maisy Schuman whenever she came into the store to see her husband.

Danny was one fellow with the ladies and another fellow entirely with his older brother, who could not seem to contain him. Danny wanted his brother to spring for a new store on the South Side. He wanted a larger inventory, big rocks for the wives of the swells who ran the oil business and a bigger array of costume jewellery for the hoi polloi. Sometimes, Ethel overheard them arguing in the back-room, and Mr. Schuman's constant theme with his brother was *let's not get over-extended; let's keep it slow and careful.*

One cold November afternoon in 1951, just after the Grey Cup but a little before the Christmas rush, Ethel was doing the cash. The last customer had gone, the sales girls had left for home, the jewellery was all locked up, Danny was nowhere to be seen, and the store had gone so quiet that the clocks seemed clamorous.

Ethel went in to say goodnight to Mr. Schuman. He was slumped in his chair, and he gazed at her through his fatigue, or whatever it was, in the dim light of the office. "Are you okay, Mr. Schuman?"

"Elly, please."

She took a chair. It was a nice old padded chair. She had not realized how tired she was until she sat down. Mr. Schuman was rifling through a drawer in his desk and out came what looked like a mickey of rye.

"Do you ever imbibe, Mrs. Mudge?"

"Ethel," she said.

He brought out two tumblers, poured a shot of rye into each glass, and eased one across his desk. He raised his drink to Ethel in a way that struck her as attentive and old-fashioned.

"I just fired Danny."

"Danny? You mean he's . . ."

"Heading back to Montreal. I can't . . . I just fired my little brother."

They sat staring across at each other in the dim light. Her first thought was that Danny would never flirt with her again and that he would never flirt with every young flibbertigibbet that came through the door. *Good riddance to bad rubbish* was her second thought. But then she realized something else: this was the first time she'd ever shared a drink with her boss, the first time they'd ever addressed each other by their first names. Danny's firing and this cozy little session, were they connected in some way?

"You've been with us here since when, Ethel?"

"Must be five years," she said.

"Five years."

"Five years and a few months," she said.

Again, the long pause, the elegant chatter of the clocks in the backroom. She had a frightening thought. Was he sending her packing as well? Was this Mr. Schuman's way of giving a girl the sack? An affectionate *bye-bye, lotsa luck*?

"Ethel, how would you like to head up the sales department?"

She felt her face blooming, and she was thankful for the subdued light. Once more, he was raising his glass to her.

"You'd get to boss the other girls around," he said, looking down at his blotting paper with a shy grin. "I still want you to do the books, but you'd never have to clean another counter. We'll get someone else for the cleaning."

"I can live with that," she said, and she wondered if she heard a note of resentment in her voice. *I will never clean another toilet.*

"Another thing, Ethel." Mr. Schuman paused. "My brother and I would have a weekly chat after closing. Sometimes Friday afternoons, sometimes late on Saturday. A chance to talk about the business. Who's working out in sales, who's not quite up to the mark. How the pieces are moving, which ones need more of a push. That sort of thing."

"Yes?"

"I hope you and I can carry on with that . . ."

His voice tailed off, and he resumed gazing at the walls.

She usually took the streetcar down Jasper Avenue to Nineteenth Street and walked north from there, but after her meeting with Mr. Schuman (correction, Elly), she felt like a brisk walk. The frosty air smelled good to her; it smelled like hope. She hiked all the way home in the dark. More than once along the way, she almost felt like singing a hymn. At last, pleasantly exhausted, she pulled out her keys from her purse, unlocked the front door of her old flat, and went inside. She smelled the stale drift of cigarettes and beer.

No. She froze inside the entrance. *No, no, no.*

He had fallen asleep on her sofa, sprawled on his belly, and judging from the dirty dishes, beer bottles, and butts in the ashtray, he had been lounging in her flat for much of the day.

"No!" she cried. "No, no, no!"

The syllables flew like tiny bats from her mouth until her panic began to subside, and she remembered something of who she had become that day.

He was gaping at her. She found herself smiling at him, a brisk and ruthless smile that a gunmoll might wield if she had a revolver in her purse. "Hardy," she said, "this is what we're going to do."

3

Some things should never happen. They are so stupid they have no explanation. Maybe they happen because you make a stupid choice. Say you dash across a busy street, you slip on the ice, and you get done in by a streetcar. Or maybe they happen because you're just bad luck. But this simply should not have happened. She had kicked out her husband and that was final. Hardy had come to collect his stuff and some of it was in a steamer trunk. She asked him to help her haul the trunk up from the basement. He was clean-shaven and sober. He was back working again, travelling the rails for the *Book of Knowledge* people. He looked nice and he seemed calm again, like nothing had ever happened. So they puffed their way up the basement stairs and lugged the thing into the living room. Right then, he apologized to her for being such a no-good excuse for a husband. She didn't know what to say, so they went through the trunk and divided up the contents. His army stuff and her items from Saskatoon. She lifted out something in a garment bag, and it turned out to be her wedding dress. It surprised her so much that she started to tear up. Hardy gave her a small hug just to comfort her, and that's all they were up to. But one minute later, they were thrashing away on the purple throw rug. When he left with his stuff, she thought, *oh hell, why not*? It was a better way of saying goodbye than the yelling match they'd had in

November. But this thing growing inside of her was not part of the plan. Men, in general, were not part of the plan. Nineteen fifty-two was simply the wrong year for any of that nonsense.

But some people just didn't get it. Maisy Schuman was always trying to line Ethel up with some dope or other, some new guy in town. Maisy had a bubbly personality, too bubbly in Ethel's view, because she was exhausting to be around. She talked too much, smoked too much, drank at parties, laughed a lot, told racy jokes and had a whole raft of friends. Every time Maisy tried to line her up, Ethel turned her down.

And now this.

The same month as Ethel's little discovery, on a Friday afternoon, Elly called Ethel into the backroom. They had their usual shot of rye, decided not to hire a part-time girl till the Christmas season, exchanged a few thoughts on costume jewellery and pocket watches, and Elly declared an end to their meeting.

"I think," he said, as they stood, "I'm getting a crush on you."

Ethel's head seemed to pop out of her neck, and for a moment, she was too stunned to speak. It was okay to have thoughts about such doings, but it was definitely not okay to express them, was Ethel's view.

"I think," said Elly, "I had better watch myself, or we might both . . ."

He held his hands like he was holding a casserole. He had expressive hands, the kind you might want for playing a piano. The hands moved together from right to left and flopped down toward the floor.

" . . . fall over the edge?"

Ethel stood there before him as though she were sitting in a movie. The sensitive guy with the toothy grin makes his pitch, they play out the scene, the music swells or something, and the patrons all go home to their humdrum lives. She shrugged herself awake and headed for the door. Just as she was turning the knob, she recovered her tongue and turned back to speak.

Elly was right there, in front of her, looking nervous and tortured and vulnerable, as though she were the boss and he merely the employee. He eased her into his arms and kissed her lightly on the lips, and as he drew her in, something between them, something in them, began to crackle like static electricity, and her insides began to quake. Then he was easing her back from his body with both hands around her upper arms, and she could not tell if he was trying to push her away or keep her right there in front of him.

"Elly, I can't."

"I know," he said and pulled her back into a long woeful embrace. "I know. Neither can I."

It was only a hug, that's all it was, and it led to nothing more. It's not like they were making whoopee all over Elly's desk. But that moment, all the same, it was disturbing. (Nice, but disturbing.) After that, they played it as though it had not happened. The Friday sessions with the tumblers of rye came to an abrupt end. Mr. Schuman went about his business in the backroom and scarcely ever seemed to take his loupe off. Ethel presided over the jewellery floor with the sales girls, and whenever Mr. Schuman came out of the backroom for some reason, he and Ethel gave each other polite nods. Work remained bearable. Life went on. She wasn't showing yet. She had gone back to thinking about Elly as Mr. Schuman.

Ethel was running late one evening when he called her into his office. She decided this time that she would remain standing. All he knew about Hardy was that he was out of the picture.

"How are you getting along these days?" he said.

She could hardly say that she was in the family way from her no-good bounder of a husband.

"Can't complain."

Mr. Schuman seemed to veer off his line of thinking. Finally, he said, "You know, Ethel, I've never forgotten our . . ."

Once more, the poor man was tongue-tied and staring at the ceiling. She wanted to tell him to finish his darn sentence and hurry up about it because she had a bus to catch.

"I haven't forgotten either," she said.

"I'm glad," said Mr. Schuman. "I'm sorry how I acted and all, but I'm glad you haven't forgotten."

She was standing just inside the doorway of his office next to the backroom. He was looking up at her from his swivel chair, and he seemed younger than Ethel rather than older. She wondered what his next move might be, and she glanced at her watch. At last, Mr. Schuman pushed his chair back from his big oak desk, stood up, and gazed at the floor.

"Maisy has cancer."

"Oh, no."

He spread out his arms as though to shrug off his news—*What can you do, eh?*—but his face began to unpack, his hands came up to his head, and his shoulders were shaking. She went over to him and drew him to her while he wept. Mr. Schuman had a held-in way of sobbing that she could scarcely hear. He was tall, bony, permanently slumped over, and almost too stiff to hold. He seemed to have no give to his body. She released him, and he pulled her back, and she held him again until his shoulders had stopped shuddering.

"What's her condition?"

"Not so good," he said. "It's lung cancer."

"I'm really sorry, Elly."

"It's the wrong time to tell you this, Ethel, but it's nice to hear you call me Elly again."

A couple of months went by, and once again, Mr. Schuman called her in. This time, he asked her to sit in the nice old padded chair he always used to offer her. He gave her a mournful sort of a smile.

"Maisy sends you her best. She's had the surgery, and she's resting at the Royal Alec. She might even be home by the weekend."

"Good health to her," said Ethel. "She's a nice lady."

"She can never know," said Mr. Schuman.

"Know?"

"How I feel about you. Ever."

"How you feel about me?" she said. "That's a funny thing to say."

"What do you mean?"

"You called it a crush, remember? Way back when? That's all it is, Elly. Gosh, I've got a crush on Clark Gable."

"You don't understand, Ethel. I think about you all the time. I don't want to, but I do. My wife has been on death's . . ." Mr. Schuman had to look away until his voice returned. "On death's doorstep and here I am clinging to this stupid hope that . . . that you and I—"

Ethel held up her hand. "Elly, most of the time at work, you don't say boo. You don't even see me. It's like I'm not here."

"Oh, I see you, Ethel. I see you all the time. I see you in my office when the door's closed. I see you at night when I'm trying to fall asleep. It has to stop," he said, head down, with one hand over his mouth.

"Has to stop?"

"This thing with you, Ethel. Don't you see what I'm getting at?"

"Not really. No."

"What I'm saying, Ethel, and this sounds crazy and unfair and stupid—"

"What, Elly?"

He raised his head and looked at her at last. "You have to go."

In years of working closely together, they had never gone to bed; they had exchanged only one kiss, and neither one of them could be said to be much in the having affairs department. If Elly ever had a wandering eye, for all she knew, it had wandered maybe only once and then fled back home before it could see anything naughty.

What a couple of saints they'd turned out to be.

Rennie Mudge was born in early November of 1952. Since this news had hit Elly's desk, Ethel had been getting monthly cheques by mail.

Severance, he called it, to pay the rent while Ethel figured out what her next step would be. Once in a long while, she and the baby would meet one of the sales girls for coffee at the Chinese restaurant on Twenty-Fourth. Ethel would get reports on Maisy's recovery or Maisy's latest decline. She died in 1953, around the time of Rennie's first birthday.

Many women in Ethel's place would keep themselves going with dreams of getting together with their former boss or meeting a rich widower or some damn thing. But Ethel had no time for that nonsense. Rather than holding out hope for a swell job with decent hours, a reasonable employer, and a bit of respectability; rather than hold out hope for something she loved to do, Ethel chose her next path by avoiding all the things she could not abide, thus avoiding the possibility that some sonofabitch might fire her. No one can fire you if you work for yourself. One day, Ethel phoned Elly at work and nixed the monthly cheques.

From the spring of 1954, Ethel began to clean houses. She was a hard worker, and she charged reasonable rates. Her employers spread the word, and within a few years, she had more clients than she could handle. It wasn't exactly rags to riches. Sometimes, she had barely enough at the end of each month to pay for a streetcar ticket, let alone a babysitter. She went grimly about the challenges of work and perhaps less grimly about the chores of motherhood.

By the late 1950s, Rennie had become a quiet, observant boy, small for his age, intense, full of curiosity. He took to school like no one ever had in Ethel's family. He was no egghead, but that boy was smart. He was her little man, her only cause, and by the time he was ten, he had become her biggest challenge.

One day, Ethel was packing her carpet bag to go and clean for a couple who lived by the river, a sloppy-looking Englishman and his clothes-horse of a wife, in a great big Tudor mansion. They never made her clean the whole thing, just the living areas. Apparently, he had a bunch of guns and hunting stuff in the basement, and he had gold bricks hidden somewhere. Rennie would be coming along with her again because he had been given the job of walking Galahad, the clients' big dog. If she didn't hustle, they would miss the bus.

Her phone rang.

"Forget it, bub."

"What'd you say?" said Rennie.

"Talking to myself. Are you ready?"

The phrase took off in her mind like an annoying song she could not get rid of. *Are you ready are you ready are youreadyareyouready*. It seemed as though she had been asking herself this question since girlhood. Are you ready for the monthlies, are you ready to call yourself a grownup, are you ready for marriage to Hardy Mudge, are you ready for full-time drudgery, are you ready for motherhood? She could not remember ever answering the question. She wondered if Rennie was dogged by similar questions.

He was looking up at her with his jacket on. "Yep," he said.

The phone was still ringing as they left the flat, and she was pretty sure who the caller was. They hurried down the street and puffed their way to the bus stop with minutes to spare. The city bus took them out to Jasper Avenue, where they transferred to a trolley and headed for the west end, the rich part of town. If you walked north, the houses went from flashy rich to ordinary, and far enough north, they went from wartime bungalows to shacks, sheds, and abandoned farmhouses. But when Ethel and Rennie got off the trolley, they went south toward the river, where there weren't any flashy rich houses, just old brick homes with huge hedges, or manor houses with stone sidewalks, or real mansions that reminded her of picture shows set in England with Ronald Coleman and all that fog.

"Rennie?"

He had his nose in a comic book. He looked out the bus window to see if they'd arrived at St. George's Crescent. "What?"

She leaned close to his right ear. She was thinking of her father and his feckless ways with money, his weakness for prospectors. "Why would a grown man have a bunch of gold bricks in his home? It makes no sense."

"I only saw three or four. One of them was little."

"But gold bricks, Rennie. Really."

"He buys stuff from prospectors. To make them with? You know, like gold dust?"

"Still . . ."

Rennie's nose was back in the comic book, a thing about GIs in a battle in Korea or some oriental place. Sometimes, her boy could be annoyingly content. He wouldn't be so content if he knew who'd been phoning them. Hardy Mudge had a talent for phoning at the least convenient time. His last call was concerning Rennie, who he referred to as *our son*. What Rennie didn't know wouldn't hurt him.

"And how did you get inside the library? It's always locked."

"I toldja. The nephew."

"What about the nephew?"

"Rodney. He went and found a skeleton key."

She did not feel comfortable asking her son where Rodney got the key from, but she would give a pretty penny to have just a little peek. No harm in that. Gold bricks? She never heard of anything so ridiculous in all her life.

When they arrived at the Eggers' house, Mrs. Eggers was waiting for a cab, dressed up all fancy in some green creation. Her husband had taken off with the car. Rennie got the leash on Galahad and headed for the riverbank. Ethel set about her cleaning according to the reward system: if she finished the upstairs, the vacuuming, the dusting, and the hardwoods before Mrs. Eggers got back, she would hop outside to the backyard and have a smoke.

The minutes flew by, and almost two hours later, she was down on her knees with the paste wax, joylessly humming some churchy thing, sweating like a marathoner. It was almost three o'clock. Where the hell was Rennie? She could almost taste that cigarette. She heaved herself up from the hardwoods, too puffed out to admire her work, and plodded into the kitchen to put away the dishes that lay dry on the rack.

The last one to put away was Mrs. Eggers' blue and white sugar bowl. That's when she saw the keys at the back of the kitchen cupboard, hanging by a tiny chain. Two of them. She recalled her exchange on the bus with Rennie. One was a skeleton key. She found herself facing the door to Mr. Eggers' library, listening to the tick of the kitchen clock. *One peek*, she thought, and opened the door.

At first, she beheld a large, gloomy chamber with the curtains drawn to shut out the light. When she hit the light switch nearest the door, the whole room seemed to awaken. Cobwebs looped down from the chandelier, weighted by dust. The books were everywhere: shelved to a great height, stacked in glassed-in cupboards or piled up on tables. So. That trampy old Englishman was a reader.

She drew open a dusty set of curtains and spotted a metal bar lying on a window ledge. The bar was so heavy she had to hold it in both of her hands. She felt a dreamlike panic flowing through her body as though something was pulling her to a forbidden place. The bar was burnished to a pale yellow lustre. She replaced it on the ledge and headed straight for the door. She reached for the light switch and her slipper struck something hard. She looked down and nudged it with her foot. It didn't move. It was a brick. She got down on her knees and gave the thing a good push with both hands. It grated grudgingly a few inches across the floor. The Englishman must have put it there to hold the door open.

She leaned out of the doorway to listen, but all she could hear was the tick-tock of the kitchen clock. She crept up to one of the biggest shelves and spied another gold brick standing on its edge to make a book-end. And another. And behind the second one, at the height of her nose, almost out of sight, was a third gold brick, bigger than the bar on the window ledge but smaller than the other bricks. She clasped it, heaved it down, and released her breath with the weight, the opulence of it. It was as heavy as a gravestone.

Ethel slept fitfully that night. There was too much to recall, too much strange and scary stuff to think about. The late afternoon came back to her like a frantic dream. Long after she had finished putting away the last of the china, the Eggers' house had remained empty. Rennie still had not returned.

Then they all showed up together and no Galahad. Mrs. Eggers was mad as a wet hen because the silly dog had gone crazy. Because Rennie had let it go for a run. That was his big crime. Galahad had gone and attacked two kids, and the cops had hauled the dog to the City Pound. Mrs. Eggers said some awfully mean things about Rennie, and Ethel told her, "Hold your horses; it wasn't Rennie bit them kids."

Mrs. Eggers glared at Ethel so that her upper lip curled, revealing her perfect teeth. "Your boy let us down. I told him, 'Do not let the dog off his leash.' He broke his promise to me."

"You raise a vicious dog, Mrs. Eggers, what do you expect? And what happens the next time that dog of yours attacks another child? Who will you blame for that?"

"You dare to accuse *me?* You are nothing, do you hear? You are vermin. You can grab your bag and your stupid boy and get the hell off my property."

So off went Ethel, lugging her carpet bag with Rennie in tow, and they almost missed their bus. Damage done. *Bye-bye, Mrs. Fancy Dress, so long, it's been good to know you.*

And there Ethel lay early in the morning, dark as pitch outside, listening to the wind. It made her shiver deep down in her body just to hear it blow. During the night, she'd dreamt about Mrs. Eggers. She would swoop down into Ethel's home like a ghost and stand before her with that hateful frown, then swoop away in her bright green dress. Would she never be free of this spiteful witch of a woman? And for heaven's sake, this thing in the bed with her, gouging her in the thigh every time she turned over.

She made up her mind to sneak it back before Mrs. Eggers discovered it missing. Old Mr. Eggers would never notice it gone because he was never one to count the price of anything, but Mrs. Eggers had the eye of a hungry bird. She probably counted up the silverware every time Ethel left her house. But after such a row, how on Earth would she ever get back in that house? Mrs. Eggers would as soon sic the cops on her as say hello. *Well, well, Ethel, and what are you doing here?*

They had never gotten along. The first time Ethel showed up with her carpet bag, she felt the woman's reproach, as though Ethel stood for something Mrs. Eggers could not abide. She wasn't just bossy and high-toned—she seemed, for some weird reason, to know things about Ethel from the day she was born. This weird resentment of Mrs. Eggers made Ethel wonder if the lady hadn't come from a troubled home.

Ethel slouched into the kitchen to make Rennie's breakfast, but all she had the energy for was a cigarette and a cup of instant. A while later, Rennie came in. He sat down at the kitchen table with a guilty look on his face.

"Sorry about the dog."

She eyed her boy. "Rennie, I'm not up to much this morning. Milk's in the fridge, cereal's where it always is."

What in hell? she wondered. *What in hell have you done? What in God's name are you going to do now?* The questions started to flow like a flooding river. Who would raise her boy, would Hardy Mudge be up to the task, would Rennie visit her in jail, would there be a—

"You don't have to be so grumbly," said Rennie.

She glared at her boy as he tore open a box of cereal. She tried to see if he was crying but Rennie had turned away. She pushed herself up from the table, butted her cigarette, and went over to the boy. She put down his box of cereal, pulled him to her, and murmured *there there there* because there was nothing else she could say, and sure as hell, she was not ready for this one.

4

At the poker table of life, Hardy Mudge had held very few aces, and Hardy being Hardy, he had not played them well. This time would be a little different, however, because this time, he had really worked things out. His ace was the key to his old apartment, from which, two weeks ago, he had been evicted for no reason at all. The barracuda landlady had it in for Hardy from the day he moved there, and now he was sleeping on his friend Mumford's lumpy chesterfield. Hardy had become obsessed with this caper, so much so that he had almost entirely quit boozing. He took his apartment key to a locksmith and had a copy made, then handed in the originals to Mrs. Barracuda.

Nightfall. Hardy is surprised at how calm he has become. Duffle bag under his arm, he takes out his key and unlocks the apartment door, hands shaking but not fumbling. His excuse is ready at the tip of his tongue. *Sorry to bust in on ya, buddy. Plain forgot to give you this here key.* No one at home. Grace of God or whatever. Much of the new tenant's possessions were still stacked in piles all over the living room. *Eeny meeny miny mo.*

Hardy glides from pile to pile, top to bottom, silent as a cat in his wool socks. The joints in his feet are cracking. He smells the sweat from his nervous pits, begins to gulp the mouldy air around him. Fifty-four is too old for this bullshit. He prays that the telephone will not ring because if it rings and he doesn't answer it, and people in the building hear him rummaging around, they'll know something is up. He also prays that the new tenant will stay true to his plans for the weekend.

Into the duffle bag goes a solid silver flute in a case, a wooden box full of cufflinks, an old pocket watch, a genuine abo-type boomerang, a piggybank stuffed with change, a nice new 1963 trophy for musical whatnot (sterling silver), a small strummy thing made from the shell of an armadillo (must be worth a few bucks), and a beautiful gold ring. The ring goes on Hardy's middle finger—not a bad fit. There's a big saxophone sitting up on a stand, bright as gold, but it won't fit into the duffle bag. That's showbiz.

He can hear someone pacing in the apartment next door, and he is reminded of how thin the walls are in his former building.

At last, there is nothing left small enough to filch. He zips up the duffle bag and has one final look around his recently abandoned flat. He pulls out some cushions from the new guy's chesterfield, and whaddya know, like some treasure in a storybook, there lies a worn canvas pouch with a bank logo. Heavy as hell. Bulging with silver dollars. *My my.* He tiptoes over to his duffle bag and lays the pouch next to the phone.

Which rings.

Holy Moses, shit. Hardy grabs the receiver. "Hello?"

"Mr. Mudge," says a lady with an English accent, "we are so pleased to hear your voice."

"You mean I'm still payin' for this telephone?"

"I'm not sure. Are you Mr. Hardy Mudge?"

Hardy now wonders why in hell he picked up the phone. So what if people in the building hear it ring? But Hardy has lived as a bachelor for many years now, and bachelors always answer their phones.

"Yes, ma'am, that's me."

"You are a hard man to get hold of, Mr. Mudge. Could you speak up?"

"I'm sorry, but I'm in a bit of a—"

"You might want to sit down, Mr. Mudge. I have something momentous to tell you."

"Shoot."

"My name is Loey Binns, Mr. Mudge, and I am happy to announce that your ticket has been selected for the Sweeps. Furthermore, I—"

"The Sweeps?" he said.

"The Irish Sweepstakes," said the woman. "Mr. Mudge, you have won a very tidy—"

"Is this some sorta—"

Once more, she cuts him off: "Mr. Mudge, there is one way to ascertain whether we are indeed legitimate. Simply bring your ticket to the nearest branch . . ." (it sounded like *brunch*) ". . . of the . . . Bank of Nova Sco-sher, and they will . . ." (something something) ". . . your winnings. Can you hear me?"

He grabs for one of the tenant's pens, she repeats her instructions, and he scribbles them down.

"Thought you'd have an Irish accent or somethin'."

"Don't they all," she said.

He thanked the woman and realized that rivulets of sweat were rolling down into his eyes. His throat was tightening, and everything from his lungs to his nostrils had gone drooly. "Sounds like you enjoy your work, Miss."

"I do indeed, Mr. Mudge. And I hope you enjoy your winnings. Men like you contribute every year to a fine cause and . . ." (*blah blah blah*) ". . . can we count on you to give some interviews, Mr. Mudge? Mr. Mudge, are you there?"

Jesus, but don't this woman go on and on. "I'm here. Haven't quite digested the news. How much did you say I won?"

"I was leaving the amount to the last. Any guesses, Mr. Mudge?"

"Not a clue."

"Your ticket on Whackfall to win, Mr. Mudge, has won you sixty-two thousand, four hundred pounds. Rounded off."

"Holy mothera Christ."

"You are a lucky man, Mr. Mudge. Have you always thought of yourself as lucky?"

"Not particularly. Say, what's your name?"

"I told you, Mr. Mudge. It's Loey Binns."

"Loey, I don't mind confiding in you. I mean, all my life, I've had to scramble for a living. It's like I've got this anvil over my head, see, and all I have to do is just get slightly out of line and down she comes to flatten me. I got this friend, Mumford, see, and he tells me that Mudge—that's my last name, Mudge—"

"I know, Mr. Mudge."

"'Course you do. 'Course you do. Anyway, this buddy, he says that Mudge is the sound of a great big anvil fallin' on my head from a hundred feet up. Not a word . . . not a word of a lie."

"There, there, Mr. Mudge, don't worry. Don't worry anymore. And there's nothing wrong with a good cry now and then. A good cry and a cup of tea. That's what my mother used to say. There, there."

"You sound like a very sympathetic person, Loey. I don't suppose you live over here, do you?"

"Oh, no, Mr. Mudge. I'm on the other side. Over the bounding main."

"Too bad. I'd love to meet the lady who changed my life, and that's no lie."

Suddenly, Loie Binns is helpless with laughter. Not a mean-spirited laugh. It's a gentle laugh. Nothing like his ex. Nothing like the women over here; they'd rather laugh at you than help you up from the gutter. But Hardy cannot dismiss the thought that he and this Loey number have a connection.

"Somebody should write your story, Mr. Mudge. It sounds fascinating. But I am going to bid you a fond farewell, and I hope your newfound luck follows you wherever you . . ."

Loey Binns chatters away, *what an absolute angel,* but suddenly, her words take root. Somebody should write his story. It would end with Hardy returning almost everything he swiped from his old apartment. Or maybe it would end with a phone call to Ethel, the mother of his son. A tearful apology and then a visit to meet the kid. They'd throw the ball back and forth, and the boy would come to know what Hardy was *really* like. The book writer would have to be somebody special . . . somebody who knew about hardship and struggle and how a man can stray and find his way back to the top again. *And goddamn it, Hardy Mudge,* you are that somebody.

5

When the phone rang, her elbow was on the kitchen table, her chin resting in the palm of her hand, her eyes fixed on the air between an empty tea cup and her latest list. She was considering a bit of breakfast, but she had no appetite.

She peered at the phone. "Go. To. Hell."

These days, the job of telephones was to interrupt people who were just going about their business. This morning, her business was to make a list before she left for cleaning. She only did them when her nerves were bad and life was getting a bit much, like her recent nightmare of Mrs. Eggers showing up at her door with the police. Anyhow:

1) phone Elly.

2) church bakes.

3) phone Mrs. Ostry.

4) new bus sch.

5) Ren pants, A & N.

She never failed to put a bracket after each number, and after each item, there was always a period. This allowed her to contain things so they wouldn't swarm at her.

She glared at the phone as it jangled in its monotonous way. It could not be anything to do with her son. Old Mr. Eggers had declared to all concerned that Rennie was blameless for letting the dog off his leash, and no one from that household had mentioned anything about a missing gold brick. But what if it was Hardy? Sad sack Hardy, phoning from the Coast, asking for a handout or a place to stay. No, that was a long shot. It was probably just a customer phoning to get a cleaning appointment or change one.

Just before the sixth ring, she picked up the receiver.

A man's voice. Familiar, but it didn't belong to Hardy. A polite voice. It said, "Ethel, I hope I've caught you at a good time."

"Mr. Schuman?"

"Please, Elly."

She glanced back at her list. *1) phone Elly.*

"How are things with you, Ethel?"

"Funny," she said. "I was going to phone you."

"You were?"

She imagined him suddenly at attention, eyes wide, mouth agape with bulging teeth. He would think, *Holy Moses.*

"So, Elly. Your nickel."

"Something has just come up . . . and I feel awkward asking you this. I mean, it's been such a long time."

"Yep."

"Here goes. Ethel, I've just lost my head salesgirl. She's having a baby, and we have . . . ah, what I mean to say is, how would you like your old job back?"

"I'll be damned," she said.

There was no way in the world she was going to take her old job back. Elly had fired her, and she had almost hit bottom, and with a kid to feed and no goddamn support from Hardy, no connection to the outside world, and a social worker snooping around every so often, eyeing Rennie for signs of malnutrition or whatever the hell those people looked for, it was simply out of the question.

"Ethel, I could give you a few days to, ah . . ."

They went silent again for a longer moment, and she could almost see Elly tamping down his eagerness. Elly held a lot of things down. Anger, desire, grief. Enough tears for a man to drown in. It seemed his whole life's mission was not to get excited. It could be downright annoying. She'd had a couple of dreams about him over the winter, and he kept saying the things to her that he'd never been able to say when he was her boss. Tender things, planning stuff with her, trips to far-off places. The dreams should have irritated her, like everything else in her life these days, but they didn't. As dreams went, they were okay.

"I'm guessing you want to think things over?" he said.

"Boy."

"Ethel, maybe we could have a coffee somewhere and talk? Salary and bonuses, that sort of thing?"

"How about next week?" she said. Her voice sounded just a tad saucy, but she couldn't stop herself. "Next week in your office with a shot of rye, Elly. Like old times?"

Ethel wondered if her voice didn't sound a little bit angry. She'd been trying for breezy.

"Maybe we could do that," he said dubiously.

"I have something to show you," she said. "And I need to bring it to your office. And it won't bite, I promise. And you'll never guess, so don't try."

Elly paused in that careful way of his as though to assess whether the pleasure or profit from meeting with her would outweigh the potential disasters. Gossip, for example, or a big scene in his store.

"This thing you want to show me," he said. "Is that what you were going to phone me about?"

"Sort of."

He suggested Friday after work, a chat and a bite to eat, and she said that would be swell.

Ethel put down the receiver in slow motion, savouring the whatever-it-was she had felt surging through her body. Mastery? Forcefulness? No, not that. Power? Vigour? No, because she was always tired. It was something like when her new friend Russell stepped on the gas.

Acceleration. Yes.

She checked her watch. She had a few minutes to eat something before she left, but damn it, she still wasn't hungry. What she really hankered for was a cigarette. She was due in about forty-five minutes for a cleaning job in Old Glenora, an easy half-day session. The bus would take her to within a block of the customer's house on Villa Avenue. The woman who hired her was not bad as bosses went. She, too, had come from Saskatoon, so she kept wanting to reminisce with Ethel. Little did the lady know how eagerly Ethel had left Saskatoon, the town where her father had bankrupted the family, the town where she had met Hardy Mudge and fallen for his jaunty personality.

But now, she had a nice yellow brick and someone to barter with. She would wrap it up in something and put it in her carpetbag. Elly would wonder, *What's in the bag?* and she would say, *Three guesses.*

Ethel was heading for the door when the phone rang again. This would be Elly with a slight change of plans. She let it ring long enough to show him that she had better things to think about than his precious job offer. She checked her watch once more and, at last, grabbed the receiver.

"Ethel, it's me. Please, for God's sake, don't hang up."

"Please, for God's sake," he cried, "don't hang up."

There was a silence at the other end, one so venomous he could almost feel it seeping into his bloodstream. Who else but Ethel could make a silence that threatening?

"Ethel, it's me, and I know I got no right phonin' you outa the blue, but please" (that word stuck like cigarette foil in his teeth), "please let me say my piece."

"You mean you talk while I listen," she said. "Tell me something new, Hardy."

"Okay, I'll tell you something new. I'm off the sauce. I'm a regular go-ta-church new man. I got a job, I'm back in business again. And Ethel, more than anything else in the whole wide world, I want . . . I want to make amends."

"Make amends with me," she said. "This I gotta hear."

"I don't mean it that way, Ethel. I mean, I feel bad about the drinkin' and all, but . . ." Hardy paused one moment for a response from his wife. His soon-to-be ex-wife. Not a sound. "I phoned you because I feel bad I was never there for Rennie. And . . . y'know . . . I want to make it up to him."

"Yeah?"

"I want to make it up to him. I want . . . I'm comin' up from Calgary on business and I want to have a bit of time with our son, Ethel. I don't intend to hang around the place. I got a hotel room all booked and ready."

Hardy had been sitting on the bed in his undershorts in the apartment of Amber Hay, his new girlfriend, smoking a cigarette and feeling stronger and more confident than he had in a long time. He had already phoned a few friends to let them know that he was back in the door-to-door game, and then he'd summoned the courage to phone Ethel before Amber returned. Amber was downtown shopping for their trip to Edmonton, so he had a nice opportunity to spread out on the bed and talk without being disturbed. He decided not to tell Ethel about the Sweepstakes ticket. Not yet, anyway. Ethel might take a notion to get greedy. Let her find out on her own.

"So," said Ethel, "you want to ride into town on your horse, and suddenly Rennie's got a brand-new dad."

"Look, Ethel, Jesus."

"The less we see of you, the better, Hardy. Do I have to spell it out for you? Do I want my son to know what his father is really like?"

"I left that all behind, Ethel. I'm sober as a judge, an no more tom-cattin' for me." He didn't think that Amber Hay fell under the category of tom-catting because, after all, he'd met her in church. "I just want a little visit with my son, goddammit, Ethel. What's wrong with that?"

"After all I've seen you do, after all this time with not a peep out of you, not one nickel and no money for the rent, you . . . you . . . now . . . want me to trust you with my boy. Well, pardon me, Hardy, if my hackles aren't risin' just a bit here."

"I know what you must think, Ethel, I know—"

"How would you ever know what I think? You were talking all the time. Do you have any idea . . ."

Hardy held the phone at arm's length like a snake handler at the end of a long day.

Rennie's mother had dressed him up in a new pair of khakis and a plaid shirt from the Army & Navy. He thought the whole thing was a stupid idea, and he told her so. "What does he want, anyway?"

"Just wants a visit. He probably feels bad about not seeing you for so long."

"What am I s'pose ta say to him?"

"You'll figure it out soon enough, kid." His mother paused and glanced out the front window. "He's never been much of a husband or a dad, Rennie, but he's still technically my husband, and he's still your dad. And just you remember, Bozo, you got a mom here that loves you. Y'got that?"

When his dad's car arrived out front, the snow was floating straight down in large, heavy flakes. His mother helped him on with his parka."You can meet him at the car," she said.

"Maybe we should let him come in?"

His mother's eyes went blank, and she sighed. "I guess."

Presently, his father knocked on the door. He walked into the narrow front hall wearing a black overcoat over a blue suit with a drooping white flower in his lapel. He was holding a black fedora in both hands.

"Ethel. Lookin well. And who might this be?" he said, checking out Rennie from bottom to top. "Who's this big guy, all grown up like a weed, hey?"

Rennie's dad announced these words like a morning deejay who had already ripped off a dozen ads in one shift. Rennie gave him a limp handshake, gave his mother a nervous jerk of the eyeball, and walked out with his father into the falling snow.

There was a dressed-up lady in the front seat, so Rennie got into the back, and his father closed the door. The car smelled sweet inside, like the fancy soap in Mrs Eggers's bathroom, only stronger than soap. It was the biggest back seat Rennie had ever seen, and in spite of the flowery blast from the front seat, he could smell the leather of the upholstery. Everything in the car smelled new. He almost forgot to be resentful, and then he *did* forget. Because the car was way neater and bigger than even Mr. Eggers's Rambler station wagon.

"Neat car," he said.

"Ever rode in a Caddy before?"

"Is this a Caddy?"

"You bet, Rennie. Purrs like a panther. Always go first class, that's my motto."

"You look like your father," said the lady to Rennie.

She had turned around on her seat and looked back, not so much to see Rennie's face as maybe to allow Rennie to see hers. She was wearing a black leather coat with a big white fur collar. When she moved her body, another warm waft of perfume seemed to float back at him. All he could see was her face like it had no body. It was framed by this white animal-fur collar. And her hair was perfect, sort of like Cleopatra hair but coal-black instead of glossy black, and flipped up at the sides with bangs at the front, and her eyebrows were painted over in black lines and makeup that gave the skin on her face a nice kind of smooth, even look. Russell Canning, his mom's new friend, would call her a real classy dame.

"I'm Amber," she said with a smile.

"Amber, Amber, Amber," chirped his father. "She's up here to help your dad in his business type-a-deal. She's my right-hand man, you might say."

"Where we goin'?" Rennie said.

"With all this gull-dang snow, I don't think we're goin' very far. How about the Pat on Twenty-Fourth?"

"How about the MacDonald Hotel?" Amber said in a purry voice.

"Ain't that just like a gal, Rennie? Go for the most expensive place in town?"

"I don't care," said Amber, "as long as I can get some cigs first." She smiled warmly at Rennie. "You don't mind if a girl has a smoke, do you?"

Rennie was so taken by her smile that he forgot to answer her.

At the MacDonald Hotel cafeteria, they ate some great big cold shrimp that were sitting in a bowl of ice cubes. They slathered the shrimp with hot red sauce, and they had some cold soup that fluttered like jello.

When Amber went to the powder room, his father moved around the table to sit next to him. They faced each other knee to knee. "Did you like the consommé?" his father said.

Rennie shrugged.

"Like your shrimp?"

"Yeah."

"That'll put meat on your bones, eh? You're gonna put on a growin' spurt, Rennie. Just you wait and see."

Rennie did not like being reminded of his small stature. He wished people would notice other things about him, but he didn't yet know what they were.

"Rennie, me and Amber are off to Las Vegas. We're gonna get married, eh? Then we're gonna hit the roulette tables for a week or two, see some sights? Wish you could come, y'know, but we'll be back in Calgary end of February, and I'll get up to see you as much as I can, right?"

Rennie was pretty sure that his dad was still married to his mom (she had said *technically*), but he did not want to say anything that might spoil his dad's good mood. "Okay."

"How do you like Amber?"

His dad gave him a big wink. It was the sort of wink that men gave to each other but didn't usually give to kids. It meant *Wow.* It meant *Yowzers.* Maybe this was how go-getters talked about women to each other. He wondered if old Mr. Eggers had ever winked like this to other guys about women. No, probably not.

"She's nice," he said.

"Rennie, does your mom, you know, does she talk about me much?"

"No."

"She doesn't talk about me? You mean not at all?"

"Sometimes she says stuff."

"Yeah, I'll bet she does." His father was gazing out the window and across the river valley. "Listen, if she ever wonders about me, I mean if she ever asks, you tell her for me," he said, jamming his thumb into his chest like a woodpecker's beak, "tell her Hardy Mudge is doin' just fine. Hey?"

He turned away from his father to see if Amber was coming back from the ladies' room. Soon, his dad would drive him home. Rennie would resume life with his mother. There would be his paper route, there would be the odd visit from Russell, and maybe Russell would take him around town in his pickup. There would be more visits to see Mr. Eggers and his rock collection. He liked to tell stories to Rennie about how he found gold up north. Anyway, Mr. Eggers and all. This meant that he didn't have time for an extra father, even a real one. And soon, maybe he and his friends would take their toboggans to the riverbank. Maybe he could buy a pair of skates with his earnings before the winter was over. Maybe he'd get some A's in his report card like last year and show his mother and Mr. Eggers. His mother would brag about Rennie to her customers. But with any luck, there would be no more visits from his dad for a long time.

Rennie would miss the Caddy, and he would miss Amber with her slow smile and her dizzy perfume and her coal-black hair. Amber seemed to send messages to Rennie from the future, something about being grown up, something about the world and all its adventures beyond his mother's dumpy little townhouse, and maybe the world would beckon to him whenever he saw an amber light at an intersection.

Rennie turned back to face his father. "Yup, I'll tell her."

6

Ethel arrived late to the jewellery store. When Elly let her in, it was almost dark. She placed the carpetbag on a chair, took off her coat and a sweater, and laid them on a counter between where the rings and the watches were displayed. She wore her light-brown, checkered skirt and a pale yellow blouse from her days at the jewellery store. From the exertion of hauling the carpetbag from the bus stop to Schuman Brothers Jewellery, she was breathing hard, and her cheeks were probably glowing.

Elly smiled at her. "So, Ethel, what's in the bag?"

"Three guesses."

It was wrapped in pillowcases like an abandoned baby. Elly lugged it over to his desk and unwrapped it slowly, with absolute concentration.

"Holy Moses."

Neither Elly nor Ethel was hungry, and they talked until well past the supper hour. She perched in the same upholstered chair that she had often sat in, and he was back in his executive chair behind the big oak desk. They sipped rye from the same small tumblers as the clocks chattered around them. Two squat table lamps offered some light, enough to see that nothing had changed in the office, except now there was a portrait of Maisy on the far wall. Ethel had forgotten how many years had passed since Maisy's death. Mr. Eggers's gold brick lay between them on the desk like a block of cheese, glinting in the subdued light of the office.

"This didn't exactly come from the mint, did it?" he said.

"Nope. He had a friend who made them. He got the gold, and his friend made the bricks."

"There were other bricks?"

"Yep," she said, as though they were talking about cheese. "Maybe a dozen. Big ones and small ones."

Elly asked if the man was still alive, and she nodded.

"Who was this guy?"

"The less you know, the better, Elly. He's an old guy who likes to spend time with Rennie. Never had a kid of his own. His wife is a wolf disguised as a woman. I'll sign whatever papers you want. This here was a gift, plain and simple."

She wanted to tell more about Mr. Eggers. How he figured out her theft of the brick, how he struck a deal with Ethel, the brick for her permission to continue his friendship with Rennie and no monkey business. Uncleing, he called it. Nothing shameful. She was even tempted to speak about the dreaded Mrs. Eggers, her Waterloo. But later. Sometime later.

"He likes your son, so he gives you a gold brick?"

Ethel heaved a dramatic sigh. "It's complicated, but it's not what you're thinking."

Elly ran his fingers over the surface of the brick. He tilted his head and peered skeptically at her. "You want me to melt it down, use it—the whole thing—to make wafers, rings, jewellery and whatnot, and you—"

"We split fifty-fifty."

"I don't know, Ethel. This isn't how we do things around here."

"Then what do *you* want? What is it you want from me?"

Elly sat up straight in his chair and stared at the ceiling, looking solemn, older than his years, frowning as though someone had just stolen something from the store. He placed his hands before him, long fingers meeting at the tips like he was about to pray for guidance. "You want to know what I want out of the bargain besides some free gold? I want you back here. That's what I want."

"Elly, can't you see? That's not going to work for me."

He held up his hand. "If I asked you to marry me, Ethel, you would turn me down. Wait, I haven't finished. If I asked you to run off with me for a romantic . . . a romantic fling somewhere, you would turn me down. Wait, please. Ethel, what if I just asked you to come back to your job? What would be so bad about that?"

She closed her mouth. She sat back with her eyes shut and breathed in and out, and when the resentment began to drift away, she realized that she was tired. That she had been tired for a long time—days, weeks, maybe years. What was it about this man's office that allowed her to admit this to herself?

She opened her eyes. "Why would you want to hire me? Just to . . ."

"Exactly. Just to have you around."

"For what?"

He smiled at her brilliantly through moist eyes. *Because. Lord help us.* This was not just a brief negotiation about a gold brick; it was something else entirely. It could lead anywhere.

"For hope," he said. "A reason to get up in the morning. Something to look forward to."

She repeated the last phrase to herself, nodding slowly and glumly as though she had read it in a book and memorized it. *Something to look forward to.* "Elly, what in the heck do you see in me?"

Something unvoiced emanated from down in his throat, an obscure shuddering sound that could mean weeping or suppressed laughter or somebody dying. When the sound stopped, Elly leaned forward over his desk, over the gold brick, too, so that it faded to the shadow of itself.

"I see *you* in you, Ethel. Isn't that enough?"

They looked at each other, and she nodded furtively in his direction. This conversation could either be their very last one or the first evening of her entire future; she hadn't the slightest idea which way this might go.

She placed her tumbler on the desk and halfway smiled at him. "Partners in crime," she said. "Hah."

"Partners in crime."

"Well. I don't know about you, Elly, but I'm feelin' kinda peckish."

7

Early in September 1983, Hardy Mudge passed away in Esquimalt. Hardy's old friend Mumford phoned the news to her on a blah sort of morning. She had been resting on the couch with hands cupped over her eyes. She had a headache, and she was bone tired.

"A bad fall at night," Mumford said. "Down a set of basement stairs. He musta gone real fast. I don't believe he felt a thing."

She would have agreed with this last part, but she didn't want to sound sarcastic. She said, "When did you find this out?"

"Happened four days ago. Our place. We discovered him on the basement floor the next morning. The wife found your phone number in his room."

Mumford reported that he'd already mailed her a copy of the death notice from *The Victoria Times*. The fellow had a deep, solemn voice, and he went on and on as if he were practising for Hardy's funeral. She thought that she remembered his name. Hardy used to refer to him after the war as a drinking buddy or some such thing.

"It was kind of you to get in touch with me," she said, which was Ethel's way of saying that this conversation was now over.

"I hafta tell you, Mrs. Mudge, I'm gonna miss your husband. We go back a long ways. He was one of the best friends I ever had."

"Well," she said, "he hasn't been my husband for a long time. I never heard a whisper from him ever since he married that girl."

"Hardy was married again?"

"I think her name was Amber."

"Oh, that one. I doubt they ever tied the knot. She didn't last very long. He always said you were his wife."

The death notice arrived in the mail the next day. When Rennie came over to her apartment for a visit, she told him the news and handed him the letter from Mr. Mumford. She retired to the couch and closed her eyes. Rennie read a few lines from the death notice and grudgingly, Ethel opened her eyes. She rose from her couch, padded through to the kitchen, and stared out the window at the blurry afternoon to check the sky. There were no clouds at all, yet there seemed to be an intangible pall over everything Ethel beheld, an unnatural gloom that made the day dark and the sun glow like a red eye in the heavens. It was the smoke, of course, from up north. She could even smell it inside the apartment. Maybe it was the smoke that was making her feel so tired these days. Breathing in all that ash or something. Ethel returned to her couch.

"Wow," said her son.

She did a quick calculation by adding seven to her own age. Hardy was the same age as Elly. "I guess he made it to seventy-four," she said.

Rennie handed her the notice.

She squinted once more at a picture of Hardy in his uniform, a handsome young man smiling mischievously as though the war was someone else's problem. Former labourer in the Great Depression, former soldier in Europe with the Canadian Light Artillery, salesman and longtime yabbity-yabbity, survived by his beloved wife, Ethel, and their son, Rennie. Something about winning a lottery. The obituary closed with some flowery stuff about life and death. *We all die in the music of our own song.*

Ethel wondered who might have written the notice. Some highfalutin friend of his out on the Coast? Some obituary fellow who got paid to tell lies? And then she wondered about her own obituary. Was that something she would leave for her son to do? *Ethel Mudge, cleaning woman, single parent, always making lists. Old before her time. Rest in peace.*

"Doesn't bear thinking about."

"What?"

"I was talking to myself," she said.

"By the way, Mom, I'm joining Mandy up north. Mom?"

She turned to her son. "Say that again?"

"I'm meeting up with Mandy this weekend. She's got some days off. How would you like to drop me at the airport?"

"There's fires up there. Why would you risk all that for one teeny visit?"

"There's no risk, Mother. She only checks out the burns after the fires have passed. She doesn't fight the fires."

"You want *me* to drive you?"

"I phoned your boyfriend," Rennie said, "but he was out."

"He's not my boyfriend. Elly and I are just old friends."

"Tell it to the Judge."

"I suppose I could drive you," she said with a sigh.

The sigh meant nothing. In fact, she was secretly pleased. Rennie scarcely ever asked her to do anything. She was always devising ways for them to spend time together. Rennie was her own flesh and blood; he had been a good son to her, but sometimes he could be so annoying. When he married Miss Nature Girl, Ethel went to the wedding with her nose out of joint because Rennie hadn't even told her they were engaged. The secret of getting information out of Rennie, she reminded herself, was not to pry. Just let him talk.

"Seriously," he said, "what does your Friday look like?"

"How should I know?"

Her son went over to the calendar and muttered something to himself about an appointment. Whisper-whisper.

She re-read Hardy Mudge's death notice referring to Ethel as his beloved wife. "What was that man thinking? Rennie?"

"Hm?"

"Calling me his beloved wife. What on Earth was he going on about? He did everything possible to destroy our marriage."

"No idea, Mom. Maybe when you're dying, you forget stuff. Maybe he was on a bender. Or living up there in Fantasy Land."

And then there was the mysterious ending. *We all die in the music of our own song.* All very nice and fancy, but what on Earth could it mean? What if you didn't have a favourite song?

She read the sentence out loud. "What do you think that means? Rennie?"

He picked up the obituary page and mumbled it to himself. Rennie had turned into a nice-looking man. A bit on the short-and-small side but handsome like Ethel's own father. His nails had all grown back again. Was it possible that girl had prevailed upon him to stop chewing them?

"It's kind of nice," he said.

On Friday morning, Ethel drove home from the airport with the familiar feeling that something was not quite right. She could not shake the feeling. She began to catalogue her various worries, her aches and pains. The smoke still lingered all through the city, but today, she couldn't smell it. Did that mean she'd lost her sense of smell? The night before, of all things, she'd had a dream about Mrs. Eggers, and it had made her feel anxious. She couldn't get back to sleep. She was dead tired, but she hadn't done anything energetic; she just felt old and used up. The week before, an oil patch worker in search of drug money had mugged an old fellow down the street. Her new neighbourhood was not particularly crime-ridden, but sometimes, living alone, Ethel did not feel safe.

She parked the car in front of her building. It seemed to welcome her. It had seven suites, two on each floor and a penthouse on top. Her own suite was on the second floor. She walked up to the main door and went inside. She was safe. So it had to be something else. Her boy was flying north to have a little holiday with his wife. And for all she knew, it would be in a small aircraft. Those little planes they flew up there, they were always crashing. You'd never catch Ethel in one of those things, especially with all the fires up there.

But that wasn't it either. Rennie would be fine. It was good to see him take a break from his work. Rennie, the big-time importer. It was good that he was his own boss. It seemed only yesterday that Rennie was living with a roommate in a dingy basement apartment. All they did for a living was buy and sell junk. And in the blink of an eye, her son was a big-shot businessman with a degree from the university. How did he afford all that high living? Not from those monthly cheques she used to send him. His most frequent answer to her question was that he had acquired an investor for his business. A wealthy type somewhere. *But Rennie, how could you make all that money from selling ashtrays and fridge magnets?* He said, *Oh, that. The usual thing. Mr. Eggers dumped a bunch of gold bricks on me.*

Rennie did that all the time. He would joke away her questions until she gave up asking. Sometimes, his little evasions made her head swim. She tried not to complain too much. After all, Rennie had bought her this big apartment, the Ethel Suite, he liked to call it. It was too big, really, but Rennie had wanted to be sure that there would be room for Elly if they ever decided to move in together. Fat chance. They liked their independence. They liked living close to each other but not in each other's pockets. When they got together, it was like a visit, and if they weren't visiting, they were gabbing with each other on the phone. He liked to phone her after lunch.

Well, then. Maybe she was still recovering from the news of Hardy Mudge's death and that cock-eyed obituary. Or maybe she had forgotten something, an appointment perhaps or a promise she'd made. These days, she was forgetting altogether too much. She wasn't always in her right mind.

Ethel went over to the calendar next to the telephone. Day, Friday the twenty-first. Month, September. Year, 1983. Rennie had scrawled a message. *Get shit now? Get shit, Mom?*

The message gave her a start. It made no sense at all. Why would her son write such a thing? *Get shot, Mom?* Was that it? Was this one of his jokes?

She changed from her shoes to her knitted slippers. She padded around to the back of her building, where the residents had planted a community garden. It was partly shaded by some old elms and maples, a nice place to sit out of the sun even on a smoky day. She lit a cigarette and stared at the scene before her. She needed to reassure herself that no characters were lurking around the grounds, that no one was waiting to shoot and rob her.

Her only company today was a ratty old husky dog. It raised its head and blinked at her from the patch of grass where it had been sleeping. It reminded her of Mrs. Eggers's big husky, Galahad, except this one didn't appear to have an aggressive bone in its body. Mrs.

Eggers had loved that dog. She was an awful person, but she loved that vicious dog. Good company for each other.

She hadn't thought much about Mrs. Eggers for some time. Ethel's nemesis, dead and gone. Boo-hoo. Ethel's great transgression. The only thing she'd ever stolen, a gold brick, and when at last old man Eggers forgave her for stealing it and didn't call the police, she felt so . . . unclean.

Could it be that old Mr. Eggers was actually Rennie's secret investor? Nonsense.

Anyway, Ethel thought at first that she'd stolen the gold brick to give Rennie a better life. She'd gotten Elly to sell it bit by bit so she could buy herself a small car and some of the things a young boy needed. But now, when she thought back on that desperate time, she wondered if she hadn't stolen it for herself. Out of resentment and desperation? To grab a piece of the world's bounty?

Ethel shook her head as though someone had just whacked her with a club. The headshaking was a recent habit she had acquired to get her eyes focused and her mind back in the world. She did not have to fret about Melony Eggers; she wasn't her cleaning woman anymore. Amen to that. And the old bat had died at last, so she couldn't accuse Ethel of making off with one of her precious trinkets.

The old husky lowered its head on the paws and closed its eyes. The whole neighbourhood, from the communal garden to the church across the way to the school on the other side of the street to beyond, was as quiet as the grave. The children wouldn't be coming home from school for a good while. The sun was still up, but for all the light it shed through the smoke, it might just as well have been the moon. The air was cool, and the blood-red sun would be heading for the horizon in a few hours. And then it would be dark, and the smoke and ashes would settle. Ethel wondered if the whole world wasn't turning to ashes.

Get shot *noon.* Of course. She had to get her flu shot at the clinic at noon, something about the lineups being shorter. Rennie had reminded her at the airport. It was this smoky veil over everything, that's what it was, as though everything all over the world was starting to die. As though life was getting shorter and shorter, and before long, she would be heading for that place that Elly had told her about, where people lived in wards surrounded by old duffers. If the smoke didn't get her first, they'd haul her off to that care home, where they spooned puréed fruit into your mouth. And then she'd die and get cremated and go up in smoke.

Well, her little gloomy spell would just have to wait. Ethel re-entered her building, sweating and puffing for no reason. She had things to do; she had no time for that nonsense. She unlocked the door to the Ethel Suite and entered.

She fell to it.

Where in Heaven's name is she now? Why hasn't Elly phoned yet? Her body tells her that she is lying on the old purple throw rug in the living room, but her mind has other ideas. Her mind reassures her that her lipstick is on, that she has changed back into her good shoes, and that she is lining up with all the others. Yes. Everyone is so quiet you'd think they were heading to the slaughterhouse, and it's just a little needle, for Heaven's sake. A tall young man offers his arm to her, and she tells him she is perfectly capable of walking to the pews. He has a goody-goody way about him that brings out her impatience.

Let me catch my breath, for Heaven's sake.

No hurry. We can take our time.

I didn't mean to snap at you. I got the heartburn and I'm feeling achy.

No offence taken, ma'am. Just remember to rest at the other end.

Seems strange that they've set up in a church.

Strange?

The clinic was always good enough for me.

Oh, of course. But the quotas are up this year.

Quotas? What quotas?

She looks up to see if he will answer her, but in the waves of dissonance that come like gusts around her flailing spirit, he has floated away. His sudden departure gives her a queer feeling. Like she is lying on a rug instead of . . . or maybe it's just the church. Because she can't breathe in a church. She hasn't even entered one for a long time. A funny thing, too. As a girl in Saskatoon, she loved to go to church, and even after she met Hardy Mudge, and he'd started balking at the prospect of sermons and singing hymns every week, she would insist on going with or without him. What a little church mouse she had been.

Her mind is wandering. She has never approved of minds that wander.

A children's choir with those little cardboard wings is singing an old-fashioned love song. She looks up at the front pews. She doesn't recognize a single soul. The people who are finished are filing into the chapel or sitting together up at the front, doctor's orders, no doubt, in their white whatchamacallits. Thirty minutes, they always say. Just to be sure.

Ethel is dying for a cigarette. The doctor, the lung fellow, he urged her half a dozen times to stop, but she is set in her ways. Old habits are better than no habits at all. Sitting next to her is a lady who looks familiar. She asks the lady how much longer.

Not long at all. I've already been.

The lady's voice echoes, and then it seems to slow down to a low groan. Ethel wants to ask her, if she's already been, why in the dickens is she sitting down here and not over there with the others. But Ethel doesn't want to sound ill-informed in case she is mistaken about something.

Perhaps we might get reacquainted, says the lady in a normal voice.

Say, are you one of those religious types?

The lady laughs in a scoffing sort of way, and her voice goes low and slow again. She is up to something, you can tell.

I used to be your boss, says the lady, smiling sadly.

Like fun you were.

Ethel peers at her with a start. Oh, my, that husky dog's mistress, Mrs. Eggers herself.

So, that's how it is, says Ethel. I suppose you've come back here to give me a piece of your mind.

You think so, do you? And what have I come to tell you?

To give it back, of course. And I can't give you what I don't have. Besides, you're not part of my world anymore. I heard about your—

Cirrhosis of the liver. It happens more often than you think.

Mrs. Eggers looks away, gazing in the direction of the stained glass windows and the empty pews on the other side of the church. Ethel turns around to peek behind her. Just in case.

A simple apology would suffice, says the lady.

An apology.

It wouldn't kill you. I'm not letting you off that easy. I don't care about any of that stuff anymore, but I'd like to see if you've got the strength to own up.

Ethel whispers to the lady, For Heaven's sakes, that happened a long time ago. I scarcely remember what year it was. And besides, your husband said I could keep the blessed thing. It was a hard time for me and Rennie, I can tell you that.

Mrs. Eggers neither nods nor shakes her head. She sits and she sighs as though she has settled in for a long conversation.

I have no time for this nonsense, says Ethel.

Still, Mrs. Eggers waits, a faint smile on her lips. She isn't wearing lipstick—no makeup at all. Ethel has never seen Mrs. Eggers look so unadorned. It's hard to see her as that show-offy wife of a rich man.

Here's something that might amuse you, says her old employer. *Those gold bricks Joseph left me? I used to think I would go and . . . you know, have a gander at them in the vault. Well, Ethel, I never did do it. They must still be there! I couldn't get myself organized to deal with them; I couldn't be bothered. I didn't even make out a proper will.*

You mean you'll never get the use of them? Why in Heaven didn't you just sell the darn things?

Is that what you did with yours?

Of course. I had some help melting it down and all that. We sold it in bits and pieces.

Mrs. Eggers smiles sadly to herself. She says, *Maybe I just couldn't bear to.*

Pretty darn typical, is Ethel's view. Wealthy people don't have to make arrangements like other people do.

Ethel says, I could've sworn you kept those things hidden in the house.

Oh, yes, that was Joseph's idea. They reminded him of his days as a prospector. But before he passed on, I got him to take them to the vault.

Now, who gets them?

Oh, Ethel, she says in a slow, echoing voice. *That's not the point . . . oint . . . oint . . .*

They sit there silently, Mrs. Eggers with that dreamy smile on her mug and Ethel simmering like a pressure cooker. She looks behind them again, just to check for . . . for . . . she cannot bear to think his name.

All right, I apologize. Are you satisfied? I did something that I'm not proud of, but there you go. Some of us have to eat—

I know, I know, says Mrs. Eggers.

Her voice is surprisingly gentle. Very strange, this new version of Mrs. Eggers. A person you can feel comfortable with, a person you can tell things to. Something in Ethel begins to relax, and her mind continues to wander.

Can I call you Melony?

You can call me Royal Bitch if you want.

Hah.

Mrs. Eggers turns around and scans the back of the church. *Ethel*, she says, *there's no one behind us. Why do you keep looking there?*

I have this notion. I can't help it. I'm afraid my ex-husband is going to show up. Don't laugh. Hardy had this habit of always showing up at the wrong time. He was such a deadbeat.

I never knew, says Mrs. Eggers.

Hardy was a deadbeat and a drunk and a womanizer. And I was stupid enough to fall for him.

Men, says Mrs. Eggers.

Oh, this one was a charmer. Full of talk. Do you want to hear something funny? I once fell in love with my boss. At a jewellery store downtown. Elliot Schuman, you may have heard of him. But he was already married.

To Maisy Lipscott.

You know him?

Mr. Schuman has done very well for himself. I didn't see his wife very often.

Maisy was a nice enough lady, I suppose. But Elly was very kind to me, and he seemed to return my affection. I mean, we never *did* anything back then, but once he gave me this big hug and I think . . . I think we both knew . . .

There, there.

He said he had to let me go.

Imagine that.

Oh, what's the use of yattering about it? I have no use for regret, I can tell you. But anyway, Elly fired me. He had to. That was a terrible time for Rennie and me. Things got tight, and then one cold day, I made off with your . . .

I see, says Melony.

I didn't plan to steal the thing. But when I saw it lying there, with all the other ones, looking so beautiful, I thought, why not just one of them for my own, you know?

Yes, yes.

Ethel's eyes keep misting up. It's annoying, and after all those years, too. And now her phone is ringing. That would be Elly. She turns back to Mrs. Eggers to say goodbye, but the lady is gone. She has simply vanished.

The children are still singing the same old love song. The last thing you'd expect to hear in a church. It smells like the fibres in somebody's rug.

Her phone keeps ringing.

Another lady in a plain white smock comes up to her and takes her by the hand, and Ethel lets out a dry cough. It has to be the smoke.

Hold on, stop tugging, she tells the new lady. I'm not gettin' any younger.

Not to worry. It'll be all over in a moment.

I know.

The new lady smiles vaguely. *You sit down right over here, and we'll deck you out.*

Deck me out?

Oh, you know what I mean. You'll walk through that door and feel like a brand-new person.

Through what door? she says. But when she looks up, the woman in the white smock is gone, and Ethel is sprawled face-down on the floor and her phone is ringing and the children are singing to her as though she is the only person in the church. She finds that she can move. She rolls over, puffing fiercely, and drags herself upright so that her nose is level with the end table in her living room. She reaches for the phone and clutches it.

"Hello, Elly?"

"My dear," he says, "have I phoned at a bad time?"

the carl quartet

I
Whutzisname Remembered

IT MUSTA BEEN AWAY BACK, God only knows. Rainy night. I found a party somewheres on Queen. Somebody in . . . I think it was the Cana Apartments. All I had was six bits in my pocket but I needed a drink real bad, so hell, why not sponge a gargle or two? Then I seen this scrawny guy in rubber boots with a forty of vodka.

You mean . . . whutzisname?

Yeah, same feller.

I used to serve him in the King George some time ago. He was a very thirsty man. Not a bad guy. Considering.

Anyhow, at this party, eh, I figure I'd hit the jackpot. We had a drink or two and then—I don't remember how exactly—but me and him get into a shouting match. Before I know it, we're outside, squaring off in front of the building. I look up, and there's the cops. Just like that, I'm in the paddy wagon. Hardly even touched the guy. Maybe I give him a poke or two. Yeah.

But what was his name?

Hell, I can remember the name of the frickin' apartments, but I can't for the life of me remember his name.

Names can be a bugger.

Anyways, here I am, near cold sober in a goddam paddy wagon. It's dark in there. But our guy, whutzisname with the rubber boots, he's in there with me, laughing. It's this deep laugh, *wowokwok,* like a frickin' warthog. I can tell by the smell he's really soaked up his share of the booze. I sez, Well, they got you too, eh?

Wokwokwok.

He's so far gone I figure he can't even hear me proper. I sez, whaddya laughin' at, pal?

Fuckin cops, he says. Tried to take my bottle away.

Right.

But I fooled 'em, he says.

Coulda fooled me, pal.

This scrawny guy, he pulls off one a his rubber boots real careful? Like if he didn't do it just right he'd lose a leg or something? Then he takes off his sock. Real slow. There's this smell, and I mean booze? Faaawk.

I says, What'd you do, pal, fall into a tubba home brew?

Wokwokwok.

Hey?

Nope, he says, I didn't fall into no tubba home brew. When I saw the cops coming, I take what's left a the vodka and I pours it into my boot.

This guy, I swear he starts to wring out his sock into his boot. He raises the boot to his mouth, and down she goes. He turns to me, he says, Still enough for a nightcap. Pal.

No.

No shit.

His name is on the tip of my tongue.

Yeah. A frickin' miracle. And you know, it wasn't all that bad? I've had worse. I swear I've had worse.

He used to drink right here, whutzisname. A pint and a whisky chaser, one after the other. Haven't seen him around for a while.

Yeah, been a while.

Maybe he's just moved on.

Yeah.

I think his name was Carl.

2
Wonderland

Don't open the window, she said, or that hellion's gonna fly.

If he flies, he flies, he said.

She said, We promised, remember? We are responsible.

It was hard to feel responsible in a dump like this. It had been a hot day, and the heat inside their friend's apartment was building. When she left for her meeting, he opened the window. The window looked out on a dry patch of lawn. There was a large electric fan on the table. He adjusted the angle of the fan to get a cross draft and pushed the high button. Sure as hell, that hairy bastard made for the end table and leaped straight out the window. Four storeys up.

He never should have pushed the high button.

He figured he had less than two hours to find that son of a bitch or think of a good excuse. He leaned out the window and scanned the yard for signs of dead or injured rabbits.

The yard was a small patch of dried grass enclosed by a chain-link fence. It was cluttered with cast-off stuff. Not a rabbit in sight. Directly below his window was a third-floor balcony. It belonged to a drunk named Carl.

He ran downstairs and knocked on Carl's door. He knocked louder, waited, and knocked again several times. Carl's door was unlocked. He rushed in, heading for the balcony, and there sat Carl with a glass of vodka, staring at a game of solitaire. He said hi to Carl, and Carl offered him a drink.

There were two chairs. Carl was slumped in one of them. The rabbit sat in the other. Neither Carl nor the rabbit seemed unduly ruffled by the situation. Perhaps the rabbit thought that this was what people did on the outside—sat quietly of an evening and drank vodka. Perhaps Carl thought that, under certain conditions, rabbits fell from the sky.

Carl drank with some guys who called themselves Alcoholics Unanimous. He told his buddies that this time, it was rabbits.

One of the guys said, Never happened to me, man. Bugs, maybe, but rabbits from the sky?

Another one of Carl's buddies seemed to object. Rabbits, man, that's just fucked-up.

You ain't seen nothin' yet, said Carl. This is just the beginning.

The rabbit's name was Mr. Stiffy.

3
What Kind of a Story

Carl finds himself hunched over on a dusty lawn chair in someone's garage, surrounded by things in containers. He does a cursory inspection of his body as though he has just walked in on this fallen version of himself. Everything in the garage is dusty—even the cobwebs look exhausted—but his eyes are receptive to the semi-dark. It beats the glare of daylight any time. Roundup. WD-40. TREMCLAD. Raid. A genie proclaiming the virtues of Lepage Sure Grip Carpenter's Glue. A rectangular can of chain oil (*You're in luck when you got a McCalla chainsaw!*). Like the glue genie, the oil-can fellow announces these words from a long time ago.

The garage must be a century old, more like a large wooden shed than a modern garage. Its rotten window ledge is a graveyard for flies. Probably there hasn't been a car in here for decades. He doesn't even know how he found himself in here, oozing vodka from every pore.

He lives alone and no longer wonders what comes next because there's nothing left to wonder about. He used to be a smart enough guy, people said. He was married once, worked hard, drove a car like anybody else. People said he was useful, smart, had a mischievous sense of humour. How on earth can a man just up and lose his sense of humour? There's a friendly woman in the apartment across the street from his whose husband goes up north for three weeks and comes home for two. He does this all year round, but our buddy here, he's forgotten whether this is an up week or a down week. What kind of a man forgets a thing like that?

A Betty Crocker calendar is nailed to the wall, and leaning in the corner, barely visible, are a garden fork, a broken rake, and a turf shovel. There's an old black telephone sitting on a shelf by his knee, up higher, an electric hedge clipper attached to a well-worn cord, and next to that, a quart sealer half-full of orange liquid. His gaze returns to the telephone. Just like the one that used to sit in a small alcove in his childhood home. The alcove was recessed and rounded at the top like a shrine.

Jesus. He can almost remember the phone number.

Carly is old enough to have a dog, but he can't have one because Mum says it might bother the twins. Maybe next year. Goody Spears had a dog; Carly's dad had a dog when he was growing up. Carly's mum is on the phone. She says, *Sure, yeah, you want a good-lookin' fella, charming . . . well, of course, all those things, wealthy, yeah, nice car . . . yes! Always listens to your . . . Gladdie, I wanted the same damn thing . . . yeah . . . uh huh . . . yeah . . .*

Carly's mum, she can go like this all afternoon, he doesn't care, Goody Spears is coming over, they're going to the varine, he doesn't have a dog no more because something happened. Carly's mum just keeps on, *blabberty blabberty*. Carly's dad doesn't talk so much; he works at the shop, he fixes radios, he says, maybe when you're bigger, you can have a dog, but Carly wants to know, what's bigger got to do with it?

. . . he has to appreciate the finer things, right, have a sense of humour,

but y'know, Gladdie, these days, hell, I'm happy if my old man takes a bath now and then, I'm happy if he doesn't drive off till I'm inside the car...

Carly's mum is making a cake, it's the Betty Crocker kind, and she lets Carly lick the spoon. The twins are too young to lick the spoon, and they're asleep now. Mum hangs up the phone. She's still laughing—

Say, young man, what are you up to?

Goody's comin' over, remember?

Isn't he a bit old for you?

Goody had a dog when he was old as me. He had a real nice little dog.

Well, he doesn't have a dog now.

She goes back into the kitchen to her cake, it's got hard maple icing and raisins.

Something has come over him, memories or whatever. He's got the telephone on his lap, crud all over it and a rusted dial. Somebody's mother smiles down at him from the calendar, but who would've put that calendar on the wall? Why would a person hang onto an old calendar whose time was up donkeys' years ago? But think. *Think,* goddamn it, what's that phone doing on his knee?

Now the knee is shaking. He clamps down on the phone so his knee won't shake so bad. He gazes back up at the 1950s mother on the calendar. She has a reassuring smile that you hope will never go away. *Carly,* she seems to say, *do you want to lick the spoon?*

Jesus, yes! he whispers to the walls and the smudged window of the garage. Because the number has come back to him. Eight—two—one—eight—two.

He tries to dial the numbers. Each time the dial swirls back, his hands are shaking, and his knee is shaking, and it's no damn good. He takes a few long breaths. He nails it on the second try.

Hello?

Can I speak to Carly, please?

I'm Carly.

Well, that's a nice name. My name is Carl, too.

The man on the phone talks like an old man, but Carly doesn't know an old man named Carl.

Honey, who's that on the phone? says Carly's mum.

No one, says Carly.

Are you going out to play? says the old man.

Carly doesn't say anything.

Carly, please. Are you going out to play? I want you to tell old Carl.

Yup, says Carly.

Carly, let me guess. Are you going out to play with Goody Spears?

Hey, how did you know? Me an' Goody, we're gonna play in the varine.

In the ravine?

Yeah, how come you know?

I'm Carl. I know everything that Carly knows.

Carly starts to laugh.

Honey, who is that on the phone?

There's this man on the phone says he's me!

What?

Carly says, Hey, who are you really?

I'm your friend, Carly, and I have to tell you something very important.

Carly is giggling. He says, What?

This is very important, Carly. Are you listening?

How can you be Carl and me be Carl?

Carly. Please. Are you listening?

Yup.

This is so important, Carly. It's more important than Christmas and your birthday and the twins' birthday all in one. It . . . it could change your whole life.

What could change my whole life?

Carly's mum, she comes into the hallway and towers over him. She's holding the big wooden spoon. It's used for icing and spankings both.

Carl, you call me Carl too, okay?

Okay, what could change my whole life?

Honey, who is that? His mum makes a grab for the telephone, but Carly twists away from her.

Shhh, he whispers to his mum. It's Carl!

Are you listening, Carly? Here's the whole thing, fella. Repeat after me, okay? Do.

Do?

Do not.

Do not?

Do not go.

Do not go?

Do not go out.

Do not go out?

Do not go out and.

Do not go out and. And what?

Do not go out and play with Goody Spears.

How come?

Please, Carly, please. Do not go out and play in the ravine with Goody Spears. Never never. Promise me, okay?

How come?

Because something bad will happen to you.

Hey, Mister, who are you?

Please, Carly, promise me!

You're not Carl. You're somebody else!

Carly, wait. I've got a little scar next to my belly button. Do you hear me? It's from a fish hook, remember?

Daddy?

No, this is not your dad. You know that. He's at the repair shop, and he's real busy right now. Don't cry, Carly. Just remember, Goody Spears is a . . . a bully, a sick boy. He likes to hurt little boys like you. You know what he did to his dog?

Carly's mum grabs the phone. Say, who is this?

Carly hears a little voice above him, like the voice of a cricket.

I hope you're proud of yourself, whoever you are, making a little boy cry. If you ever show up—you're what? You're trying to warn him? Say, what kind of a story is that? He does, does he? And how would you know?

The little voice above him keeps chirping away in his mum's hand, but Carly can't quite make out the words, something about a dog, it's like the words are mostly in cricket. He looks away up. His mum is nodding, and then she stops nodding. She looks down at Carly with a great big worry on her face.

4
Just Supposing

A scrawny man in his seventies contemplates some dishevelled columns of cards on the table. He half-listens to a song from the kitchen radio. From that famous guy who died. Nice that a famous guy can sing a brand-new song on the radio after he dies. Nice for the famous guy, anyway.

I'd like to write for prisoners who need a new guru,
I'd like to write for hopeless drunks, I'd like to write for you.

No one has dropped in or phoned him lately, but that doesn't seem to matter. What matters today is this impasse he has come to in a game of solitaire because the three of clubs is proving to be elusive.

He's thirsty. Not thirsty as in days of old, with all that hell-bound hilarity. A glass of water sits above him next to an empty flower vase. The glass reminds him of that other thirst, where a funny sort of magic could pop up and take over. He has conquered that thirst and continues each day to keep it at bay by avoiding his former haunts and his drinking buddies. Sobriety is its own reward, but with its arrival, the magic has vanished. Solitaire is his only addiction, and solitaire becomes boring after about the tenth game. The game, therefore, is its own aversion therapy.

He congratulates himself on this insight.

The dead guy on the radio growls out his words, a voice from the bottom of a gravel pit. Brand-new song from a dead guy. In a dreamy moment, Carl wonders if that isn't a sort of magic.

My poem might mean something, but I'm not allowed to
know it,
It needs a new cryptology; it needs a better poet.

Eyes still on the cards, he fumbles for his glass of water and topples the vase. It shatters on the floor.

Shit.

Fumes from the shards of pottery rise from the floor, and from the fumes, a genie appears. Or else it doesn't appear. It depends on your perspective.

What is your wish?

Slowly, Carl awakens from his torpor. He peers at the genie, an old-fashioned sort of fellow in a yellow golf shirt and pale blue Fortrel pants. He returns to his cards, sighs, then takes a second look at the genie.

I get a wish?

I grant you one wish, says the genie in a voice grown haughty with boredom.

I thought you guys always granted three wishes.

We used to. A trace of desolation appears on the genie's lips, his eyes. We're not so much in demand these days. I'm not sure anyone believes in magic anymore. To tell you the truth, I think we're getting replaced by smartphones. My people think of it as downsizing.

The genie takes a long breath and releases it. So. One is all you get. You can ask for a woman to love or a bag full of gemstones. You know, the usual.

Carl nods wearily at the shelf from which the vase has toppled, perusing the chapters of his life. Divorced by the first wife. Lost the second one, the nice one, to heart problems. He has turned stingy, has no place to spend his old-age cheques. He has survived a brutal cancer, and even though he looks like road kill, his cancer is in remission. A passionate love affair, what would that be like in his present state? Maybe he should wish for a stretch of good health and the return of his old energy. But then he might start drinking again, and he wouldn't get the wonderful woman.

He looks down at the shattered vase, a wedding gift from his second marriage. He'll have to clean that up. He may be living like a bachelor, but these days, he likes his digs to be tidy.

You seem bored with your life, says the genie.

Wokwokwok!

Seriously, Carl, you seem bored.

I do okay.

Playing solitaire in the middle of the day? In your pyjamas? You call that okay?

He has forgotten that he's still in his pyjamas.

What about engagement with life? says the genie. What about your friends, your community?

What about them? Are you doing any better? You don't even wear swami clothes. Is your phone ringing off the hook? You got a whole raft of swami friends? A swami lifestyle?

I'm not a swami, I'm a genie. There's a vast difference. And it's you we're talking about.

Carl stares with renewed curiosity at the genie. He doesn't seem like a bad guy, just a bit of a dullard. He has a disenchanted look about him, as though, for him, depression is the norm.

Carl says, This doesn't count as a wish, okay? This is just supposing. What if my wish was to ask you to join me here? Keep living in this house, and we could shoot the shit now and then. I'd get you a new vase, that goes without saying.

In bewilderment, the genie looks around the room. Carl can tell that the genie has probably never had to field this one before.

We could talk about genie stuff. We could talk about, say . . . what's that thing that happens when you return as a rabbit?

Reincarnation? says the genie.

Yeah! We could talk about things like that.

We don't do reincarnation. That's for swamis.

But surely, Carl shouts, surely you know stuff that I don't have a clue about? Genie stuff?

No need to get excited, says the genie. Calm down. What about the yearnings of your heart? What about passion and love and lifelong companionship?

What do I call you?

We don't give out names, says the genie.

Look, fella, I got nothing against love and passion, okay? But I don't think I'm up for that anymore. I'm barely alive. I've been through some hard times. Tell you the truth, I've been to hell and back. Booze, sickness, bad company, bad decisions, wife's dead, you name it. It's over for me. And I've finally . . . you know . . .

Laid your ghosts to rest? says the genie.

You could say that.

The genie is looking at his watch. Maybe he has to strike a deal with a new client or just relocate to a new vase. Carl looks away, and the memory of a smile appears on his lips.

I know something that might help me on my way, he says.

Tell me your wish, and it shall be so, my good fellow.

I would die for a three of clubs.

And lo, Carl's wish is granted.

reincarnation

July 5, 2019

VERONICA CALLED ME LAST NIGHT. I had spent a nothing day stuck in my head, so I picked up my phone.

"I know this is a bit weird," she said, "but they need a swami."

"What do I have to do?"

"I don't know. Swami stuff. It happens next month."

"So, like, I float out of a big vase and do magic tricks?"

"No, you idiot. That's what genies do. Swamis tell fortunes."

"Isn't that what gypsies do?"

Veronica cracked up. Smoker's laugh. It blasts out of her like exhaust from a bad muffler, and she gasps to get her breath back. I could almost smell the smoke. But good to hear. For months, she's been working on a committee to organize a reunion at Lowland Composite High. And this time, there is no question that I will do her bidding. This venture out into the world feels like I'm about to parachute from a plane. And I've never been good with heights. I have picked the wrong month to try to quit my panic pills.

Last week, finally, I asked Veronica where the money had come from. Couldn't stop myself, just blurted out the question. She was still puffing and wheezing from the stairs. She peered disapprovingly into the unclean corners of my flat. She handed me my meds.

"Who paid my share of the billings?" I said.

With all those medical personnel, all my drugs, post-op care, it had to be a lot of money, and Medicare and insurance would only go so far on such a new procedure. I persisted with more questions. Was it some sort of medical foundation in the States that topped up the funding? Was it something like the Canadian Wish Foundation? Who had paid such a large portion of my bills?

"It's all been taken care of," she said.

"You always say that. I don't think I believe you."

She glared at me for a long, indecisive moment. She has a very expressive face. If she lost a hundred pounds, it would be a pretty face. This particular glare seemed to beam out a conflicting range of emotions. Including anger. And then I knew.

"Oh, fuck no," I said.

The glare persisted. "Oh, fuck yes."

"How much did it all cost?"

"You don't want to know," she said at last.

"But where did you get all the—"

"Not from Daddy Dearest," was all she said.

My sister has recently turned thirty-two. She and I have always been closer to each other than to our parents or anyone else. We are equally skeptical, equally sarcastic. I think we interpret the world for each other. If this were a journal and not a diary, I would write, *Veronica is lovely and plump because you can't have too much of something nice.* But this is my diary. In the last five or ten years, she has gone from sturdy to fleshy to bulky to fat. At first, she smoked cigarettes to lose weight, but now, she just smokes a lot. Like me, she goes through life dismayed about a lot of things, but there are always these jokes. She cracks them to get through the day.

"Your garret could use a vacuum cleaner," she said.

Veronica is very bossy, but even more so around me. She seems to think that I need a manager. And maybe sometimes she's right. I'm as smart as she is, but, as she puts it, I don't seem to have a rudder.

Veronica doesn't lack for rudders. She is so take-charge she makes our parents look adolescent by comparison. She could have been a professor or the CEO of some big company; she's that smart. But Veronica has chosen an unremarkable career as an agent with a small insurance franchise. She does mostly homes and vehicles. She likes to meet her clients in person and talk with them face-to-face as often as she can. Some of them she thinks of as family, and perhaps they think of her in the same way, because her connections with them make for a pretty active social life. Her small office is plastered with snapshots of her clients' children.

July 10, 2019

Got my courage up and had a look at Veronica's two photos. Before photos. The close-up one shook me to the core. The whole unbearable thing came roaring back, but not a word about it in my diaries. Can't believe I was too cowardly, too depressed to write some of it down. I acted like people in the aftermath of a nuclear meltdown. There are certain places you don't go walking.

The photos remind me of a Hallowe'en horror mask. The skin on most of my face was pale and shiny with angry red craters here and there, my features rearranged or missing. A slash for a mouth that I could open just enough to take in the straw. Ravaged eyelids, melted brows. Made me look like I'm in a permanent state of alarm. Where my nose used to be, two holes remained. Ears missing. People assumed I was deaf. I had just turned twenty-seven. I remember thinking my life was over.

When Veronica brought me the envelope containing the photos last month, she must have thought I was ready to revisit my mangled mug. Maybe she was tired of my whining and wanted to show me how far I'd come. I resisted opening the envelope till today. Had to sit down.

Two years ago in Saskatoon, while I was in the burn unit, Veronica began checking online for procedures available to Canadian casualties like me, and one night, she managed to make contact with a hospital that promised so many miracles that, at first, we were both dubious.

"But Garvey," she said, "they could totally re-make your face."

I just stared at my phone. I had to say something to my bossy older sister. She has always been there for me. Protector of my troubled youth when I was too small, geeky and friendless to fend off school bullies. But bossy, yes. Veronica the Insister.

I asked her what I was supposed to do.

"Let me take your picture."

That's what did it for us. Their response to our application was pretty quick. It brought Veronica puffing up the stairs. Instead of her usual complaints about my third-floor flat, she was smiling.

"They want to model your new mug on the face of a celebrity. Your choices are Donald Trump or Donald Duck."

Then it was off to Toronto. On the morning of my procedure, I tried (yet again) to pump Veronica for info on her arrangements. It's hard to talk through a mangled mouth. *Sherioushly!* I kept saying. She was deliberately vague.

"There's a committee that decides," she said. "Canadian surgeons are learning this procedure, and they need a new burn victim. The more grotesque, the better."

It seemed I had won a beauty contest. I was only the fourth patient in Canada to have this procedure. The team amounted to six or seven surgeons, one from the States, and a large complement of medical personnel. Veronica and I flew out together and went straight to St. Martin's Hospital, where transplant research for burn victims had been going on for some years.

In the first phase of the operation, the surgeons scraped, teased out, and lifted the tatters of my face. Hours later, they replaced it with the face of a young athlete from a terminal ward. He had willed his body to the hospital's parts department, as Veronica put it.

The second step was to bring down the new face like a rubber mask over my skull and begin the anti-rejection drugs that would allow the face and skull to bond. In less than a month, the numbness began to recede. I could place my fingers on my new cheeks and feel them. My earbuds fit perfectly. My new mouth and bionic jawbone began to acquire a jerky mobility. My face lacked the proper musculature and, therefore, the expressive range of its former owner. Day after day, my face has remained mostly in neutral, which makes it a good face for being aloof. No stretch there. And now, miracle of miracles, I have the beginnings of a crop of whiskers.

"Happy now?" says Veronica.

"Happy?"

"Grateful, then?"

"I'm more afraid than anything."

Veronica stares at me as though she were searching for a better person.

July 14, 2019

My face reminds me of someone I've seen before, but I can't quite make the connection. No one but Veronica will know it's me. She has promised. I will be the most mysterious swami that Lowland High has ever had. This doesn't help my nerves in the slightest.

July 17, 2019

My shrink tells me that she's proud of me that I finally looked at my pictures. Proud of me! She likes that I've been able to revisit the trauma of the operation and the despairing times that preceded it. I've never let her read my diary. She tells me that's okay. Just go back further in my journaling. I trust my shrink, I like her, but at times, she gets a bit fervent. Go back, she says, to the time that led up to the accident. Write it all down.

Here goes. My accident came on the heels of my breakup with Orchid late in 2016. We had been in the same class in our last year at Lowland High. A few years on, we got together. In high school, she had been Marian Price, but in this phase of her life, she was just Orchid. I must admit, I've never had much luck with people who boast only one name. Orchid admired me for my aloof and disapproving ways, my important-looking books and mags. She liked the fact that I had broken ties with my parents. I was only a sessional lecturer in the psychology department, but she thought of me as a professor. I felt unworthy of her body, which had much to recommend it. She didn't seem to mind my begoggled looks and geeky smile. She once said I looked ANIMATED when I spoke about my graduate work. But I was bewildered by her devotion to such things as spiritual healing, self-help books, and online Buddhism. When she talked about these things, she went all fluid and fuzzy. She told me once that if crystals could be used for healing, they could be just as handy for reading auras and horoscopes. Apparently, in some circles, you can still get away with that kind of thinking. But I was determined not to seem judgmental about her beliefs.

She loves me, she loves me not, she loves me, she loves me not. With Orchid, that was my daily mantra. How pathetic is that?

"You could be a fortuneteller," I told her.

She gave me her skeptical look. "That is so not me."

"They make a lot of money," I said, beaming at my suggestion. "That's why they're called fortunetellers."

She did not appreciate my sense of humour, or anyone else's, it seemed. That was Veronica's view of things.

There wasn't even a breaking point. We had never really argued. Maybe just disagreed a lot toward the end. I went down to Regina for a few days to do a workshop on professional ethics. When I came back, Orchid had moved out. She had dumped me for a man who could channel angels and prophets online.

I was stunned by the fact that I'd never sleep with her again. I started walking through the streets at night. It was a way of getting out of my flat anonymously, and walking somehow diverted me from thoughts of ending it all. Finally, one stormy evening in November, I got a case of the stupids. I borrowed Veronica's Honda Civic and, fuelled by determination and ecstasy, I sailed unbuckled into a blizzard on Highway 5. The Honda collided with a snowplow, jolting my skull against the windshield. I woke up to the sensation of a man grunting, dragging me from the burning car as my face crackled and bubbled. Body bruised, face fried. Never even thanked the guy.

During my first year of recovery, I got my voice back. A low, gravelly sound. This development was no comfort. I had adjusted to silence in the presence of visitors to the burn unit. During that time, with the exception of Veronica, I felt disinclined to speak to anyone. I thought of my smartphone as a table ornament. When the gravelly voice proclaimed itself to me, I persisted, at first with some success, in the pretense that I was mute. This allowed me to disengage from conversations with my blustering father and my pill-popping mother when they flew out from Victoria for a visit.

Sitting in silence in the presence of people eager to prattle, or deliver monologues, or commiserate with me—this felt like a return to my troubled adolescence when I used to flee to the boys' washroom in the basement of my old high school and lock myself in a cubicle. In Grades 10 and 11, hiding from my schoolmates and teachers became an acquired skill, a specialty of mine.

July 24, 2019

My shrink's name is Sara. She insists that I call her that and stop addressing her as Dr. Glassman. She's not a psychiatrist, she's a psychologist, so forget the doctor stuff. She *really* likes that I'm about to come out of my closet and play swami at my high school reunion. I'm scared shitless about this sudden exposure to my old high school connections: the awful memories, the assholes who taunted me. Sara told me to go back to my diary and re-encounter my time at the school. I hate to let her down, but it's too depressing to revisit those memories. I told her this, and she said, *This is your recovery. Try something else, but keep writing your entries.*

Same day

Gazed at my new face. I'm not used to it yet. Who is this guy in the mirror looking out at me? Reminds me of a movie star, but not a movie idol. More like what they call an actor. I don't see many movies, but I think he played villains.

July 26, 2019

My recovery.

Returned to Saskatoon after a long stay at Toronto St. Martin's Hospital. I had this new face to get used to. I was afraid of leaving my flat. (That hasn't changed much.) Afraid of traffic and noise. Afraid to fly to Victoria and make nice with my parents. Afraid that I might run into Orchid and her loony boyfriend.

I've never been an extrovert like my sister. Even at age twenty-nine, I tend to be shy around people. And now, in the city of my various humiliations, I am even more of a loner. I always tended to keep friends at a distance, but I never wanted to feel this alone.

My job helps. I do the night shifts out in the industrial burbs, sorting mail at a Canada Post depot. I like the absence of conversation.

My collision was like a death. People here have forgotten about me. My accident was noted briefly in the *Saskatoon Star-Phoenix*, but there was no coverage of my big operation in Toronto, my big chance at a new life. As far as I could tell, no one had ever heard about it except readers of the *Toronto Sun*. This was strangely comforting because although I felt a terrible isolation, I welcomed my newfound anonymity. Maybe the other way around: although I have welcomed my anonymity, I still feel a terrible isolation. I have resolved that there is nothing to be done. My latest mantra. Even now, in the grip of all this apathy, I look at my new face in the mirror as though I've taken on a roommate, and we have to make friends with each other.

July 28, 2019

The counselling process with Sara is going smoothly these days. I write my entry and we discuss it the same week. She's still okay with not reading my entries so long as I keep up with the writing. So. Here goes nothing.

School Days, School Days. Lowland Composite High School was a 1920s-era brick edifice in a middle-class neighbourhood. Its basement housed a boiler room, an industrial arts shop, a detention room, and a large classroom for girls who took typing and shorthand. The academic classes were taught above ground on the first and second floors, and so the school became a class-divided territory between a minority of students who went down for training and discipline and a majority of students who stayed up for enlightenment. The washrooms in the basement were dimly lit, the plumbing badly rusted. The air that lingered in the boys' washroom was laced with the aroma of various excretions.

In my many flights of fear, boredom, and misery, I perched, knees to chin, on a toilet adjacent to the sinks. I felt a scurvy sort of belonging there in the basement washroom, and I soon learned things about my fellow students and a handful of teachers who frequented it. I was a whiz at math, French, Social Studies, etc. But in my first two years at Lowland High, while vultching in my cubicle, I also learned about sex: forbidden sex, awkward sex, sometimes coerced, and sometimes (though less frequently) romantic.

I remember a bully who used to grab girls and hustle them into the boys' room for some aggressive snogging. I remember the girls' volleyball coach, known to all of us as Mr. Fingers. He, too, had his favourites for boys'-room recreation. I remember Ernie Marshall, an arrogant jock who loved to humiliate outcasts like me. He and his teammates did a swarming in my dark domain. They picked on a gay kid, and I heard it all. It was more about humiliation than bloodshed. They cut his hair and let him go.

August 5, 2019

BEWARE THE SWAMI!

Too much has happened over the last two days. I have to get it down on my laptop before I forget the details. My diary. Always the best of friends we are, but even more so right now.

I walked over to Lowland High by myself. I wouldn't let Veronica drive me, but she was there to greet me in the front lobby. We agreed that I would be Veronica's friend Rupert. Beats Garvey all to hell. She gave me a tour of the gymnasium and the classrooms nearby, where a large crew of ex-Lowlanders were finishing preparations. The school has a new name, Mildred Kerr High, and it's had a big facelift, but it smells the same.

The reunion would take place on Saturday and Sunday afternoons. It was going to be huge. The organizers had decided on a circus theme. There would be games of chance, demonstrations, troubadours, cosplay. Some of the school's cheerleaders would do their old dance routines. But according to Veronica, their designated swami had fallen ill. My job would be to sit in a tent where people would donate money to the school's scholarship fund and get their fortunes told. The routine had something to do with reincarnation.

"Tell them they'll return as a brain surgeon or a priest," said Veronica.

"Or a snake," I said.

"Or a snake. Why not?" she said, with a despairing glance at the ceiling.

A colleague from Veronica's insurance company got me rigged up in my tent. Jade Kratchmer, a former cheerleader. Still quite lean and lovely. I recognized her from my solitary years at Lowland High. She smeared my face first with cold cream and then with brown makeup. It was oddly pleasurable, the feeling of her fingers on my new face. No one had touched my face in ages. She told me I reminded her of that movie star who killed himself last year. We couldn't remember his name.

"And now, Rupert, it's time for the sexiest part of all."

She brought out her university convocation robe, a bright green cloak with a gold silk mantle. By now, it was plain as day that Jade Kratchmer was flirting with me. She placed an orange turban on my head. She and Veronica gazed at me approvingly.

When we were alone, I said to Veronica, "What if someone recognizes me?"

I can't believe I said that.

The lineup began to form after lunch. Aided by a Hollywood-Arab accent and a large round light fixture from Veronica's apartment, I moved into my role, telling people about their reincarnations or predicting their fortunes. After a dozen or so of these, I realized I was enjoying myself. All my studies in psychology, all of my detached observations of people throughout the years, a favourite course in criminology, all of this seemed to enhance my role as swami.

Without warning, Ernie Marshall walked in. My favourite tormentor, circa 2005. He had gained a lot of weight, but he was instantly recognizable. The same swagger, the same easy good looks, the jaunty charm. Veronica ushered him in, beaming conspiratorially. After a moment, his wife joined us, and Veronica slipped out of the tent.

I invited Ernie to sit down. His wife stood expectantly behind him.

"Gimme the goods, Mr. Swami."

I looked into my crystal ball, and I gave him the goods.

"Your name," I whispered. "I can't be sure, but it has military associations, yes?"

"Not bad," said Ernie.

"Very good," said his wife.

"What about my first name?" said Ernie.

"First names are harder," I said. "But you find yourself on the path of earnest atonement. Ernest? Could that be your first name?"

"Wow," said Ernie's wife.

"What's this atonement bit?" said Ernie in an unusually shy voice.

I returned to my crystal ball. "I see a young man. A small young man . . . with long hair, surrounded by big fellows in a dungeon. Your atonement concerns this young fellow and perhaps others like him."

"A dungeon?" said Ernie.

"The image is not clear. But his captors have swarmed around him, and they want to cut . . . ah, this is strange. They are cutting his hair. A frightened young man, what people in your country call . . . a gay?"

After an incredulous silence and some nervous mutterings, Ernie Marshall retreated.

I hesitate to reveal this episode to Sara because it might reflect badly on me. I especially hesitate to reveal my intense feelings of excitement, the extreme sense of gratification that I felt when Ernie Marshall and his wife exited my tent, that aroused look of curiosity on her face. Yesterday, I was self-exiled, fearful, despairing. Today, I sensed a power pulsing through my veins that I had never felt before.

Not long afterwards, without any warning, Orchid and her otherworldly boyfriend entered my tent. I was speechless until Orchid placed her hands on my crystal ball.

"Take your hands off the Galinda," I said.

She withdrew her hands as though my crystal ball might electrocute her.

"The what?" her boyfriend said. He was a tall weed of a man with a shiny pelt of long hair and some hair beneath his lower lip.

As far as I know, there is no such thing as a Galinda.

"Who shall be first to hear their destiny?" I peered up at Orchid. "Madam?" I said, and she sat down, peering suspiciously at me.

"You may now touch the Galinda."

Our fingers met from each side of the globe.

"You are suspicious of fortunetellers?" I said, and she shrugged at me.

"Ah," I said, looking into my makeshift globe, "you present yourself as a flower."

"Huh?"

"A tulip, perhaps?"

"Oh, my God," she said. "How could you possibly . . . like, my name is literally Orchid!"

"Wow," said the boyfriend, and he moved closer to me, gawking at my crystal ball. Veronica's crystal ball.

"And a spirit hovers over your sleep at night," I said. A wounded spirit."

She trilled out a nervous laugh.

"There was an accident, perhaps?"

"No," she said, "I've never been in an accident."

"Perhaps this wounded spirit was a friend? Ah, now I see it. A lover, a solitary man, a tortured soul, yes?"

"Oh, fuck," she said. She glanced at her boyfriend a moment, then returned her gaze searchingly to me. "This guy I was dating, he was, like, really into me, and I'm like, *You're too intense*, and he just drove away one day and disappeared."

"Ah, but the Galinda," I said. "There was an accident?"

"Oh yeah, that too. His name is Garvey."

"His name *was* Garvey," I said. "He is gone from the Earth. He has passed in sorrow from this world and risen to the seventh sphere, this Garvey. He tries to speak with you at night from the seventh sphere."

"Holy shit," said the boyfriend.

"The seventh sphere?" said Orchid.

"This means," I said, "that he is, ah, how should I say, favoured by the gods."

"What about me?" said Orchid.

"You walk in the shadows," I said. "And you walk with a pretender."

Orchid recoiled and withdrew her hands. Suddenly, she seemed to resent me every bit as much in this role as she had done when we lived together. She rose awkwardly from her chair, and they both stared in wonder at me.

As they backed out of the tent, I cried out, "My child, you are fading, fading. Oh, my child, you are lost."

It was hard to keep from laughing.

The afternoon unfolded pleasantly. I revelled in the memory of Orchid and her boyfriend fleeing my precious Galinda, backing out of the tent in . . . awe? Fear? Psychic disorder? All of the above? Don't I wish. There were men that I recognized from my old toilet-perching days. I outed them as best I could in front of their wives. I should have been alarmed by my little orgy of revenge, but I was exhilarated.

But who can I tell this to?

I was exhilarated until the Insister drove me home. OMINOUS SILENCE in the car. At last, Veronica told me that I could forget about being a swami on Sunday.

"Am I being chastised?" I said.

"You're being fired."

She told me that I had behaved mercilessly and that she was ashamed to be my sister. That arrogant jock, Ernie Marshall, for example. He was, in her words, *a nice guy*.

"He was a bully," I said. "At school, he treated me with contempt. He and his lout pals."

"He coaches kids in his spare time, bantam league hockey. His players come from reserves. He even buys their equipment for them."

I sat there for some time, staring ahead of me while Veronica fiddled with her rearview mirror. I offered her an excuse or two, and I apologized. She nodded but did not turn to face me.

"I hope you didn't tell him who Rupert—"

"Garvey, you have just asked the wrong question."

I've rarely seen the Insister as angry as this. She tore a mighty strip off me from head to toe. She unmasked me, you might say.

"I was just having a little fun with those idiots," I said. "I thought it was all kind of funny. I didn't mean to *hurt* them. Why are you so—"

"Those idiots, Garvey. Some of them have grown up. Young people do grow up. They grow up and they marry and do jobs and raise kids, and I doubt they hold grudges all their lives. You, by comparison . . . today, you reverted to adolescence. Did you see how distressed Orchid and her boyfriend were? No? Well, I did."

"I was putting them in their place," I said.

She turned and looked right into me. "When I took you through that procedure, I gave up half of my life. I thought you'd come back a new person, a kinder person. I thought you'd drop the aloof bullshit and get off your ass and . . . I thought I would come to feel proud of you again. Garvey, I used to be proud of you. Instead, you've come back as an asshole."

Her tearful tirade went on longer than I have recorded here.

As I got out of her car, Veronica said, "By the time you reach thirty, you will have to face some big questions. What have you done with your life, and who the hell are you going to be? Call me when you have some answers."

And then she drove away.

August 7, 2019

My precious solitude has become boring. My diary is no longer a refuge; it's a chore. I'm back on panic pills. Veronica may well be gone from my life, but I still have Sara. Admittedly, my orgy of revenge was a bit over the top. Have I been reincarnated as an asshole? Have I regressed morally? Scary questions. Can I use my gifts for good causes?

To be or not to be: the scariest question of all.

marty opens the door

SAILOR SHOWED up on Sunday morning in Marty's backyard, and Marty opened the door to greet him. Sailor was looking up at Marty's roof. From the patio, he pointed to a set of wooden stairs that led to the second floor.

"See that screen door up there?" Sailor said.

"Yeah."

Sailor pointed to the back door. "See that lock there?"

"Yeah."

"Both these doors, the one up there and this one, eh? Take about two seconds to break in with a crowbar. You got an alarm system?"

"No," said Marty, and he wondered if Helen would have revealed this much.

"You could get them doors secured real easy. Safety locks. Cost ya hunnerd, maybe two hunnerd bucks."

"Thanks," Marty said without much conviction.

Marty led the way behind his house to a half-ton, a loaner from his brother. He pointed to a concrete slab that lay in the bed on top of some cardboard. The slab had a two-line motto: *Mom & Dad/close to you*. It would lie over his parents' ashes, which he had recently interred in the little cemetery.

"You okay with this?" he said to Sailor.

"No sweat."

The graveyard was a good twenty-five kilometres away on a bench among sand hills and coulees southwest of town. When they reached it, Sailor rolled out of the truck and paused to check the lay of the land. "Jesus."

"This is it," said Marty.

"Middle a nowhere. My God."

"Yeah, well."

Marty knew that he had found the perfect spot to bury his parents' ashes, and Helen had also given it the thumbs-up. Seeing his parents' plot yet again made him all the more certain. The two men ambled through the barbed-wire gate and into the graveyard, gazing at the old markers.

"Ask ya somethin'?" Sailor was gawking at a gravestone that read *Clarence Eversham, 1842-1903, RIP.* "Why in the Christ would you want to bury someone in this godforsaken place?"

"Oh, you know." Marty tried to reach for a simple explanation.

"This your folks, right?"

"Right."

"Didn't you get along with them type deal?"

"Oh, no. I mean, yes. We got along okay."

"I mean, if you didn't get along with them, I'd understand. My old man beat on me as regular as pissin'. And my mother was a frickin' klepto. I'd understand, believe me. Dumpin' them off here, I mean."

Sailor went over to the bed of the half-ton and climbed in. He nudged the slab with the toe of his boot. He was looking down at Marty from several feet up. He had a voice like a blaring horn. "Marty, I could get you a deal on a plot *right in town* for seven hunnerd bucks. Are you sure you want to leave your folks' ashes in this rat hole?"

"Well, yeah."

"Remember, Marty, this is a one-time gig, right?"

"Right."

"Because, Marty, once I lay this baby down, that's it. Too late to say yer sorry type a deal."

"Sailor, I loved my mom and dad, and I'm sure. I like it out here."

Sailor shrugged, hopped down from the truck, took a breath, and lifted the grave marker with scarcely a grunt.

During the winter before the laying of the slab, Marty had run into Sailor downtown and the two men had gone for coffee. Sailor had been an inmate of the prison where Marty had been hired as a program facilitator. A four-year stretch for breaking and entering. Sailor had straightened out his life to some extent. He seemed to sport the tattoos, the muscle shirts, and the duck-ass hair as souvenirs from a former life. He had an ugly three-inch scar on his forehead. Whenever Sailor got agitated, the scar seemed to deepen from pale to deep pink.

The two men kept running into each other and having coffee together. They had both left the prison within the same year. Sailor was now a handyman (a contractor, he called himself), and Marty had become an addictions counsellor for a rehab agency. Scarcely any of his clients had criminal backgrounds. Once he'd purchased the slab for his parents' ashes, Marty had phoned Sailor for the chore.

Marty's father had just died, and Marty was getting a handle on his new job. His father had asked to be cremated, and Marty had obliged. There was a memorial service on the Coast, where Marty's parents had lived, and Marty had driven back to Saskatoon with his father's ashes to have them interred with those of his mother, who had died a year earlier. Using the seatbelt, he'd managed to strap his father's urn to the front passenger seat. He'd had to travel without Helen, and it was a two-day drive home. Marty had passed the time listening to the radio, catching brief glimpses of the scenery, calculating the kilometres between rest stops, and talking to his father's urn next to him in the passenger seat. It was an unusual sort of trip.

I know, Dad, you think I'm a bleeding heart for working in corrections. I know you still think Helen should quit her teaching job and she and I should have some kids. You know, Pop? You were never big on understanding me, never too eager to see things my way. You once said if I ever got a real job, you'd fall over with surprise? Well, I got a job, Pop. A real job. Don't interrupt. Maybe I don't golf at the country club like my bigshot brother, but I'm not the screw-up you said I was. Sure, I ran in circles for a while, but I grew up, Dad. Here I am, a grownup man.

When Marty got back home from laying the slab with Sailor, he was feeling proud of himself.

"You guys got it done?" said Helen.

Marty shrugged. No big deal.

"Your friend Sailor is quite the looker."

"As good-looking as me?"

"A few tattoos and a few scars, and you'd be right up there." She kissed him. "I don't know. Maybe you could go for the ponytail?"

"There's a message for you," she said a week later. "From your good buddy Sailor. I think he thinks you're his father."

"Haw-haw."

The message was a reply to a suggestion of Marty's that Sailor help him shingle his roof. Sailor had done roofs before and he'd be a lot more agile up there than Marty, and Marty would save some money. Soon after he answered Sailor's call, Sailor brought two men to Marty and Helen's house: a native fellow with some front teeth missing and a shaggy gut-hung fellow named Kroker who lumbered around like a lineman on a football team.

Sailor did the introductions. "Winston here, he's good with heights. He and I can do all the nailing, and Kroker can haul up the shingles and crap."

"Nice to meet you guys," Marty said and shook their hands.

Kroker lugged a big double ladder off the truck and around to the backyard and adjusted it as though it were a Lego set. The men came and went that day and all the next week according to their own mysterious schedule. They showed up late in the mornings, and the shingling progressed slowly on the second-storey roof.

Toward the end of the job, Helen got nervous at night. She kept the blinds down in their bedroom and checked and rechecked the locks on their doors. Something had happened between her and Sailor, something weird, and she didn't know what to make of it. Probably nothing. But now she was having nightmares. In one of them, Sailor was out at the old country graveyard digging a hole for her and Marty. Presumably, they were already dead, but they looked on, and she made suggestions to Sailor. *Not so close to Marty's folks. Over there a ways.*

"I don't know about these guys," she told Marty. They were in bed reading, and Helen looked too edgy for sleep. "I'm glad Sailor helped with the burial and all, but I'll be happy when this job is over."

"Well, we're almost done. Sailor's already talking about another job across town."

"Hear, hear."

Marty sat up in bed and readjusted his pillows. He'd been about to turn off the light, but now he knew he wouldn't sleep for a while. The wind was up, rattling things around in the alley behind their house, and now Helen was getting antsy.

"What were these two new guys in for?"

"Winston, something to do with cars. He'd lift them and drop them off at a garage out in the country where someone else repainted them. Finally, they caught up with them. He's never done anything . . . you know . . ."

"And Kroker," she said. "What was he in for?"

"Oh, well, that was a bit more serious."

"Never mind," she said. "I don't want to know."

"I didn't realize these men were bothering you."

"They weren't *bothering* me."

"I mean, I didn't realize they were weighing on you. That's all. I thought you were cool about them doing jobs around here."

She took a breath before she spoke. She had to arrange her thoughts so that she wouldn't sound resentful or shrill. She was thinking about the incident with Sailor. Which might have been nothing to worry about, but now was not the time to bring it up. She would have to put this thing aside. She had to sound rational.

"Look, Marty, when you went off to work in the pen each day, I didn't say boo, right? I had to bite my tongue."

"Right. And when I quit out there, you were pretty relieved."

"Of course, I was. I didn't have to worry all the time that something was going to happen to you. I didn't have to worry anymore that you were so . . . *connected* to these people. Jesus. And now, don't you see, these characters think we're their friends. They'll be coming over for beers pretty soon. They'll bring their buddies. They'll be looking over our stuff to see how much they can get at the pawn shop. I didn't sign up for this."

"Look, Helen, honey, I didn't realize you were so uneasy. We'll bid them goodbye the second the roof is done. No more handyman jobs, no more coming over here. You can rest easy, okay? I just didn't know they were bothering you."

"I didn't *say* they were bothering me."

Marty raised his index finger. It was a cross between an order to cease and desist and a white flag, a peace sign with one finger. "Has this got anything to do with Sailor?"

Helen shot her husband a quick look.

"Last winter, we had coffee downtown," he said. "Sailor was shaking. He'd fallen off the wagon. He started owning up to me like I was some kind of Father Confessor. I've done this, I've done that, I'm not worthy to even have coffee with you. That kind of thing. I have sinned against God, he said. Can you believe Sailor saying shit like that?"

"Marty, you hear this stuff all the time."

"I know, I know, but don't you see?" Marty raised his hands to the ceiling of their bedroom, proclaiming, like a man immersed in a vision. "He's changed. He's back in the program. He's working, for God's sake."

Helen's attention drifted for a moment. "Did you lock the back door?"

"Yes, as usual."

Helen sighed and fell back on her pillow. What she *wanted* to tell him was the thing that happened last week. It was a hot day. She had been weeding in the backyard, and she was wearing shorts and a halter top. She heard a noise up above her. Sailor was hunkered over on the edge of the second-floor roof as though he thought he could fly. He said, *Helen, didn't you ever want to just go wild?* His entire face had broken into a weird smile that had nothing whatsoever to do with joy, and the scar on his forehead was glowing hot pink.

I don't know, Sailor. Just don't fall off my roof.

The fanatic smile vanished. Clearly, she had said the wrong thing.

The wind had set the leaves to trembling in their backyard, and something was rattling in the lane.

"Are you sure you locked the back door?"

"Yeah. I'll check."

Marty got out of bed and worked his slippers on. He wanted to continue with their dispute, but the words that would ease Helen's mind just would not come. He could not tell Helen that Sailor was like the prodigal son to him. *He was lost and now he's found.* Marty descended the stairs to the main floor and shuffled through the kitchen. He squinted out the backdoor window into his yard, and he saw someone standing alone in the wind a half-dozen yards from his house.

He opened the door, leaned out into the night, and said, "Sailor, is that you?"

gordon's idea

I

IN HIS DREAM, he told Kimpy that he wanted to go home.

You are home, silly.

He tried to explain to her that he couldn't possibly be home if it didn't feel like home. He knew he shouldn't whine too much. Kimpy had already heard enough of this in the past year, and she found his self-pity annoying. Best to say no more.

When he opened his eyes, it was dark out. Kimpy was still somewhere in the room, which made him feel as though he was still dreaming.

"You've got to get out of yourself," she said. "You're living too much inside your mind, so you have to externalize. You can't get your old job back; we both know that. You can't get me back, either."

"No need to belabour the obvious."

"Think about other things, Gordon. Jobs you need to do around here. Or think about something you'd *like* to do. Spend some money on clothes. Go to a restaurant. Don't be so stingy on yourself. Get out that old fly rod. You might have more energy inside than you realize."

He tried to interrupt her. "Where on Earth do I get the— "

"Or do something for someone in need," she said with just a trace of impatience. "You know, sign up for the Food Bank. Visit our daughter. Volunteer your services at that church west of Broadway. Or go to a palliative care centre. They might need volunteers. And at coffee at the Co-op, sit next to Grace Moony. You know how much she likes you. And get walking again, long walks in the sunshine. Just don't slip on the ice."

Kimpy seemed to enjoy these middle-of-the-night sessions, during which she became the mother and he the child.

"Now, on the other matter . . ."

Kimpy paused for a moment, allowing Gordon to focus on the other matter. He knew what was coming.

"I've said this before, but why don't you join a ballroom club? All kinds of people your age join ballroom clubs. Don't give me that look. Gordon, do you honestly think they join up just because they're crazy about dancing?"

Kimpy ended the conversation by drifting out of the room. An annoying habit, but perhaps she had a point. Or perhaps this ballroom business was driven more by exasperation than common sense. Because the thought of toiling and sweating with some hopeful widow across a gymnasium floor, just the thought of it, made him groan. Kimpy's advice was frequently good, but she was not infallible.

The bedside clock said 3:13 a.m. His insomnia was back in control. If he remained beneath the covers, he would progress into ever-gloomier thoughts. He could feel them lining up to interrogate him.

Gordon grunted his way into a sitting position at the edge of the bed. The next step would be to wiggle into his slippers, but he lacked the necessary excuse to do so. The wind rose outside his bedroom window. *February*, it said. *Here come the blahs*. His feet were getting cold, so he pulled on his slippers and padded down the hall to his study. He walked tiredly, like a quarterback who had been sacked once too often.

Thus resumed his insomnia routine. He settled down facing his laptop, the same one he had used since the latter days of his teaching career, the days of frantic emails from students in his brave little brigade . . . his noble band of . . .

He opened his laptop, and it sighed at him resignedly as though an old rodent had been hibernating there. At first, the screen was too bright, and aqueous floaters began to inch across like transparent worms. Owing to his latest depression, Gordon had not checked his email for two or three days. Five vertical blue bullets had arranged themselves like happy faces for his attention. The last one down was —*my God.*

"Richard Simon."

He leaned toward the screen and forgot about his empty bed, his insomnia, and the dark world beyond his study. *Greetings and salutations, Young Gordon. It occurs to me that I've been a less-than-active correspondent.* He still wrote as he talked, the well-bred formality of an emcee presiding over a banquet. And Gordon was still Young Gordon. In fact, he was but a few weeks younger than Richard Simon. *I've had a bit of cancer, and for a while, it looked scary. But I'm back on my feet again, and I'd love to chat with you.* He gave Gordon a phone number. *Remember, we're early risers out here and early to bed. Two hrs difference. Why don't you ring us about three or four pm SASK TIME?*

It was always *ring us,* never *ring me.* But Simon was divorced. Gordon had picked that up from other sources because many people told Richard Simon stories, even those who had never met him. But Richard was still "us." And why "SASK TIME" in upper-case letters? Because Young Gordon was so clueless he needed to be prompted by some . . . some . . . superior entity?

Gordon wrenched his mind away from his briefcase full of dark assumptions, past grievances, exhaustion, and a whole range of nullities, and he stared out into the dark beyond his rattling window. It was cold out there. Between gusts, it was as quiet as a country graveyard. Soon, it would be March, but this February, there was almost no snow in Gordon's yard. The ice that remained had melted, then frozen, and melted again and frozen, and left a massive dirty glaze up the streets and out across the prairie. Saskatchewan had turned into the largest, dingiest curling rink in the country.

And Richard Simon had had a scary cancer. His old friend in Vancouver, his fishing buddy with the baseball cap, who always looked elegant and scholarly, even when gutting a trout, who got drunk decades ago the night he was elected president of the university students' union and, from memory, gave an impromptu speech by Warren Harding, something about a return to normalcy, and cracked up the entire room of supporters. That fellow. The politician. His zealously right-wing friend and fly-fishing buddy, his rival in love, the only famous person he had ever known, had had a scary cancer.

Gordon fell into a sudden dread. What if he phoned good old Richard only to discover that they had nothing to say to each other?

Their friendship had begun in the early 1950s in Social Credit Alberta. During their early teens, they discovered that they happened to read the same magazine. Their parents had probably given them subscriptions to *Outdoor Life* at roughly the same time. They read the fly-fishing stories first, in which pipe-smoking sages guided their readers up the Beaverkill or down the Battenkill or somewhere in Western Montana for brown trout, brookies, or rainbows. Young Gordon (awkward, overshadowed by classmates, bored silly with school, always on the outside of things, listening, reading, dreaming) could match Richard Simon (born leader, precociously bright and witty, fastidious dresser) factoid for factoid on such things as tippet strength, the superiority of pheasant hackles, record size and location for eastern speckled trout, and how to calculate the weight of a fish by measuring length and girth. At age thirteen, they enlisted in fly-casting and fly-tying classes and rode the bus together on winter nights across Edmonton to Eastwood School. They learned how to cast in a basement gym, dropping flies onto the circles beneath the basketball hoops. Yes, Gordon Carter may very well have been an uninspired drudge in Grade 8, but he was a polymath in fly-fishing school, his brain a great dry sponge that soaked up trickles, streams, and rivers of trout lore. And Gordon Carter remembered everything.

It was this vibrant memory, enticed by visions of mountain streams, that accompanied Gordon to the phone in the late afternoon, Saskatchewan time.

"You know what I've been missing?" said Richard.

"This has to be something to do with trout."

Richard broke into his old falsetto chuckle. "You read my mind, Carter. I miss our fishing together. I truly regret not fishing with you since . . ."

"1964, I think it was."

"Was it that long ago? Surely not. What about that time you came out to Vancouver during your Easter break?"

"That was 1969," said Gordon, "and we fished in your rowboat on Horseshoe Bay."

"And nearly got wiped out by a B.C. ferry, as I recall."

"Yes, indeed. But that was for salmon on spinning rods," said Gordon, "and that doesn't count, does it?"

This last remark was more purist-to-purist than man-to-man, a reminder that fly-fishing for trout was at the top of a hierarchy. Did that mean that Gordon was some sort of elitist? And did that also mean that he was a failed socialist? Perish the thought. Both men paused in conversation, each waiting for the other, with twelve hundred kilometres of telephone poles between them.

"Seriously, Richard, what sort of shape are you in?"

"I'm coming around," he said. "No more radiation, no more chemo. Thank God for that. I'm gaining some weight, I do a bit of walking now. They won't yet say if it's actually *gone* or if it's just hiding somewhere. But I can live with that. If it feels like I'm on the mend, then I guess I'm on the mend. Appetite returning."

"You used to have a great weakness for pancakes. Slathered all over with everything bad. And you never gained a pound. Remember Flapjack Charlie's?"

"In Jasper? You know, Carter, damn it, you are right. How do you remember stuff like that? Anyway, Jasper. That is why I emailed you.

I'm coming out to Jasper in June for a keynote at the Lodge. Political thing. They want me to talk about the good old days."

"Such innocent times."

"Right again, Young Carter. Bloody good to hear from you."

"Likewise, Old Simon."

"Anyway, Gordy, do you think you might join me for a bit of fishing?"

Almost four months later, Gordon descended to the basement to find his fly rod. He had come to dislike the basement, with its network of cobwebs and the sour smell of alkali and bleach. He found the rod in its case, tucked in behind a jumble of dusty golf clubs inherited from Kimpy's father. He had not brought out and assembled the rod for a very long time. Decades. Various sportsmen in Saskatoon had assured him that there were trout streams to be found in his adopted province, but none of these men seemed to own a fly rod. They fished with spinning rods; they owned big Lunds with outboard motors and wheeled them on long trailers with pickup trucks to a variety of northern lakes. Up there it was all about jigging for walleye, casting big spoons for pike, trolling with down-riggers for massive lake trout. Fly-fishing was for introverts, bookworms, tree-huggers. Fly-fishing was for the sort of man who felt little inclination to watch hockey games.

Once, encouraged by Kimpy to go it alone, Gordon drove to a recommended stream several hours northeast of Saskatoon. By this time, he had discovered a fly-fishing club in town. A lovely woman in the Bugchuckers Club told him that the stream had been stocked with brook trout. It descended through a heavily treed valley, a place that looked very wild to Gordon. There were no streamside paths and little evidence of previous anglers, no discarded leaders or packaging. Very few bootprints. Just the heavy bush and the boreal forest waiting to be entered.

He parked his new Corolla near a small bridge, donned his

waders, assembled his fly rod, doused himself with mosquito repellent, and plunged into the trees beside the stream. The more he trudged, the heavier the undergrowth and the harder it was to see any activity on the water. He thought for a minute that he had found a path, but it turned out to be a game trail.

He fought his way out of the bush and found access to the creek alongside an old barbed-wire fence. He set up his rod with a floating fly and tried to wade upstream, but the bottom of the creek was too soft and perilous for wading. He finally thrashed his way to a beaver dam that widened out before him. A sudden splash at the edge of the reeds made his heart lurch, and he pulled out some line for a cast. Just as his fly hit the water, an animal grunted close by, and Gordon pulled in his line.

Oh, shit.

He tried to reckon how close the animal might be. It started to snort and huff like a bull or a large hog. What were domesticated animals doing in the wild? He lurched out of the stream, plunged back into the willows, aspens, and thorn bushes, and headed in the direction of his car. His fly caught on a branch, the leader snapped, and he left his fly behind.

He found himself in a clearing surrounded by black spruce. He could hear the stream to his right, so he assumed that beyond the clearing, his car would be parked by the bridge. He inspected the trees all around him and listened for the animal.

Shrouded among the branches and shadows of several big spruce was an ill-defined mass of deeper black. It had a light brown snout. As he strode across the clearing, the snout followed his movements and began to huff repeatedly. Gordon bulled his way through the trees and into some low bushes. There, he beheld his Corolla parked by the bridge.

The bear emerged into the open and fled in the other direction. It was visible for only a second or two. It looked big and astoundingly black.

He drove home to Kimpy, who laughed uncontrollably at his account.

Gordon planned other excursions with his fly rod, but they never materialized. He became a vicarious trout fisherman and continued to attend the Saskatoon Bugchuckers Club, a friendly group of several dozen men and a few brave women. He stocked up more than once on flies and leaders, but his flies never saw a trout stream. His greatest enjoyment at the Bugchuckers' meetings was hearing their stories: uncatchable lunkers in the Cypress Hills, northern ponds filled with wary trout, wolf scat and wolf sightings, bears that prowled by the campers and tents for food at night.

When the first stroke hit Kimpy, she had to quit her teaching job, and Gordon became preoccupied with her recuperation, her physiotherapy sessions and doctors' appointments. He was too disheartened by Kimpy's decline to consider a return to his favourite obsession. He had given himself over to her care, and even then, she urged him to try another trout stream. The best he could manage was frequenting the aisles of The Fishin' Hole, a store he had befriended when he arrived in Saskatoon. The fly rod was consigned to the basement with the unused golf clubs, and there it remained until a few months after Richard Simon reappeared from the past.

In mid-June, Gordon drove his now aging Corolla to Jasper and stayed in the cheapest motel he could find. He motored to the Jasper Park Lodge the next morning, and there was Richard with his fly rod and a small backpack. They shook hands for the first time in decades. Gordon's friend had always managed to remain fairly lean, but this time, he was scrawny and pale. His hair was starting to make a comeback, but Richard did not seem to realize how skeletal, how stooped, how sepulchral he looked.

Once again, their old rapport returned quickly, their old trout obsession. "Why don't we give Patricia Lake a try?" said Gordon.

"No bodies this time?" said Richard.

"Promise."

For years, Gordon had scarcely thought about the body. One spring, when they were in their late teens, he and Richard had discovered a man's corpse on a game trail overlooking Patricia Lake, picked clean by wolves or coyotes. They led the Mounties back to the scene, and the Mounties took some pictures and conveyed the skeleton back to Jasper, complete with a few scattered bones, torn clothing, and a.22 rifle. According to a story Gordon read in *The Edmonton Journal*, the man had been suffering from depression. One day in late fall, he had shouldered a rifle, hiked up the long road to Patricia Lake, and then, presumably, pulled the trigger. Gordon sometimes wondered if the man hadn't contracted an incurable disease and chosen to end his life on his own terms on a bright autumn day in a beloved alpine setting.

"If you felt like walking," Gordon said, "we could take our old trail to the end of the lake." There was a meadow that came to the edge of a small bay with pale-blue water in the shallows and a deep drop-off about twenty feet from shore. The meadow allowed for a decent back-cast. And if the small bay didn't work for them, there was always the stream that flowed out of the bay. If Richard had enough energy in him, they could walk a little farther, if need be, and check out their old stream with its beaver dams full of brook trout.

They drove to Patricia Lake, parked near a small aging lodge, and wandered down the hill to their old meadow. It was still intact after all these years. Gordon pulled off his hat and wiped his brow.

"Look at you," said Richard. "Where did you get that mop of white hair?"

Slowly, the men wandered down to their favourite boyhood spot, Richard with a new baseball cap and Gordon with his well-worn Tilley. The old path seemed wider, perhaps more heavily used, and badly eroded, and it forked into the bush and aimlessly returned to the main path. The bay at the end of the lake seemed smaller than they remembered, and the meadow had been trampled from too many picnics. When they got right down to the end of the lake,

Richard was puffing and coughing, and he had to sit down on a fallen tree next to the bay.

"Young Gordon," he said when he'd caught his breath, "if I should kick the bucket in the next while, bury me right here. Just dig a hole. God, it couldn't be more beautiful. Nothing has changed since we were high school kids."

Gordon said, "I think the last time we fished here was in 1959. You were already in first-year university."

"In October, Gordy, we'll both be sixty-five."

"Don't remind me."

Richard sat in the shade and stared out at the deep blue water in the bay and gazed up at Pyramid Mountain and back down at the lake as though he were searching for a glimpse of the boy he used to be: Dick Simon, the great enthusiast, the great purveyor of optimism when optimism was in vogue. "Gordy, what's missing here?"

Gordon disliked the name Gordy as much as he did Young Gordon, but he scarcely ever complained about it. He gazed across the lake and up at Pyramid Mountain, with its copper and bluish-grey slopes, and down at the deep-blue water and the pale-blue shallows. Neither man had begun to assemble his fly rod. "I give up."

"Gordy, I haven't seen a single rise."

Gordon gazed at the water before him. If he were writing for *Outdoor Life,* he would have called the water in the shallows gin-clear. Back then, that was the required adjective. Crystalline, limpid, pellucid words such as those never stood a chance. Too highfalutin. Had Gordon ever pursued writing rather than teaching literature, *he* might have been too highfalutin.

"There are no fish," said Richard.

"By God, you're right."

A year or two back, an old friend from Alberta had told Gordon that the fishing in the parks had gone belly-up, but fishermen always liked to complain—while at the same time staying mum on the subject of their own favourite fishing holes. Gordon might have done the same thing in his Alberta fishing days. Could it be that the friend had been telling the truth? In the old days, always in late May or

June, Richard and Gordon could spot schools of brookies and occasional large rainbows tailing slowly past the shore, poking around for caddis casings and dragonfly nymphs. In the old days, there were trout rising all over this bay. How sadly out of touch Gordon had become. How sadly troutless this beautiful world seemed now.

The men took out their bag lunches and continued to survey the water as they ate. Several whisky jacks came to visit. They perched on branches close to the log where the men sat.

Richard broke off a piece of his sandwich and flicked it in the direction of one of the birds. "There used to be ospreys here."

"They know better than to come here now," said Gordon.

They assembled their fly rods and tried a few casts out beyond the shallows, but this was done without conviction. It was the first time in many years that Gordon had tried casting flies. He was reassured to discover that he could still do it. Good old muscle memory. He kept on casting until his casts grew longer, they both did, and Gordon became aware of something he could not quite admit to his friend: in spite of the absence of their beloved trout, he was, for the moment, no longer depressed. He was more than halfway back to his old self.

They trudged up the same path to the lake's only pier and up a set of wooden stairs to the bungalows that had always perched above the lake. There was an office in one of the cabins. A woman behind the desk with long tresses of white hair smiled as the men approached. "Are you the guys with the fishin' poles?"

Richard and Gordon stared at the woman.

"Elsie come in here for coffee and said she seen two guys with fishin' poles."

"That's us," said Gordon. "Fishing fools."

"If I'd a-seen you, I coulda told you." She was shaking her head. "No fish in this lake. Hasn't been for years. No fish hatchery, no stockin'. No more fish, no-how."

"What happened to the hatchery?" said Richard.

"A virus disease type-a-deal. Killed all the hatchery fish. That's what some people say."

Gordon and Richard had bought park licences, so there had to be some fish somewhere. They had always found trout in the park. The white-haired woman followed them out to their car to have a smoke. They asked her where they might try their luck.

"Better try Maligne Lake. Rent a guide. Cost a month's wages, but you might catch somethin' up there."

They drove back down the winding road to the Jasper town site. Gordon was determined not to hand over a fortune to fish with a guide. No doubt, Richard would offer to spring for the guiding fees, but Gordon would not allow such charity from his friend, especially from this particular friend.

Richard was checking his brochure for fishing in Jasper Park. "It says here, Gordy, that Maligne Lake isn't even open to fishing for another month."

"Richard, remember Lake Edith? With those nice old cabins around the lake?"

"I do. It used to have some big rainbows."

"Did you also know that it has a feeder stream? Spring-fed, beautiful water."

Richard turned to face Gordon with a puzzled expression.

"And in that stream, Richard, every spring, those rainbows would come up to spawn. No walking necessary. We could park close to the lake."

"Aha."

"And how is Kimpy these days?"

Gordon was staring at the feeder stream that trickled down through a bed of multicoloured pebbles into Lake Edith. The stream was exceedingly low. It was hard to imagine that anything might have spawned in such a trickle of spring water. Richard's question caught Gordon off guard; he had expected it much earlier in their conversation.

And now, Kimpy was there before them, one hand raised to shade her eyes, the other pointing up at something. It might have been a mountain bluebird.

"She passed away more than a year ago."

"Oh, dear me."

No other men of Gordon's acquaintance would ever say *Oh, dear me.* It was a phrase that their mothers might have uttered. But Richard Simon could say it and get away with it because he was Richard Simon, a gentleman of the old school.

"I always thought that divorce was the most painful thing I've ever had to endure," said Richard, "but this . . . this must have been . . ."

"Yes, it's been hard. She had a couple of strokes, and the second one was particularly . . . difficult. Our daughter came to stay with us during the last . . . you know, and she and Kimpy spent some nice time together."

Then daughter Janet, apparently wavering between tender condolences and the urgencies of her own life, rejoined her family in Winnipeg, went back to her job, and became the busy daughter once again. He could hardly blame her.

As Gordon and Richard gazed at the azure lake, the head of a sea lion bobbed up not fifty feet away. Correction. A masked man in scuba tanks and a wet suit. He made his way to the beach, sucking and blowing air as though through an echo chamber. He trudged up the beach and shed his equipment.

"See any fish down there?" said Richard.

The man stared at Gordon and Richard as though their very presence on the shore warranted some degree of incredulity. "One of the guys said he saw a little one up by the narrows. Probably a frog or something."

Gordon frowned at this observation, which sounded as though the diver hadn't done his homework. "But surely there could be some natural spawning in the stream. No?"

The diver seemed to be gazing at the two men over a gulf of centuries. "It's a brand-new world, man."

A new world? That was an absurd thing to say. As far as Gordon was concerned, it was merely 2006.

Richard joined Gordon for supper at the Athabasca, an old hotel and pub, a favoured watering hole of theirs in the early1960s when Richard, Kimpy and Gordon all had summer jobs in the Jasper Rockies. Gordon had expected to be hit with a wave of nostalgia, but when their beers and their supper came, the re-decorated pub seemed too altered for him to revisit his youth. At least the hunting and fishing corpses were still hanging on the wall.

"I'm terribly sorry about Kimpy."

"Oh, Richard, you weren't the only one to romance her. She had a lot of attention in those days."

"Not that," Richard replied. "I mean, I have regrets about that too, but I meant her death. It's hard to imagine the world without her. She was so beloved."

"She was that."

The old friends went silent and returned to their beers. Gordon stared at the walls of the old pub, the trophy heads of moose, mule deer, bighorn sheep, black bear, and a huge, badly mounted rainbow. He would bet a wad of money that this rainbow had come from Lake Edith. From the days when trout were everywhere. He closed his eyes and rubbed them and glimpsed an image of Lake Edith, a greenish-yellow projection on the inside of his eyelids as indistinct as a drift of smoke.

Then, a memory, slick like an icicle, slid into his heart. Taking turns with daughter Janet and Kimpy's friend, Lila Green, to sit with Kimpy as her lungs rattled through the night. He felt weary, as though he were spiralling back down into that grey landscape of his recent past. The Stupid Room, he liked to call it. He was heading once more for the Stupid Room.

"You mentioned some regrets," Gordon said. "About Kimpy?"

Richard looked up from his plate and paused. "Back then, things went by so quickly. I think I was smitten by her, but I had no time to be smitten. It's like I blinked one day, and she was with this guy or that guy, and I was in Harvard."

"She was pretty keen on you. I was jealous of you for that."

"Well, Gordon, she married you."

The men went silent and Kimpy walked by, and she seemed to muse at both of them from the corner of the bar. She was young again and smiling dolefully as though she felt sorry for all the sad and yearning men of her acquaintance. Then she put her hands on her hips and started to tap-dance. She angled her body left and then rocked it back to the right as though she were floating inches above the floor. She'd always been a damn good dancer.

"Where did that name come from? Is Kimpy short for something?"

"It was a nickname," said Gordon after a pause. "Remember the woman who made the espresso and slung beer in that jazz basement? On the south side, the Yardbird Suite? Zuzu, I think it was. She gave Kimpy that name."

"I think I remember," Richard whispered.

Rhonda was Kimpy's given name. He used to think the name had something to do with her hair, which was resistant to any kind of curlers, salon treatments, ironing (for sheen), or dippity-do (for body), resistant to the point of rebellion. She would sleep all night in curlers, then brush out her curls in the morning, and the curls would unfold into a slow droop all day long as though, one by one, they had succumbed to apathy. During their courtship in the late 1960s, Gordon discovered that in the *OED*, there was no such word as "kimpy." Her nickname meant nothing except what her friends could ascribe to it. The unbearable Winston Towers claimed that Kimpy meant unkempt, as though the wind was always blowing her around in the dust.

Gordon was still in Edmonton, doing his master's degree, and Kimpy was teaching elementary school, recovering from a breakup with a married man. They ran into each other one Saturday downtown in the Java Shop. She brought her coffee over to his table. "Gordon! Of all people. I haven't seen you in so long."

"Not since Banff."

"Oh, God, don't remind me. Gordon, you were so noble."

She was referring to an encounter they'd had with Winston Towers, whose name and lofty height reminded Gordon of a high-rise. Winston was an occasional and sometimes dissonant presence in their social circle, the son of wealthy parents, a jock, an outspoken racist, a patrician in training. Winston Towers was the only one Gordon ever knew who played polo.

The encounter happened in the mezzanine of the St. George at about one in the morning, as student après-skiers straggled in and out of the hotel. Gordon had been drinking with some fellows in a pub down the street on Banff Avenue. He left the pub feeling aimless and sleepy and headed for the St. George. On the second floor, near his room, he encountered Winston (Kimpy's ex-boyfriend), Richard (Kimpy's current boyfriend), and Kimpy (everyone's fantasy girlfriend) engaged in a tugging match. Richard held one of Kimpy's arms while Winston yanked at the other, and Kimpy was getting vocal about the situation when Gordon stepped in. He stationed himself between Kimpy and Winston, and he glared up into Winston's face, from which there came a bracing exhalation of booze.

"Winston, let go of her," Gordon shouted. "Kimpy wants to go with Richard. Let go of her."

Winston must have known that, in order to dismantle Young Gordon, he would have to release Kimpy. He did so, and Gordon awaited the inevitable blow from Winston Towers, but it never came. He was not sure why Winston held back from demolishing him. Was it that Kimpy would witness the slaughter and condemn the bigger boy? Was it because Winston was outnumbered? Was it because Gordon was a pacifist, and no one ever attacked a pacifist because it was deemed unmanly? Was it because Winston had never in his life seen Gordon bear his teeth? Was it because Winston had been caught red-handed trying to force his ex-girlfriend into a hotel room?

At any rate, Winston Towers sulked down one corridor, Kimpy

and Richard went hand in hand down the other corridor, and good old Gordon was left to imagine what transpired in the privacy of their room.

"You were such an angel," Kimpy said.

"I hate being called that."

"But you are, Gordon, you're an angel."

"Angels might come in handy now and then," he said, "but let's face it, you're never going to bed with one."

A sunrise bloomed on her face, and Gordon smiled. "Kimpy, I believe that you are blushing."

"Oh, stop it." She released a despairing laugh and covered her face with her scarf. At that moment, Gordon found a small measure of courage.

"How would you like to go to a concert with an eligible bachelor?"

He glimpsed something worn-down, something low-spirited, in her face. World-weariness, was that it? Kimpy had grown impatient with the attentions of A-Type men. This she had confided to Gordon. Most of them she'd sent packing before the fireworks began, confident young men, for the most part, on the run from one job, one city, to a bigger one. Or on the road from commitment to brief love.

"Yes," she said, "I'd like to."

Gordon and Richard's conversation moved into a second pint. Gordon asked Richard, "What happened with you and Michelle? I'm not trying to be nosy. I was just wondering."

Richard looked at his glass of beer for a moment. "It wasn't her fault," he said. "Michelle and I had drifted apart. Provincial politics took me away from home all the time. And on the road, there were . . . you know."

"Distractions?"

Richard seemed grateful for the word, and he smiled. "I was no angel."

"You mean," said Gordon, "there are such things as right-wing groupies?"

"They're just like left-wing groupies," said Richard, "only they dress rather smartly."

"I always liked Michelle. I remember when the two of you first met. You were an ad for romantic bliss."

Richard had no reply. He rubbed his hands together, dislodging some crumbs, and he peered at his friend. "Gordy, I think it was the biggest mistake of my life. I have no excuse. Sure, I was bored with . . . with . . . but that's no excuse. Boredom is never a good excuse. You shouldn't let yourself be defined by boredom. I think I loved women a little too much. I had affairs because it seemed so easy. But after a year or two, the press, the lefty press, I mean, got hold of it and just ate it up."

"You referred to 'us' in your email."

"Yes," Richard said and exhaled at some length. "I'm involved with someone. She's terrific. She puts up with me, so she must be terrific."

He cast a glance at the waiter, who was in conversation across the floor beneath the antlers of a bull moose. The two old friends lapsed into another thoughtful silence, the man with no woman for his bed and the man with memories of too many women. Gordon found himself fighting back a wave of resentment.

"Not to change the subject, Gordon, but why did you retire early?"

"My principal urged me to resign. It was time, I guess. I had made some stupid choices. Questionable choices, I guess you might say."

"Are we talking foolishness of the flesh here?"

"No, no. I had a bunch of precocious Grade 11s and 12s, and some of them were idealists. The stuff I taught them, Dickens, Thoreau, Margaret Atwood. Books that were bursting with idealism. They just ate them up. It surprised me because these days, it's hard to get students away from their computers to read books that matter. But these young people were the exceptions. Some of them reminded me of sixties protesters, except more nerdy and less pious. Sometimes, the conversation would turn to misogyny, or racism, or gay-bashing, or social justice. And one of the complaints that kept coming up in class was, *Why don't they do something about this?* My answer to them was, *You might ask that question of yourselves.*"

"God, Carter, are you still an idealist after all these years?"

"Of course."

"No offence, but I thought people grew out of that stuff."

"What stuff exactly?"

"Saving the world. Saving the planet. Bleeding the corporations. Socialism."

"You should try it sometime. I could give you a primer on socialism through the ages."

"You taught socialism to your students?"

"I sometimes think they taught it to me. They didn't call it socialism, no one does these days, but most of them were suckers for social causes. Anyway, we formed a kind of lit club, my favourite little zealots and me. They called themselves the Here and Now."

"Not exactly grounds for dismissal."

"There's more. These kids wanted to change the whole social order. I challenged them to pick their battles and to start off small. Something with large implications, but a battle with limits, one that they could win."

Richard's head cocked forty-five degrees to the right. This had always been his skeptical look.

"Yes, Richard, I aided and abetted them. But I also did my best to put limits on their activities. I showed them that there were lines they shouldn't cross."

He gave Richard an apologetic smile. Gordon was remembering Sooey Guenther. A whiz-kid with a buzz cut, short and chunky, built for heavy causes. Her mother was a great reader and very pretty. She used to flirt with Gordon but did so, apparently, without intent. Sooey's father flew helicopters for a living. Among many other things, Sooey was a grammarian. She wore heavy boots, and she had a potty mouth and a disturbingly loud voice, but on the page, she insisted on proper grammar.

He remembered Sooey and the Here and Now club sprawled all over the floor of the school's newspaper room. Sooey, telling a story.

"I walk down Broadway, and there's this big sign saying 'Buds.' I'm like, what is this, a florist?"

"No," said Charlie Coulson, a young drummer with a garage band. "It belongs to a guy named Bud. It's a blues bar."

"I *know* that, Charlie. But it doesn't say that. It says Buds, the plural of bud. Our man Bud forgot the apostrophe. So he's advertising what, a fucking flower shop?"

"Or a weed shop," said Ronen Margolis, who smoked weed in the school washroom and still won chess tournaments all over the province.

"Yeah," said Sooey, "and in the staff room? The fucking Teachers' Room? There's this nonexistent word on the door of the little boys' room: *M-E-N-S*. The frickin' apostrophe again. I'm like . . . this is our school, and we got teachers known as mens in the crapper."

Much laughter and applause. Even Gordon was applauding.

Another girl in the group spoke about cottage-dweller signs out at Wakaw Lake. The Smith's. The Melnyk's. The Johnson's. What's a Smith? What's a Melnyk? They all knew what a Johnson was.

"The frickin' plural possessive. I mean . . ." Sooey glanced up at Mr. Carter, who she referred to as the Gordster, as if to say, *Stand up for the frickin' language, Bozo.*

The Here and Now group rose to a frenzy. This was a small war they could win. They wanted to go guerrilla and do some sign-changing. Gordon saw visions of spray paint and vandalism all over town.

"You have to think about what happens when you get caught," he told the group. "You don't want to get expelled, and I don't want you to, either." Gordon was also thinking about how he would not like to get fired over this campaign. But like his students, he was inspired by it.

"We can do it at night."

"My parents are both lawyers, so what's to worry about?"

"We can wear those headlamps."

"I am so totally on board."

"They wouldn't expel us if we concentrated on the downtown."

"Or over on Broadway."

Gordon went along with it. He and Kimpy even went for night walks to photograph the newly improved signs. Sooey branched out and became a specialist in rewording offensive graffiti on two of the old bridges connected to Saskatoon's downtown. Much of it had the tone of Hollywood Satanism. "Charles Manson is God." "Hells Gate." "Kill the Bitches."

"These slogans really creep me out," Sooey confessed to the group. "I think there's like a clubhouse for perverts under one of those bridges. You know, lurkers?"

"Do you go about changing these slogans alone at night?" said Gordon.

"No, I take my brother with me."

Sooey's brother, Bungo Guenther, was a standout left guard on the Mildred Kerr High School football team. When it came to opposing linemen and lurkers, he had aggressive inclinations. Bungo thought the lurkers should all be run out of town. But with her brother's vigilance, Sooey Guenther was able to get creative beneath the bridges of Saskatoon. "Charles Manson is God" became "Charles's Mansion is sold." "Kill the Bitches" became "Fill the Ditches."

According to Sooey, her brother Bungo had a different idea of how society might be reformed. He and his buddies wanted to set up a sting for the lurkers under the Broadway Bridge. Tough love, Bungo called it.

"If you see Bungo before I do," said Gordon to Sooey, "tell him no. No. No. Under no circumstances should Bungo and his football bros do their interventions under the bridge. No vigilantes from Mildred Kerr High. This is how young men get convictions on their records and sometimes go to jail."

"Bungo thinks he's doing us all a favour," she said.

After a few days of brooding over it, Sooey came around to Gordon's way of thinking. They both prevailed upon Bungo to nix his version of tough love, and Sooey and her comrades in the Here and Now got on with the term. June exams were looming, and their club disbanded for the year. But Bungo Guenther could not leave his idea alone. He phoned a couple of TV stations in town and told them that on Saturday night, a citizens' group would gather to do the work that the Saskatoon Police Service would not: oust the alleged perverts from beneath the Broadway Bridge.

On the appointed night, Bungo and some righteous jocks, emboldened with beer, lumbered beneath the Broadway Bridge and found a couple of itinerant men asleep on cardboard mats. Bungo's reformers assumed the role of bouncers, and the men pushed back. There was a struggle, and no one seemed to know who did what exactly. But one of Bungo's friends got a knife in the thigh, and one of the street guys went to hospital with a spinal injury.

"My name appeared in the *Star-Phoenix* a couple of mornings later," said Gordon to Richard.

"Oh, no."

"As an instigator. It seems that one of the football guys disapproved of my club rules and ratted on me."

Richard regarded Gordon with a mournful gaze that looked like equal parts sympathy and disdain. Or perhaps Richard recognized something else. Perhaps those newspaper items about expensive dinners, affairs, and exclusive parties had returned to haunt his friend. His love of women and his political downfall had gone national.

"Serious question, Gordon. What is the appeal of this moral fervour? Why would you let yourself get sucked in?"

"I loved these kids. They were good people. I thought I could help to channel their idealism into something that would be a learning experience. And I, too, am a grammarian."

"Channel their idealism? Gordy, that's just the socialist in you. A good learning experience would be to get them thinking about employment. Standing on their own two feet. Learning how to speak in public or how to start a business. The last I heard, vandals and graffiti guerrillas don't get very healthy salaries."

Gordon drained his pint and carefully placed his glass on the table. "In a world where the gap between rich and poor has become distressingly widened, Richard, I don't think healthy salaries are very high on my list. Pedagogically speaking. I don't like the idea of pointing my students to the corporate trough. I tried to get them to raise the bar for their future. And if things are ever going to change, Richard, it's people like Sooey Guenther who will lead the way."

"Sit down, Gordon. Sit down."

Richard said this with admirable restraint, and Gordon sat down, glowered at his empty glass, and at last faced his old friend.

"Do you think," Richard said, "we might be allowing our ideologies to speak for us?"

"Never," said Gordon, and he allowed himself a smile.

"Let me just say this," Richard continued. "I do have sympathy for what you idealists try to do. On my side of the aisle, we called them bleeding hearts. But I liked their sincerity. I liked their compassion. As an elected representative, I put my own ideals to work in different ways. But that doesn't mean I didn't admire those folks in opposition for their moral courage."

"Once," Gordon replied, "I read a book by Ayn Rand."

Richard tapped the fingers of his right hand on the palm of his left. This was known back at university as the Silent Clap, Richard Simon's ironic gesture of approval. "Well done, Gordy. Nice to know you've taken a walk on the bright side of things."

"Actually, I read two of them," said Gordon. "I read them to suck up to a girl I was eager to get to know."

Richard was staring at his pint.

Gordon held up an index finger. "I have to admit, I have a soft spot for those few conservatives who have the wisdom to know what's worth conserving."

With a melancholy gaze, chin in hand, Richard drifted elsewhere for a moment and then returned to the conversation. "Carter, did you say those *few* conservatives?"

Gordon leaned forward and spoke in a hushed voice. "Yes, goddam it. But those people now, who vote for conservative parties just to preserve the . . . the . . ."

"Status quo?" said Richard.

"I guess so. But just what do these *new* conservatives actually fight to conserve? Their fast-buck lifestyle? The serene rhythms of their daily lives?"

"Jesus, Gordon, be specific. Who are these people?"

"Developers, realtors, suburbanites, nouveau riche, over-paid executives, politicians who blow with the strongest wind. I don't know. I don't understand them. By the way, Richard, I include you on my very short list of worthy conservatives. In case you wondered."

With his pate and his attenuated neck, Richard gave Gordon a slight bow.

Gordon looked down at his empty glass and said, "We all thought you'd run for the Big Job. Back then."

Richard looked skyward and gazed bleakly at nothing, then turned slightly away and peered at Gordon from the corner of his eye.

Gordon said, "We all thought that if Dapper Dicky Simon ran, he would win."

"Well, Young Gordy, that's a sad story for another time."

"Would a third beer help?"

"I think," said Richard, "I'm going to ask you to drop me off at the Lodge. Sometimes, my energy level just drops out of sight."

On the drive back to the Jasper Park Lodge, they were both silent. Gordon fetched Richard's gear from the trunk and walked him as far as the grand lobby. It hadn't changed much since he worked there in the summer of 1962.

"Gordy, I think I won't see you for a while."

"For a while. But Richard, I want you to keep improving. Get healthy, stay healthy. We have to show those trout who's boss."

"What trout?"

"We'll find some."

"As in days of old."

"Promise me we'll do this before too long?" said Gordon.

They shook hands, and Richard Simon walked away through the lobby, turned, raised his hand, and sent Gordon a formal wave. He had the solemn look of a magician leaving the stage. Gordon sent up a quick prayer that he would see his friend again. On the road back to his motel, he growled at himself again and again for losing his temper, for going too far.

2

That night in Jasper, after taking leave of Richard Simon, Gordon fell into a feverish dream that had some semblance of a plot. There was a drummer in a band with a countrified deep-South voice. He sang something sad about how the sun didn't shine no more, and the rain fell on his door. Another fellow in the band, the guitar player, looked out into the audience, spotted Gordon, and told him to get ready.

"Get ready for what?" cried Gordon.

The guitarist said, "Get ready, goddammit."

"I am ready," shouted Gordon. "Stop telling me to get ready when I'm ready."

"Ready for what?" said the guitarist.

"I haven't the faintest idea," said Gordon.

"Two privileged white guys went into a bar," said the guitarist. "The first guy, he says to the bartender, 'What's to say yes about?'"

"What's to say yes about?" said Gordon.

"Yeah. The second one, he says, 'Not much these days.' "

" 'No,' says the first one. 'It's all no no no.' "

"The second one says, 'You got that right.' "

Gordon tried to interrupt the guitarist.

"If you need the octopus," said the guitarist, "it's on Page 31."

"Why would I need an octopus?" Gordon cried, but the guitarist had fled.

A thunderstorm had gathered, people were running for shelter, and there was Kimpy yelling, *Get ready!* Gordon called after her but Kimpy kept on going. She was carrying a load of groceries in two plastic bags. He wanted to run after her, but he had to prepare for his English class, and he hadn't even pulled his pants on. His students were already flooding into the classroom. How could you teach a class if your heart was this heavy? How could you teach a class when you didn't have your pants on?

The voice of the thunder roared like the God of Revelation. It said, *Gordon, wake up. Ready yourself.* Gordon woke up with tears in his eyes.

In the shadowy pre-dawn, Gordon imagined that he was being forced to shoulder the burdens of Job. He yawned at the idea, but the more he mulled over the Job connection, the more Gordon was inclined to reject it—because probably it was Richard's turn to be Job. He wondered if Richard Simon would even make it through the year. Gordon had lost his wife, his occupation, and perhaps his reason for being. But Richard stood to lose absolutely everything. The Book of Job had always ranked as one of Gordon's favourite reads. A stimulating read. Good old Jewish despair, good old existential ponderings. But now, it seemed to Gordon that being Job was just a sad rite of passage for almost everybody. Perhaps the corpse Gordon and Richard had discovered when they were teenagers had succumbed to that rite of passage. Perhaps in a few months, a year, Richard's new partner in Vancouver would become Job. Perhaps half the people in Gordon's Grief Circle were shouldering the despair of Job. All of humanity seemed to be grieving with Gordon as he loaded his car for the trip home.

Back on the road to Saskatoon, from the foothills to the prairies, Gordon reviewed what awaited him in the old frame house that Kimpy had loved so much. He would resume his numb-hearted wandering through their home, wondering where his life had gone and whether there was anything left to look forward to. His insomnia was sure to return. Each morning, he would tell himself that he must be up and doing. For one thing, he had to finish his taxes. He was several weeks behind the deadline.

Should he sell the house? Of course, he should, but he couldn't. And he couldn't tell anyone why he couldn't sell the house because it would sound too weird. *Sorry, folks, but my wife is still hanging around here.* For comfort, he would have conversations with Kimpy and wonder, later on, if he were going mad. There would be the daily battle with himself to go outside and take a walk by the river. There was his Grief Circle, and there were friends he could phone, of course, but he had fallen into a kind of hibernatorial state, and he could not bring himself to pick up the telephone. No one wanted to keep company with a gloomy insomniac. His favourite colleague at Mildred Kerr High had passed away two years ago. His colleague's widow, Carly Daschuk, a family lawyer, had suggested after one of their sessions with the Grief Circle that they get together for coffee. Just the thought of phoning her inspired dread.

Gordon pulled in on the Alberta side of Lloydminster to fill his tank where the gas was cheaper. With his hand on the hose, gasoline pulsing through it, he looked around him with sluggish disapproval. He had not always disdained what people called progress, but today, he despised it. Lloydminster was booming. It gave Gordon the impression of a bright, massive, treeless mall in a state of perpetual construction. He paid for his gas and pulled out into the traffic.

A woman on the sidewalk carrying two plastic bags filled with groceries walked just ahead and to the right of his Corolla. From the rear, she looked like Kimpy. He drove slowly past her and caught a glimpse of her face. She was much too young, and her nose was—

Whump! A sound the head makes when it whacks the backrest and again when it whips into the steering wheel. The clustered isles of his brain rattled and juiced against the inside of his skull. All he could see in front of him was a rusted grey tanker truck. Which he had just rear-ended.

Blood was seeping from his nose. He sat embracing the steering wheel and glanced to his right. The woman with the groceries was glaring at him. Disapprovingly. She wore a lot of makeup around the eyes. He looked to the left. A short man had clambered down from his truck, and he was knocking on Gordon's window. The man yanked open Gordon's door and said something to Gordon. Something about the fucking road or the switch or the traffic or the switching. Yes, the switching of the lanes in the lanes of the lanes.

"You all right?" said the man.

"My head hurts," said Gordon, "and my heart is broken," and he tumbled back over a steep cliff and into a wondrous oblivion.

Gordon woke up wearing a hospital robe and lying on a cot in the emergency ward. His nostrils were encrusted with blood. His neck was throbbing deep down, and something pounded on the doors of his temples. A doctor came in, a stern, attractive young woman. She gave Gordon a brief examination and assured him that he'd been lucky.

"You may have had a concussion," said the doctor, "but your nose is not broken."

"Am I good to go?"

"As long as you don't attempt to drive, you're good to go."

The doctor parted the curtain that surrounded Gordon's cot. She turned back to him. "I believe you have a visitor."

There stood the fellow whom Gordon had rear-ended, a small, unshaven man with intense black eyes. He sounded like a heavy smoker and growled his words, leaning toward Gordon as though they were organizing some sort of mob caper.

"Well, sir," the man said, "the good news is there's hardly a scratch on my unit. My honey wagon is steel-plated, see? But your car's a write-off. Yessir, totalled and towed."

"A honey wagon? Did you just say a honey wagon?"

The man nodded.

"Just my luck," Gordon murmured, mostly to himself.

He apologized to the fellow and wondered out loud how he might get to Saskatoon.

"That's where I'm goin'," said the man. "You can ride up front with me. We'll pick up the contents of your vehicle and then one more little detour along the way. That okay with you?"

Gordon nodded to the man, and the man extended his hand. "Al Postnikov, at your service."

By mid-afternoon, Gordon and his truck-driver Good Samaritan were heading south on a gravel road that Gordon had never driven. Presumably, they were headed for a septic tank or a septic dump. The sky was heavy with rain clouds that glowered over the greening crops and parkland. The rain would hit them soon. The whole scenario was unfolding in a fog of unreality. After a long bout of yawning, Gordon fell asleep, woke up, and apologized for having drifted off.

"I must be dull company," he told the man.

Mr. Postnikov did not seem to mind. The owner of the honey wagon described to Gordon where they were going and how, after his brief dump, they would make their way to Saskatoon.

"I am very much indebted to you," said Gordon.

"No big deal."

Gordon asked the man how the sewage dumping business was going these days.

"No idea," said Postnikov.

"I daresay people treat you with the same ambivalence that they treat dentists and doctors. Am I right?"

"Huh?"

"No one wants to deal with them, or you, until there's a crisis. Then you pump out their tanks, and they're, you know, renewed for another stretch."

Postnikov shrugged his shoulders and geared down. The tanker lumbered off the gravel road onto a dirt trail that led to a narrow lake and a picnic ground. He turned the truck around and backed down to within a few metres of the lake.

"You gotta promise to not say nothin' about this, okay?"

"Surely you are not going to dump that filth into the—"

"No filth in this baby. I got ten thousand fingerlings."

"What?"

"Trout," he said, leaning in Gordon's direction. "Shitload a' rainbows. They call me the Stocker."

3

Gordon was sitting in the kitchen when he heard the letter carrier's rattle at the box. He was in no mood for a chat with Marg, his mail-woman, or even for an exchange of good mornings, so he waited till she had turned away. He put his cup of tea down and crept out to the front steps.

He was wrong. It wasn't Marg the mailwoman. The mysterious visitor was in his or her car, which looked somewhat like *his* former Corolla, and was driving rapidly down the street.

Which reminded Gordon that he needed to go car shopping.

Something was sticking out of his mailbox. He reached for it as though it might harbour some hornets or a large spider. Protruding from the opening was a bouquet of freshly picked flowers, what Kimpy used to call brown-eyed Susans. The person had attached a note. All the note said was, *It's summer!* It had to be a woman, Gordon deduced, because men tended to avoid the use of exclamation marks. At least in correspondence with each other. And they don't usually give each other flowers.

A few days later, Gordon discovered a card in his mailbox, a hand-crafted one. The stranger had gone to some trouble to colour it and paste on some fruit stickers. The message inside the card read *I hope you're having a good week. You looked a little downcast at the bakery.* It was signed, *One of your admirers.*

By the end of July, there were two more cards.

He tried each day to think of who it might be. Sooey Guenther's flirtatious mother? (He'd forgotten her first name.) Or Marg, the letter carrier? A nice young woman, very sturdy. Terribly chatty. And there was Mona down the street, who had taken to shovelling his walks the previous winter. She owned a nice little house, and he was pretty sure that she was single. And there was a white-and-green frame house just down and across from him. Students rented there. Sometimes, one or other of the girls waved hi to him. But he didn't even know their names. And these notes did not have a youthful touch. Might it be Kimpy's old friend Lila?

Gordon returned to these questions a few mornings later as he pulled on his socks. He picked up his left shoe and stared at it. Someone from his Grief Circle? Carly Daschuk? Yes, that was a possibility. And there were other widows in the Grief Circle. Or could it be an ex-student of his who might have read about Kimpy's passing? Or Grace Moony from the coffee shop at the Co-op? Sending him flowers might be something she would do.

He pulled on his left shoe and tied the lace. He picked up his right shoe and paused once again.

Or a former teaching colleague? He'd had a pleasant relationship with Rebecca Summers when they taught at Mildred Kerr High, but as far as he knew, her condition had flared up, and she was confined to a wheelchair. There would be no way that Rebecca could manage his front stairs—

A metallic clunk from the direction of his front porch. With his heart pounding and one shoe in hand, he hobbled downstairs. He flung open the door and heard the receding purr of a car down the street. A Corolla! He opened his mailbox, a large metal affair ideal for holding newspapers and large envelopes, and looked inside. Another bunch of newly picked daisies had been stuffed inside the box. They were somewhere between pink and purple. There was a note in a small envelope. It said, *How's fishing?*

He stumped into the kitchen, put on his remaining shoe, opened a high cupboard, and found a vase, and when the phone rang, he dropped the vase on the floor. It splintered into dozens of bright shards.

"Hello?"

"Greetings and salutations."

"My God. Richard Simon."

"I thought I'd touch base with you. See if you've recovered from our heroics in May."

He told Richard about his accident in Lloydminster. His search for a new car, his latest foray into modern automobiles with bags that inflated upon impact—what were those things called? Richard had caught him off-guard, and for a moment, he didn't know what else to talk about.

"Richard, how are you in the health department?" he finally said.

"Well, that's one of the reasons I called. "My cancer is still hanging around, but I'm still in the game. It's a sarcoma, and it sort of moves around."

"A sarcoma."

"Yes, it's a cancer of the connective tissue inside. My doctors have managed to shrink the two biggest tumours, but smaller ones show up now and then, and we're back to square one."

"Richard, it's hard for me to tell if this is more bad than good or more good than bad. News, I mean."

"Of course. It's constantly changing news. But since we got together three months ago, I've started to walk a bit more each week. I'm still not sure if I'm walking more because I feel somewhat better or if forcing myself to walk each day makes me feel better."

"I think, Richard, that the very thought of fishing with me again is the source of your newfound strength."

"Ha. Carter, you might have a point there. But a year ago, I didn't think my chances were great to get this far, and now . . ."

Gordon waited for Richard to finish his sentence.

"Now I'm learning to live with my mortality. It almost feels like progress. And speaking about our old friend mortality, Gordy, tell me . . ."

"Yes?"

"I can't help wondering whether you're back in the game again. Back in the female companionship game."

"Oh, that game. I think I'm out of that game, Richard. There will never be another Kimpy."

"I feared you might say that, Young Gordon. I know you can't replace Kimpy, but I also know that waking up to a splendid woman can do wonders for a man's outlook on life."

Gordon answered his old friend, his old rival, with a long sigh.

"Sorry to bring up such a touchy subject, Gordon. What I really wanted to say is that . . . thinking about another fishing trip with you, Gordon Carter—and I mean this—is quite the incentive."

"Thank you, Richard."

"Have you managed to wet a line since our Jasper trip?"

"Not exactly. I returned to the Bugchuckers Club for a visit. Heard some tall tales. I guess I've become a vicarious flyfisher. For the time being."

"We'll have to change that, Gordon, but perhaps not this summer."

Richard might just as well have been talking about Gordon's love life. The prospects of going for trout or going for female companionship were about equal. Both men tried to keep the conversation going, but something between them appeared to be stuck. The argument they'd had—was that still lingering? The old envy problem? Or was it the bloody telephone? Gordon had never liked the telephone. He was a reluctant chatterer.

Their conversation ended politely. Gordon swept up the broken glass, carried it out to the alley, and dumped it in his trash can. He returned to his backyard, pulled a lawn chair into the shade, and stared vacantly at his abandoned garden. Kimpy's garden, going weedy. It was a hot afternoon in mid-August; the wind was shaking the trees and stirring up dust in the alley, and the sun was glowing orange through the dust and the trees. Gordon couldn't quite move on from his brief chat with Richard Simon. Who was now learning to live with his mortality.

His phone rang again, and he dashed inside and grabbed it on the fourth ring. It was Janet. She wanted to know how he was coming along, always her first question.

"Oh, you know," he replied. "Some days I'm feeling fine, and some days I'm in the . . ."

"The Stupid Room," said Janet. "I hate to think of you just sitting around being gloomy."

"It's never as bad as you think," he said. "I'm better than last year."

"I should hope so. Dad, I've been talking with Marvin, and please don't be offended by this, but we think you might consider a move to

Winnipeg. Hear me out, Dad. We now have a big guest bedroom, and you wouldn't have to sell your house. You could leave the house or rent it to someone and come here. You could even just try it here for a month or two. Apparently, they have fly-fishing in Western Manitoba."

"Janet," he said, "you're a peach of a daughter, but I don't think I could possibly live with you two. Tell Marvin thank—"

"Grandad, I think you can live with me. We could take you sopping for ice cream!"

The new voice was Tansy, who was apparently part of this conspiracy.

"Are you sad, Grandad? If you're sad, you can take us for a ride. We could go to Calgary."

"What a nice idea," he said.

"They got dinosaurs in Calgary."

"I never knew that, Tansy. Dinosaurs. I hope they're the friendly kind."

"We don't want an answer, Dad," said Janet. "We just want you to think about it. Everything . . . everything is negotiable. Just think about it."

Gordon ambled out to the backyard and pulled up a lawn chair. Something inside him re-asserted that he did not want to go and live with his daughter's little threesome in Winnipeg. But how might he explain this reticence to Janet? How could he tell his daughter that he preferred his sometimes gloomy existence in Saskatoon to her bustling life in Winnipeg? For tell her, he must.

As Gordon slumped in his chair, gazing at the embattled perennials, he puzzled about the latest note from his mysterious admirer, a woman who must have known that he had been a keen angler. Maybe he still was. Maybe if the fishing prospects improved in Saskatchewan or in the national parks, he could try it again.

A voice from the Stupid Room seemed to say otherwise.

But gradually, a new idea sprouted from the weeds in Kimpy's garden. It was a big idea that seemed to glow with flashes of consequence and destiny. He knew that he should get up and do something useful, but he could not abandon his new idea. It was so big in its implications that he had to remain in his chair to watch the whole thing unfurl. His big idea smiled down at him.

One morning, after a better-than-average sleep, Gordon decided to shop for flies and leaders. He had not purchased anything at his favourite store since before his trip to Jasper. But if he and Richard were to meet again for another go at the trout, perhaps in the following spring, he would need to be ready.

He drove his (bewildering) new Corolla to The Fishin' Hole, an anglers' oasis out on Circle Drive. He was friendly with the staff there. After Kimpy passed away, he had gone there a few times to escape his empty house. He had rarely bought anything, but he'd managed to renew his acquaintance with the sales crew. There was an austere sort of pleasure walking up and down the aisles, gazing at stuffed trout, fly rods, trolling motors, and photos of great lunkers caught by local anglers. Absurdly cheerful and charged as they were with mercantile intentions, these items and the accompanying images nevertheless carried an enshrined, totemic power. They reminded Gordon that in spite of his fallen state, a good and healing world, afloat with clear water and piney breezes, was out there waiting for him. On every aisle of The Fishin' Hole, if he chose to, he could buy his way to success and happiness. He could become one of those happy, pipe-smoking men he used to read about in *Outdoor Life*.

Up until the time of her strokes, Kimpy had had an equivalent ritual when she went owly from too much winter or when her energy was low. She would drive to an all-night drugstore and check the shelves for shampoo, lipstick, nail polish, or movie magazines until the feelings that impelled this ritual went away.

Gordon approached the cashier and stood in line while two aging flyfishers ahead of him grumbled about the sad state of fishing in their province.

"You spend an hour driving there, and a buncha kids are racing around with those jet skis? They got this angry sound?"

"Like two-ton hornets."

"Hah. Or somebody's got his stereo blasting noise that some people call music."

"Or there's no gull-damn trout anymore."

"Time to call the Stocker, that's what I say."

The tall man breathed out a weary laugh. "Does that guy actually exist?"

"You got me there."

"I met him once," said Gordon.

The two old anglers turned around to scrutinize him. He recognized the taller of the two. He thought his name was Horner.

"You actually met him?" said the tall man.

"I did," Gordon replied. "He told me his name."

"You wouldn't have an address for him, would you? Hell, I could use a few hundred rainbows for my dug-out."

The shorter one wheezed out a laugh.

When the old fellows had paid for their fishing gear, a bald man at the till greeted Gordon. They had known each other for many years. The man leaned over confidentially.

"You've actually met Postnikov? Gordon, you're in a very small minority."

"We've travelled together," said Gordon, *sotto voce*.

"Did he ever tell you where he gets his brown trout fingerlings from?"

"No," said Gordon. "Not from around here, that's for sure."

The bald fellow pointed to a photograph on his corkboard. "Now that's what I'd call a brown trout. Hey?"

Gordon had to lean over the counter. He found himself squinting at a young fly fisher with dark curly hair. He was hefting a lunker well over two feet long, a male in pre-spawning form, copper brown with bright red blotches among the black, a kyped lower jaw, and a pale orange belly. He'd caught it in a creek in Western Alberta the year before he and Kimpy moved to Saskatchewan. In a flourish of angler vanity, he had given the photo to The Fishin' Hole staff for their display board.

"Boy," Gordon gasped, "I should have let that one go."

"Fried 'er up, did you?"

"We baked it. Fed a dozen neighbours, with lots left over."

They had rented some cabins, together with friends, on the Clearwater River. Kimpy had snapped the photo. He gutted the trout, and Kimpy made the stuffing. She chopped up some onions, celery, and mushrooms and sautéed them in the cast-iron pan. Threw in salt, pepper, curry, fresh dill, and sage. She dumped some dried breadcrumbs into the hot pan and stirred up the mix. When the stuffing had cooled off, she filled the brown trout's bounteous cavity. She packed up the trout in aluminum foil and put it into the oven. The prodigious brown baked for about an hour, and its heavy fragrance drifted to every corner of the cabin.

The old photograph took him back to their courting days when he and Kimpy would pack up the tent and go on road trips through the western provinces and the northwestern states. They would sleep naked in a double bedroll. In Gordon's mind, the lovemaking and the fly-fishing seemed to thrive together.

"Back there," the bald man whispered as though he were alluding to a poker game. "In the storage area. *Shhh.*" The man grinned knowingly.

"What?"

"Just go back there. You'll see."

Gordon trudged to the rear of the store, pushed open a swinging door, and entered a dimly lit storage area. He stepped between two stacks of cardboard cartons and peered into a dingy office. Two people were talking in subdued tones. Gordon crept nearer to the office and saw that one of the speakers was an unshaven little man. He growled at the woman and passed her a cigarette. She looked like Audrey, the receiving clerk. She was chuckling at something the fellow had said, and there was a trace of intimacy between them. The man wasn't really growling. His natural voice was a growl. He turned to face Gordon.

"Al Postnikov?"

The man squinted up at him as though Gordon might be some sort of investigator. Then he broke into a crazed smile. "Hey, buddy. You bang into any trucks lately?"

Why, Gordon asked, were they whispering?

Al shushed him with his finger. "Why d'ya think?" he said. "The Stocker keeps a low profile, eh? I'm not exactly certified." He snickered over his own remark.

Audrey abandoned the two men to run out back for a smoke. She and Gordon had had many a chat over a broken rod or an obscure fly pattern. She lived at Pike Lake and commuted to work each day because she loved to come home to lots of privacy, the small lake, plenty of ponds, and aspen groves. Could this be where the mysterious Stocker was hanging his hat? Gordon sat in Audrey's chair, and he and Postnikov leaned toward each other in the manner of desperate men.

"I'm looking for someone to do a job," said Gordon.

"You wanna hire me?"

"Yes. Al, you see, I have this . . . I have this big idea."

4

Gordon's big idea had several components to it, and one of the most needed components was money. For the past two or three years, in a routine manner, Gordon had banked a goodly chunk of his pension cheques. His favourite teller, a voluble big woman with ornate nails and meticulously applied makeup, told him in August that his accumulated term deposits came to more than thirty thousand dollars.

He wandered dolefully out of the bank and back to his house. It seemed odd that, in the midst of his long period of grieving, he had actually been accruing some money. Wasn't a discovery like this supposed to make people happy? *No*, Gordon thought. But at least he had the funds for his new big idea.

Check.

A second component of this idea was the need for someone to live in his house for maybe a few weeks. Sooey Guenther came to mind. Since his forced resignation in 2004, she had kept in touch with Gordon. Sooey was popular now, a young woman with several constituencies to call upon. Bookish friends, lesbian and gay friends, cycling and jogging friends, progressive political allies. And Gordon could not imagine Sooey or her friends throwing wild parties in his house. Sooey had contempt for noisy, inarticulate drunks who went to wild parties. Her brother Bungo, in other words. Gordon phoned her one evening in early September.

"I need someone who could be responsible for the house. To stay for free, of course. He or she would need to bring in the mail. That sort of thing."

"Hmm."

"A sensible young person," he said. "Someone who wouldn't wreck the house?"

"Sounds like someone I know."

"Would I know her? Or him?"

"Yeah. Goes by the name of Guenther, and these days her parents are, like, driving her crazy."

Check.

A third component of Gordon's big idea was Gordon himself, an improved, healthy version. A Gordon Carter who could walk a great deal more than the distance from his house to the bakery four blocks away. This Gordon would need to walk up a mountain trail, if necessary, and pretend he was the old Gordon with the brown curly hair who had dragged his canoe over Alberta river portages, propelled his belly-boat into the wind, and walked to work in the morning and back home at night. The Gordon who once carried Kimpy all the way downstairs to their car and drove her at frantic speed to Emergency.

Gordon began a regime of walking well down into the river paths and up again three days a week. At first, this tramping around was an agony, and frequently, he had to stop at his favourite bench on the lower trail and have a rest. On alternate days, he took his much-neglected bicycle out on the Meewasin Trail. He peddled a little farther each day. He began to eat better and lose weight, and by late

August, he began to look forward to each engagement with the bicycle.

Check.

The fourth and greatest component was Al Postnikov. The Stocker was his own greatest gift.

Check.

Well before sunrise in late September, the two men headed west on the Yellowhead in Postnikov's honey wagon. They reached a tiny settlement east of Hinton, Alberta, by around three o'clock. Postnikov parked his truck on a trail in the bush some distance from the Obed Lake Resort. He gave his horn a few blasts. He climbed up on the truck and opened a big hatch.

A sturdy old fellow with chaotic white hair strode stiffly down the path to a chicken house near Al's truck. He gawked up at Al and nodded glumly. "What the hell are you doin' here?"

"I'm very well, thank you," said Al, pawing at the blackflies.

"S'pose you want some fish."

"Hell, no. I'm here for the conversation."

"Three thousand browns? Is that what you said?"

"That'll do."

"It'll cost ya."

"There's a surprise."

The old fellow leaned a dip net against the truck and unlocked the chicken house, which proved to house no chickens at all. Postnikov turned to Gordon, who was also swatting at blackflies. "This here's Bindle. We call him Under the Table Bindle. Sweetest guy I know."

Soon, Postnikov had paid Bindle and he and Gordon were back on the highway. The tamaracks were turning from green to blinding yellow, the aspens had lost many of their leaves, and the late September skies were gathering legions of rain clouds. Postnikov seemed unaffected or unaware of the mustering clouds. He was preoccupied with one of his trout-infested monologues.

"I don't care what anyone says." He turned to glower at Gordon. "No way can you put frickin' brook trout in Patricia Lake. Never again."

"I was just asking," said Gordon. "The brookies did very nicely when I was a— "

"Of course, they did well. They did way too well. Remember that stream that runs from Pyramid into Patricia and out the other end?"

"Yes. I used to fish that creek."

"Cottonwood Crick. Flowed into the Athabasca River. Well, them brook trout. Exotic species, right? Invasive little fuckers. They clean out all the bull trout eggs, clean out the cutthroat fry. All because guys like you and me wanted to catch some brook trout like those buggers down east, eh? No frickin' way."

"So how can we bring back the—"

"Rainbows, man. Rainbows. They belong in that system, and they don't wipe out every other goddam fish in the neighbourhood. If you want brookies, you have to show me a lake that don't have no outlet stream. Otherwise, you're wastin' my time and your money."

When they reached the park gate, Gordon began to fidget and look around for park rangers and police vehicles. Postnikov pulled over to the through lane, drove slowly, and waved at the fellow in the kiosk. The young man checked out the logo on Al's tanker truck. It read B&B Septic Service. He seemed to be frowning. Al rolled on through.

"He let you go," said Gordon.

"Them guys always do. I smile and wave, and they wave back. They're not too fussy about climbing up behind."

"Climbing up behind?"

"To check the honey wagon."

"Oh," said Gordon. The man was a genius.

Postnikov shifted gears, and the water in his tank swooshed and sluiced as though the tide was coming in.

When they arrived at Lake Edith, there was no one in sight. The cabin owners had been gone for several weeks, and the old log structures stood stoically along the lakeshore as though they contained the ghosts of giggling children, outdoor cooking, and beers with the neighbours. The truck lumbered up at last to the edge of the lake.

Kimpy was waiting for them, her hands covering her lips and her eyes wide with surprise. She wore her char uniform, a plain black dress with white frills at the sleeves and collar, and her black-and-white sneakers. He hadn't seen her in that uniform since the summer of 1962, when Richard was a travel agent, and Gordon was a driver for the Jasper Park Lodge. But right now, Kimpy was lingering at the shores of Lake Edith because she got it. She got Gordon's little caper, and she approved. She raised her fist. *Go, Gordy.*

His job was to walk back up the road and watch for park vehicles or snoops while Al tended to the three-inch hose that ran from his tank to the lake. When Gordon came back from his vigil, Al was standing up inside the open tank, sweeping the last of the fingerlings through the drainage hole and down through the hose. They emerged squirming from the other end and finned cautiously into the shallows, three thousand of them. In the clear water, even at five or six inches, he could see that they were brown trout. The wisest, wariest fish of them all, the truest trout of them all, the dark golden denizen of English chalk streams, boggy Scottish creeks, German meadow streams, and northern Russian rivers, the prodigious ambushers who lay under stream banks and fallen trees, waiting.

"Guess what they stocked this lake with back in the 1920s," Al said.

"It was always rainbows, wasn't it?"

"Brown trout. Hell. They grew like hogs, and they lived three times as long as a rainbow. Massive buggers."

Gordon was caught up with the wonder of men like Al Postnikov and Bindle, fly-fishing zealots who pumped trout fingerlings into sapphire-blue lakes. Al watched from shore as the young browns had their first feed in their new home. They were going for tiny flies on the surface, jassids, or emerging midges. Gordon wondered if Al might return and check on their growth, these perfect, flashy beings.

If so, Gordon might just ask himself along for the trip. Wasn't Al Postnikov a little bit like God?

Well, no. Because God would never have charged Gordon Carter three thousand bucks per lake.

"Carter, hey?"

Gordon awakened from his reverie.

"Go check the road. I gotta bring in the hose and turn this baby around. Shout if you hear anyone, okay?"

Gordon ambled up the road, shaking with wonder.

Postnikov drove the empty truck to a campground south of the Jasper town site on the Banff-Jasper highway. Their campsite was as far into the trees as Al could manage. Because it was late September, there were only a handful of campers and tents scattered among the aspens and pines. The two men worked in the semi-dark and the light rain to set up Al's big tent, an old canvas affair, an outfitter's tent with a hole in the roof for a stack from the wood stove. The tent bore fragrance from decades of smoke. They hauled two camp cots and their sleeping bags inside. The Stocker lit the stove, and they had beer and sandwiches for supper.

"You know, Al, we could have driven into town and eaten at a restaurant. My treat."

"How? With that big sucker of a truck? Big ol' negatory, Carter. What we're doing isn't even close to legal. Low profile. That's the Stocker's motto."

It was still raining steadily in the morning. Over a breakfast of cereal and instant coffee, they talked about a large pond they had both known from their separate experiences in Jasper Park, known as Iris Lake. Before the trout stocking had been phased out, there had been good fishing there. It had always sported a good population of brook trout, and neither of them could recall seeing an outlet stream. This meant that the trout staged near shore just before spawning every October. Gordon had once seen them there in the fall, and he'd never forgotten the sight. They were staging over a gravelly shore as though this stretch was the next best thing to a stream.

Gordon managed to prevail upon the Stocker to give Iris another look, so they needed to get some brook trout fry. They gassed up the truck just outside of Jasper and drove west through the rain. Postnikov took the Yellowhead into British Columbia, to a bush farm deep in the backcountry. The farm had a sad-looking house with fake wood siding and several large outbuildings some distance away. A stream flowed through the middle of the spread and meandered beneath a large barn and out the other side. At Postnikov's request, Gordon waited in the truck while his partner in crime went in search of the farmer. Al emerged from the barn and signalled to him. Gordon held a newspaper over his head and jogged through the wet grass.

Inside the barn, Gordon beheld the flyfisher's equivalent of a pirate's hoard. At the upstream end of the barn, there were several long, parallel troughs dimly illuminated by overhead lights. The troughs were filled with fluttering water—thousands of trout fry. The outflowing water emptied through the screens and into an artificial pond, which drained out of the barn.

"Gordon, I want you to meet the best trout freelancer in the business. Fred Smolt."

Gordon looked up from the nearest trough at a tall, pudgy, smiling man with a helmet of wavy hair. He wore a dark green shirt, muddy green pants, and rubber boots. Fred's benign smile reminded Gordon of a kindergarten teacher. "Is that your real name?"

"What do you think, Carter?" said Postnikov.

"This place is amazing. It's just amazing."

"We like it," said Fred in a blissful, subdued voice.

"We?"

Fred Smolt extended his hand toward the troughs in a wide sweeping gesture. "Me and my little friends."

Gordon gave Postnikov a meaningful look, and he turned his gaze to Fred Smolt. "Would some of your friends today happen to be brook trout?"

Fred did everything slowly. His relaxed demeanour was catching. Slowly and carefully, the men went to work on one of the outer troughs. They scooped roughly two thousand brook trout fry into a heavy-gauge plastic bag more than half-filled with water and ice. They puffed out the remainder of the bag with oxygen from a pressurized tank and tied off the end with duct tape. They loaded a second and third bag in the same manner.

"Al, I could give you a deal on some cutthroat," Fred remarked entreatingly. "I just got these from . . . from one of my people?"

"Not this time, bro. We're working down around four thousand feet."

"No harm in asking."

They lugged the three bags of trout fry into the back of Fred's station wagon and bound them to three wooden pack-boards. Al asked Fred if he could leave his honey wagon by the gate, and Fred assured him that no one would notice it or ask any questions if they did. Gordon wondered out loud if the pack-boards in the station wagon were designed for mules and packhorses.

"Oh, yes," Fred replied. "These frames are older than we are."

"And at the other end," Gordon said to Al, "are there some—"

" 'Fraid not, Carter. When we get back to the park and them trails, we are the mules."

Their first drop was at Iris Lake, a half-hour walk from the Yellowhead Highway. The three of them unloaded at the trailhead, and by late morning, they were heading up a hikers' path through a forest of yellow tamarack and white spruce. It was chilly and damp. The rain had stopped, and a light mist floated all around them. Gordon had not seen the mountains in two days. He was last in line, and within the first hundred metres or so, he began to gasp and wheeze at an alarming rate. At least he wasn't chilly anymore.

"Bearshit," Postnikov growled, and he veered to the right.

"Bear poop," said Fred in his kindly voice, and he, too, veered to the right.

It lay in the middle of the trail, piled high and massive. The three of them stood around to admire the bear scat, and only Gordon was puffing beneath the weight of his pack-board. "It's blue," he said.

"Blueberries," Fred replied. There was a note of apology in his voice as though, on occasion, nature comported itself in shameless ways.

They sloshed forward another kilometre up the trail, and Gordon began to perspire as he never had in all his life.

"Not far to go," Fred called back.

They hiked up over a rocky ridge, and below them lay Iris Lake, a large, marshy pond covering perhaps a hundred acres. Postnikov raised his right arm for silence. "Keep the frickin' noise down from here on," he whispered. "You never know who's wandering around."

They trudged through the pines into a weedy, mossy bowl surrounding the pond. Gordon wondered if it was really the bears that Postnikov was edgy about. They arrived at last at a small bay and a muddy access to the pond. Gordon recalled the boats that used to lie by this bay, small punts chained to the trees, but the only evidence of them now was a few old grooves in the sandy clay carved by the keels on the edge of the pond.

Fred helped Gordon to shed his pack-board, and as the men opened up the bag, Gordon sat puffing and sweating on a fallen tamarack by the edge of the pond. He was too fatigued to stand up and watch the release. He closed his eyes, breathed in and out, and smelled at last the larchy perfume that drifted past his nostrils. His exhaustion made him oddly contented.

There were two more bags of brook trout fry to deliver, so Gordon arose from his fallen tree and shouldered his pack-board once again —his gloriously unburdened pack-board. He had to hurry to keep up with Fred and Postnikov, and he wondered what it might take to get into that kind of shape.

The path did not inspire much confidence. It was little used and almost as narrow as a game trail. It wound up through the trees, rose and fell over several ridges, and snaked around some of the largest boulders. One did not pass through the trees and boulders; one walked in and out, up and down, all around them. Owing to the omnipresence of thick forest and mist, the light was dim and foreboding, but as they moved higher up the trail, the mist seemed to recede, and the forest began to thin out.

"Can I give either of you fellows a hand?" said Gordon, puffing and wheezing once more.

"Keep your voice down," said Postnikov, signalling with his right hand.

It seemed that they had all been enlisted in a war movie: Postnikov, the cigar-chewing sergeant in command; Fred Smolt, the young medic, the idealist. Gordon would be the new kid, fresh out of basic training, learning how to smoke and cuss. Taciturnity was the key. Gordon had never been very good at taciturnity, but he could try. *Ya may notta heard, fellas, but there's a war on.* Kimpy would have been amused by the entire caper.

Around noon, the men arrived on the shores of a larger, deeper pond. Unlike Iris Lake, which was surrounded by marshy weeds, grass, and cattails, this pond had a rounded shape with several small bays, and the shore was studded with huge boulders covered in moss. Only a metre or two from shore, the pond went deep and dark. The water was unusually still, a perfect mirror for large boulders. The pond had an otherworldly, mystical appeal. And like Iris Lake, according to Fred, it had no outlet stream.

Gordon asked what this large pond was called. Postnikov said it didn't have a name, and Fred said that was a shame.

"Such a pretty pond," Fred declared. "I didn't even know it was here."

"Hardly no one knows it's here," said Postnikov. "The odd hiker, maybe. It's not even on the survey maps. And that's the whole point."

There was a small beach below where they stood, contained by a four-foot bank. The three men descended to the beach and gathered by the shore to help each other with the two remaining bags. In this tiny bay, the shoreline and the shallows were awash with white sand, but farther out, the water lay dark and deep. The trout fry flowed out of their bags, and a few dozen casualties floated belly-up. The survivors fanned out, inch-long explorers in a place as new as the trough where they'd hatched out. They darted and drifted, darted and glided, and soon they began to feed. Hundreds of brook trout fry began to rise up and suck in morsels too tiny to see. Pond plankton, Al Postnikov called it. The tiny fish rose like bubbles, dimpled the surface, dived down, flashing over the sand, and cruised like predators in training. Fred and Al gazed at the fry, hands dripping and strangely silent.

"It never gets better than this," said Al.

"Exactly," said Fred.

"Well," said Gordon, "there is the fishing."

In one chilly, rain-filled week, working from Fred's concealed barn, the men stocked four ponds and five lakes. The last stocking was the toughest challenge of all, a high mountain cirque lake half an hour's drive south of the Columbia Icefields. The lake lay well above the treeline. Cutthroat country. They each carried a small bag of Fred's cherished cutthroat (which cost Gordon an extra two thousand dollars). Their trail took them through the forest and then sharply uphill into a high meadow. Gordon made it to the lake without having a heart attack, for which he was secretly proud, and he realized that, at last, he was getting into hiking shape, or what might pass for hiking shape among sixty-five-year-olds. He felt that he was about halfway there, whatever that meant. But this high lake was the last trek of their great adventure.

The rain had been descending on them in misty droplets. Around lunchtime, just after they had dumped the cutthroat, the wind came up, the droplets turned to rain, and the rain turned to sleet. The men arose quickly from their snacks, packed up, and, as the sleet turned into snowflakes, trudged down the mountain. They managed to stay warm as they strode all the way to the station wagon. Fred drove them back north on the Banff-Jasper highway, and when at last they turned west into British Columbia again, the snow had returned to rain, and the road back to Fred's trout nursery was wet and gloomy. But not entirely gloomy for Gordon. He was starting to feel like a teenage dissident in the Here and Now Club. But his brief reversion to youthful resistance, his little adventure, was coming to an end.

Postnikov turned to his friend in the front seat. "You should move back to Alberta, Freddie. Else any day now, you'll be sproutin' ferns from the armpits. The other place, too."

"Then why, old comrade," said Fred, "did you flee Alberta?"

"Fewer regs in Saskatchewan fisheries. Fewer conservation officers. Cheaper to live at good old Pike Lake." Postnikov turned to Gordon, who was starting to nod in the back seat. "Carter here. He did the same thing, eh? Hightailed it to Saskatchewan."

Fred glanced back briefly to Gordon. "But why?"

"It's a difficult question to answer," said Gordon. "I grew up in Edmonton in the 1950s. Later on, I met my wife there. For me, it was like growing up in a town called Success. It was the fastest-growing city, the Gateway to the North. Back then, they called it the Oil Capital of Canada. I didn't like Edmonton's big ego. I didn't like the Social Credit government. Does any of this make sense?"

They had both wanted to leave Edmonton. Kimpy told Gordon that she wanted to shed her skin like a party dress and grow a new one. *I want to be a new person,* she said. *And I think I want a kid. Did I just say that?* Another challenge was getting permanent teaching jobs in the city. They wanted a new start in a newer, slower town, so they took jobs in Saskatoon and left Edmonton with few regrets. And got jobs and got pregnant.

"It makes sense to me," said Fred with a yawn. The rain seemed to inspire yawning, and they all had a go at it.

Postnikov recounted how he and Fred had grown up in Jasper.

"We both got jobs feeding the fish at the hatchery," Fred remarked. "Back in the late 1950s?"

"We were just sprouts," said Postnikov. "Thirteen, maybe fourteen."

"You fellows must be almost as old as I am."

"Yes," Fred murmured, "and we hated junior high school about equally."

Gordon perked up. "Do you remember the time that man's body was found up near Patricia Lake?"

Fred and Al shared a nervous glance in the front seat.

Al spoke at last. "You gonna tell him, buddy, or should I?"

Fred sounded either bored or glum; Gordon couldn't tell which.

"His name was Abe Collins," Fred began. "He was a very kind man, a gentle fellow. He managed the hatchery. A rumour went around that he was gay, except back then, they didn't use that word. People began to whisper that he was *taking advantage* of the boys he hired at the hatchery. People say to this day that it was a fish disease that killed the hatchery, but the hatchery began its big decline when Abe Collins got pushed out. Amen."

This was the first time Gordon had witnessed Fred go on at any length about anything. Fred maintained a dispassionate gaze as he drove through the rain.

"What a sad story," said Gordon.

"By then, Al and his family were living in Edmonton," Fred went on.

"Yep," said Al. "I missed all the flack when the shit hit the fan."

"One day, Abe just walked up the valley and blew his brains out." Fred stared glumly ahead as the rain pelted his windshield. "What can I say? He was my friend. He was a friend to all of us. Back then, people saw no difference between a pedophile and a gay man who just, you know, enjoyed our company."

"A friend of mine and I found the body," said Gordon. "It was the spring of 1959."

Fred Smolt turned to stare at the Stocker, and the Stocker stared back.

"Say that again?" said Postnikov.

Gordon repeated his revelation.

"You found Abe's body?" cried Fred. "You and your friend found him?"

"We hopped out of there as though we'd seen a ghost. We went straight to the Mounties in town."

"The story was in the Jasper paper," Fred whispered. "Almost half a century ago. I still have a copy of the article. I'll bet your names will be in that article."

"I got holda the same article," said Postnikov. "I never threw it away." The Stocker turned around and stared at Gordon. "Can you beat that? You, of all people. The guy who rams my honey wagon."

Fred Smolt continued. "When it happened, like I say, Al and his family had moved away. So he missed all the sadness and the gossip. It was a terrible time. I always thought I could have done something, like tell people what Mr. Collins was really like, but I didn't. No one ever asked me. I can't go back there without feeling regret."

The rest of the drive back to Fred Smolt's farm was in silence. He slowed the station wagon at his gate and drove to the house. The men left their pack-boards outside for the rain to clean off the silt and mud, and they tramped inside. Fred lit a fire in the kitchen stove. The three men threw some sandwiches together, and Fred brought out the beer.

"So," Gordon said to his two conspirators, "is it mere coincidence that we're all here together, talking about this good man, Mr. Collins?"

Gordon had been thinking about his country, how most of the population had gathered in a long, messy line a hundred or so miles above the American border. How he kept running into his students in the stores downtown and in airports all over Western Canada. How old stories kept getting re-told by old acquaintances at every reunion. How people and stories kept coinciding, and how the stories seemed to change with each teller. Unlike Gordon's version, a high adventure where two boys find a corpse, this one was intimate and sad. Almost too real, a modern tragedy.

"Your little accident," Fred muttered. "With Al's truck? It was fate. It was a case of fate, pure and simple."

"That friend of yours," said Postnikov. "You still in touch with him?"

"Sort of," said Gordon. "He was my fishing buddy when we were a lot younger. In fact, if you fellows wouldn't mind, I'd like to name our nameless lake after him. The deep one we stocked with brook trout? Above Iris?"

The two friends nodded.

"You guys may as well know this. The work I'm paying you for, it's sort of a surprise for my friend, Richard Simon. A tribute, I suppose. I'd like to call our unnamed brook trout lake Simon Pond. Unofficial, of course. Keep it off the map. Would you fellows be all right with that?"

"Is he in some kind of trouble?" Fred asked.

"He's battling a bad cancer," Gordon muttered. "Actually, I think I owe him a phone call."

Upon Gordon's return, Sooey Guenther welcomed him with a big hug. She related how great it had been to have a place of her own and how *friendly* and *accepting* and *open to diversity* his neighbours were. But when she left the house, Gordon was left with the sound of the wind, a clamorous dry wind, moaning through the branches of the elm trees. It hummed something vaguely funereal. The temperature was hovering around three above, the sky dishwater grey. Saskatoon always had days like this in October: leafless elms, clouds from horizon to horizon, temperatures progressing from chilly to cold, and light receding rapidly each day. The Land of Dying Skies.

He half-opened the Venetian blinds to let in just enough light through the front door window without being seen by people passing by. He stationed himself in his front hall and dialled Richard's number. His heart was thumping.

A woman answered the phone.

Gordon introduced himself to the woman, whose name was Jane.

"Richard has mentioned you," she replied. "He's resting right now, but you could try him a little later if you want. Say half an hour?"

"How is he doing?"

"Oh," she began in an anxious, cheerful voice, "he has his good days."

She told Gordon about some recent procedures, a battery of tests coming up, and their visits to specialists over the past few months. "He gets tired," she said, "and that might be the new meds that he's taking." As she spoke, Gordon's heart pounded continuously. He slumped down on a chair in the hallway and closed his eyes, and Jane carried on with the details of Richard's changing condition.

Gordon heard a noise and opened his eyes. A woman was stuffing something into his mailbox. He could only see her through the horizontal cracks afforded by the blinds, but not well enough to recognize her. She was wearing a faded blue denim jacket. She retreated slowly down the front steps. He crept toward the blinds. She might have been ash blonde. She had a narrow back.

"Turn around," he whispered as she walked toward her car.

"I beg your pardon?" said the woman named Jane.

"Nothing," said Gordon. "Just someone at my mailbox. I hope you're bearing up all right."

"Oh, yes," said the woman. "I used to work in critical care. I guess you could say I'm a veteran."

When the conversation ended, Gordon's heart began to calm. He walked outside and gazed up and down the windy street. Thousands of elm leaves were swirling around. This time, his mailbox produced a tiny box of Belgian chocolates and a small note in a matching white envelope: *This is your welcoming committee! I hope you had a happy trip. If you're still wondering who the mystery gal is, just check me out someday at my favourite place. Hint: It might also be one of yours as well! Warm wishes, Mystery Gal.*

Gordon strolled back inside and collapsed on the living room couch. Richard Simon was dying, but before he got sick, he'd had the good sense to hook up with a nurse. He might never see Richard again, but someone had his friend's back. And Gordon was being stalked (Courted? Comforted? Riddled to death?) by a well-meaning admirer. How lonely she must be.

The wind rose, and the leafless trees began to sway. The hallway seemed to darken as Gordon gazed around. Kimpy had drifted into the darkened hallway, but this time, he could barely see her. Ghostly. She looked ghostly.

"What should I do?" he said.

"I don't know, Gordy. I think it's up to her, don't you?"

"I suppose you're right. How would you feel if . . . if someday I invited her in for tea?"

"I think you should *at least* invite her in for tea. Give the poor gal a chance."

"But here's my worry. I don't think that I have any . . . I don't have any heart left. I'm . . . don't you see, Kimpy, I'm . . ." He began to thump his chest as though he were knocking on a stranger's door. "I'm dead in my heart. It's not *in* me to have another . . . you know."

"There, there."

"You spoiled me, don't you see? I could never love another woman."

"That's so sweet, Gordon."

"I'm all dead in here."

Kimpy waited until he had blown his nose and regained his voice. "Maybe I was lucky, Gordon. Maybe I died before my heart did. And you were right there to the end. Just like that Jane woman."

"Jane and me. We're angels, you know."

"Ha. Anyway, you might just be exaggerating, Gordon. You might fear that your heart is dead, but how can you know for sure?"

Kimpy paused for a moment, and Gordon wondered, as he'd been doing lately, if people went somewhere after their death. Was Kimpy's energy issuing here from some other dimension? Could it be that something in Kimpy had found a way of returning to the place she had nurtured, the place that had nurtured her for so long? Not just a thought lodged in Gordon's memory, but the spirit of something, like an echo of something that kept returning? And was that the state where Richard Simon might soon find himself? Not one echo but two, singing a duet? Richard and Kimpy, back together again? *Dream on, old pedagogue.*

Kimpy said, "What's that you're holding?"

"Nothing. Just some chocolates."

"Try one, Gordy. Try one just for me."

Gordon tore open the box and inspected his gift from Mystery Gal. He picked out a round one and put it into his mouth. He rolled it about with his tongue and bit down on the chocolate, and it flooded his mouth with a burst of strawberries. He chewed slowly, surprised that it tasted so good. Should he try a second one? He checked his watch. His half-hour had elapsed. He picked up the phone and dialled.

Richard answered on the second ring. "Greetings and salutations, Young Carter," he declared. "How are you faring these days?"

"That was going to be my question. I just met Jane over the phone, and she filled me in."

"Well, I suppose Jane filled your ear with all the gory details? She does tend to exaggerate things, you know. But I'm feeling just fine today. I've had my nap. Ready for a stroll around the block."

"That's good to hear, old buddy." Gordon paused briefly. "Richard, I have something to tell you, and I don't quite know where to start."

Richard did sound well. He was always good at dissimulating, painting an optimistic picture that urged people away from disturbing news. He could spread optimism at the drop of a hat. He could make others feel better in his presence. Gordon had almost forgotten how considerate his friend was, how kindly toward others. Gordon released a polite strawberry belch into the phone.

"My story has something to do with our mutual addiction. How people like us come together at the strangest times. And it has a corpse as well. I've had a bit of an adventure in the mountains. You might say. In your honour, you might say."

"Well, now you have my curiosity going, Gordon. Why don't you just start at the beginning?"

Gordon popped another chocolate into his mouth, chomped it rapidly, and started at the beginning.

5

For decades, the Bugchuckers Club had been meeting once a month in a rented hall near the airport. Gordon's attendance had become intermittent over the year, so on this occasion, in early November, he felt like an outsider. He wandered from conversation to conversation without saying much of anything. It seemed that half of the members were aching to gather information on trout, the where and the how of catching them. The other half of the membership was eager to answer these questions, to pass on their wisdom about things of utter importance: Were the rainbows in Diefenbaker any good to eat? Was it true that you could catch four species of trout at Zeden Lake? Why would they do that? How do you tie an authentic seal bugger? How do you fish those creeks in the Cypress Hills with that jungle of tall grass, for God's sake? And cougars, aren't there cougars down there? Are belly-boats as safe as they say, or is that just so much spin? Where can I take my kids to learn fly-casting?

Eager conversations like these hummed and roared around the meeting room for well over an hour, and after a while, they managed to distract Gordon from Jane's latest news in Vancouver.

Jane Simon. She and Richard had married in the last weeks before his death. She had wondered, over the phone, if Gordon might come to the celebration of Richard's life. *He asked me, just before the end, if you'd say a few words.* At that moment, Jane's voice had faltered, and Gordon could feel the measure of her devotion to his old friend.

Yes, absolutely. It would now be Jane's turn to be Job.

Richard Simon was gone from the world. *Goodbye and tight lines.* This time, Mortality had snagged a big one.

"How do I get started again?" Gordon asked an old fellow who had gathered a crowd. His face was familiar.

Gordon's question seemed to fly from his mouth as though he were calling for a life jacket. They re-introduced themselves. The old fellow's name was Jimmy Horner. He was well over six feet tall, and people at the Bugchuckers Club seemed to defer to him for piscatorial wisdom.

"Say, aren't you the fellow I saw at The Fishin' Hole last summer? We were waiting in line. You told me you knew the Stocker personally?"

Gordon's little stocking initiative in the Rockies came back to him, and he smiled. It seemed like a long time ago. He had tried to run down Postnikov again, but no one at Pike Lake had seen him or Audrey for weeks.

"You want to get started, Carter? Come up north with us next June. A bunch of the members have a family fish-out. Bring the missus."

"I'll have to find one first," said Gordon.

"I see. Well, all you really need is a fly rod. Still got your fly rod?"

"I do indeed," said Gordon. "I can cast a line but that's about the sum total of my knowledge. My trouting brain is very rusty."

"You're a member here, aren't you?" said Horner.

"I used to be a regular. I try to show up once in a while. I've seen some familiar faces tonight."

"I thought so."

"Welcome back," said another man. "Gordon, isn't it?"

Gordon shook the new man's hand, but he didn't recognize him.

"Welcome back, Gordon," said an old fellow beside him.

He found himself surrounded by well-wishers, all of whose names had escaped him. He felt as though he had just come back to a church after a long absence.

"Didn't you teach at Mildred Kerr High?"

"I did," said Gordon to a short bald fellow with a familiar grin, an extrovert's grin. "Guilty as charged."

"Guilty nothing," said the bald fellow. "My son loved your English class. Remember Ronan Margolis?"

"I do indeed," said Gordon. "Ronan's very bright. How is he doing these days?"

"He's got his nose in the books these days," said Mr. Margolis.

"Bad habit," said Gordon. "The next thing you know, poor Ronan will be playing chess."

Some people chuckled at Gordon's little joke. He caught himself enjoying the exchange.

"My neighbour's daughter took one of your English classes," a woman said. "She thought you were a pretty cool teacher."

"I loved the job while it lasted," Gordon replied.

Jimmy Horner wanted to know something that had been bugging him for a month: if the Stocker was a real person, why in hell didn't he join up with the Bugchuckers Club? Mr. Margolis wanted to know how retirement suited Gordon. Another fellow wondered out loud if Gordon was planning to sign up for a fly-tying workshop. The volume of the conversations and the laughter had risen, and Gordon had to shout to be heard.

"I had to start up again," said a woman. "I couldn't find my fly rod, but one day, I was looking for something else in the garage, and there it was."

Her face was familiar.

"Miranda, is it?"

She nodded, and he asked her if she was one of the women who had cared for Kimpy in the hospital.

"No," she said, "I own the bakery on Broadway. Your wife was one of our customers. Everybody seemed to love her. I'm not sure if you remember, but I'm also the gal who fishes down on Bone Creek. You asked me once about stream fishing in the province?"

Gordon had all but forgotten that conversation, but something she said rang a bell. He fixed on the word *bakery* and then on the word *gal.* "You wouldn't happen to grow daisies in your yard, would you?"

She was a few inches shorter than Gordon, her formerly blonde hair turning white. The skin on her face was delicately lined, and it was dappled with many a washed-out freckle. She had a welcoming, open grin. She seemed replete with curiosity. She moved and spoke quickly and seemed to possess a good deal of nervous energy. She had a nothing-to-lose way about her, which made him wonder where all that courage came from. She was probably well into her fifties, and she would have been cute as a child, looked cute as a high school girl, cute as a young woman, cute in middle age, and destined to be cute in old age. *Cute. A word very much out of favour*, Gordon thought. And what exactly did cute mean? He would never be able to tell her that she was cute unless, perhaps, he did so with irony. She wore scarcely any makeup. She was as unadorned and trim as a daisy. Why had he never really fixed on her before?

Miranda Clifton was the daughter of Jimmy Horner, who had recently become president of the Bugchuckers. Miranda and her ex had owned the bakery on Broadway, and under the terms of the divorce agreement, she had walked away with the bakery.

Gordon and Miranda had a pleasantly charged conversation while all around them, the laughter and the fishing wisdom swirled. It got so loud that Gordon had to interrupt Miranda occasionally to urge her to repeat what she said. This was embarrassing for Gordon because he did not want to come across as a faltering old duck in need of a hearing aid. He tried to read her lips so that he wouldn't have to interrupt her again. She said, or seemed to say, *Why not try it?*

She was waiting for an answer.

"I don't know," he said, hoping for clarity.

It could be fine, her lips seemed to say. She smiled at him.

What could he say? Maybe she wanted to have coffee sometime, or maybe she wanted to take him fishing or try the fudge on the table next to the fishing photos, or maybe she wanted to take in a movie, or maybe she was trying to hustle him, maybe her husband was a decent guy who got burned in the settlement, or maybe he was the asshole and she the victim, but Miranda did not act like a victim; she acted like the sort of woman Kimpy would like, but you never can tell about these things—maybe she was too much of a Daddy's girl, Daddy's little fly-fishing adoring-type daughter, maybe long-term relationships were not her thing—stung by love, never to love again, or maybe that was Gordon, destined to live out his days in the Stupid Room of a house that felt less and less like home, and maybe

Miranda—who was *still* waiting for an answer to her question—maybe Miranda was one of those aggressive psychotic women who stalked men who wanted to disentangle themselves from her.

Gordon, look, he said to himself, *you are being very stupid.* There stood, quite possibly, the only person in the world he might take to Simon Pond for brook trout, the only woman he might bring home for tea. She had fetched a card from her pocket, and she was holding it in front of him. But what the hell was Miranda asking of him? What would Richard do at this moment?

Gordon knew what Richard would do.

He took a big breath, released it slowly, and said to Miranda in high volume, "Yes, absolutely. Why not?"

mallow's course

BACK IN THE 1980S, when I was still an eager scholar, I went to a conference in Chicago. My arrival there coincided with a bout of insomnia, and, tossing my way through the night, I was reminded that in this city, I might at last catch up with Eleanor Nix. I had heard somewhere that she'd moved here in the late sixties to become a medievalist. I was there for a conference on courtly love. In spite of my failure to keep in touch with her, I grew hopeful that she and I would get re-acquainted. She was not one of the presenters, but perhaps she would attend some of the sessions. If not, perhaps I would get news of her. On the first day of the conference, I kept seeing large women drifting in and out of lecture halls who, from odd angles, might indeed be Eleanor.

Where did this anticipation come from? Was I homesick and seeking a friendly face? Was it merely because I'd found myself in Eleanor's domain? Perhaps I was in need of some connection to my (admittedly unremarkable) past. If she and I had been able to Google each other back then, perhaps one of us would have done so.

On the night of the conference's final banquet, there was a big reception. I remember saying to myself, *This is it, Jane. Eleanor Nix, now or never.* I was sitting on a large sofa next to a gathering of conference people. Along came a tipsy old fellow with a young woman in tow, perhaps a graduate student. She could not disguise her discomfort at the spectacle this old buffoon was creating. They sat next to me. The old fellow was shouting to be heard above the chatter of academic voices, leaning forward, scrawny and florid-faced, aiming his nose at her breasts.

"Open wide!" he croaked to the young woman.

"Open wide?"

"Wide wide wide."

That raspy old voice, that downright blatant leer. My old Professor Mallow, in the flesh.

Two decades before the Chicago conference, I had taken his class in Duckton, Oregon, a university town with a California feel to it. Mallow's class was known as the Wipeout Course, the most daunting hoop to jump through in the entire graduate program, its official title something like "Methods of Literary Scholarship and Criticism." There were no essays to write, only a final exam. To pass this exam, one had to demonstrate a knowledge of almost every reference book and scholarly periodical in the library. One also had to be well-versed in several conflicting theories of modern criticism.

Mallow was the department chairman, a dapper little eighteenth-century scholar with a studiously acquired accent, somewhere between Home Counties Brit and Southern genteel. He chain-smoked throughout the question period of each lecture, dropping sexual references like a chef depositing anchovies on an otherwise plain pizza.

On my very first day of grad school, I was one of roughly a hundred students in an amphitheatre, all of us waiting for Professor Mallow to appear. He arrived five or ten minutes late, placed his briefcase on a table, and squinted up at us through Coke-bottle glasses.

"Would all the ladies be kind enough to cross their legs?"

His voice was so hoarse and gravelly that I wondered how many years of nicotine and bourbon his body had welcomed.

"Yes. Good."

An incredulous silence.

"Now that the Gates of Hell are closed, I think we can safely proceed."

These days, if Professor Mallow had tried that witty opener, and if indeed he had escaped tar and feathering, he would have been sacked. But those were the good old sixties.

In grad school, I sailed through the library, a purposeful vision in white and grey, my hair cut short and serviceable. And that is where I met Eleanor Nix. She and her friends seemed, in all probability, even more bookish and untried by life than I. Eleanor was their leader, a big, billowy, freckled girl of twenty-five or so with a capacity for hard work and a solid academic record.

I refer to Eleanor as a girl because, like me, perhaps, she seemed to be on her way from girlhood to ladyhood without the intervening complications of womanhood. She dressed primly as though to suggest that her body was in perpetual service to her mind. She had not the slightest air about her of carnal knowledge and never encouraged off-colour humour. I used to notice her friends in the hallways. Among them all, there seemed to be a tacit contract of celibacy.

I needn't have brought my winter clothes to Duckton. The winter in Oregon amounted to a few months of rain, and then spring blossomed in early March with jungles of pink and green all along the road from my apartment to the campus. The wind ushered in salty air from the coast. I soon bonded with Eleanor's friends, several women and two men. After classes, we would browse among the shops. Warm nights, salty breezes, specialized book and music stores, coffee houses, all-night restaurants.

Eleanor's word for these things, so new to her, was liberating. Duckton itself was liberating. As to what it was liberating from, she never elaborated. From my memory of things back then, liberation had less to do with love-ins, drugs, or articles in *Playboy* or *Playgirl* and more to do with Vatican II and Martin Luther King. In 1965, it seems to me, all the Beatles wanted was to hold your hand. So, I found myself in the company of Eleanor and her friends, who never seemed to consider wetting their toes in the troublesome slough of their desires, and that was fine with me.

Surely, my own life in graduate school had been as celibate as theirs, but at least I nourished the occasional unchaste thought. I had a dream once about a bearded fellow named Mr. Mordo. I must have given him D. H. Lawrence's face. We had some naughty times before the night was over. But if I remember correctly, most of my unchaste thoughts were of the nostalgic variety. I had broken my engagement with Adrian Fermin a month or two before heading out to Oregon. For mysterious reasons, we had been drifting apart. Among his own friends in Hartford, Adrian was his gregarious and witty self, but in my company, he had begun to lapse into long sulks, during which he smoked a pipe. My favourite refrain at the time was that old standard: *Is there someone else?*

One night, we had a tiff and decided to call things off. I was well rid of him, but something down inside of me took its time forgetting Adrian Fermin.

Early in the fall at Duckton, Eleanor invited me to attend a study session with some of her colleagues who had all known one another from the previous year. If I remember correctly, there were seven of us, including myself. I've lost track of their names, except for the two men, Martin and Jerome. The idea of the meeting was to share information in order to cut down on the amount of legwork necessary to contend with Mallow's Wipeout Course. We would each peruse about a seventh of the relevant material, summarize our findings on four-by-six-inch file cards, and, at the end of each month, trade notes.

Most of my days and nights were spent on campus poring through my share of the scholarly journals and books for which we would be held responsible in Mallow's exam. He must have been aware that the majority of grad students in our program were devoting most of their waking hours to his course. The other professors would receive the remaining tatters of our energy. The failure rate in Mallow's course was over fifty percent. You were given three chances at the final, and then, if you hadn't passed with a B or better, you were sent packing. Ah, those were the days.

Eleanor Nix's friend Jerome had already written the final twice and failed twice. On the eve of his second try, he told us, he was so tense that his shoulders had frozen into a buzzard hunch. He went over to the student infirmary. The nurse on duty asked him to describe his symptoms, and each time he tried to respond, he dissolved into tears. At last, he managed to say enough so that the nurse could assess the problem. They poked a needle into him, some sort of muscle relaxant, and his shoulders fell back into place.

Jerome Kopella. He was shorter than Eleanor, considerably smaller, and the two of them went everywhere together like a precocious boy and his favourite aunt.

One day after classes, my file cards and I were on our way to the library to find out what *The Journal of English and Germanic Philology* was all about. I spied Eleanor heading in the same direction, lugging an impressive stack of books in her great, soft, freckled arms.

Let's see. When I conjure her up, she is wearing a newly ironed blouse with a round collar. I recall a circle pin on one of her lapels. Black or grey culottes and loafers. If she conjures me up at all, perhaps she sees a grey wool suit, straight long skirt, high-buttoned blouse. And sensible shoes.

"Need a hand?" I asked her.

"No thanks," she replied cheerfully, marching toward the entrance to the library. She had an impressive turnout; her feet flapped outward as she walked.

"Where's Jerome?"

"I don't know. Why?"

"He wasn't in class today, and you're the logical one to ask."

"I suppose I am," she said. She broke into a girlish smile. "No announcements yet. But hope springs eternal."

"You mean you two are engaged?"

"Well, not formally. Fingers crossed."

And there it was, love blossoming in the stacks. Sometime in the future, Jerome Kopella and Eleanor Nix would be man and wife.

Later that day, I found Jerome in a carrel, toiling over his notes. He looked woeful. "Oh, it's you," he said. "Is she coming this way?"

Jerome was in a terrible state. After spending some time working through the stacks and taking notes, I went back to his carrel and suggested lunch. His gloom seemed to be on display for my benefit.

We took our food to a table in the student cafeteria, and looking down at his soup, Jerome revealed the reason for his despondency. "Have you noticed anything weird about Eleanor?"

"She mentioned that you two were almost engaged, but that is not what I would call weird."

Jerome looked up. "That is weird."

I waited for him to continue.

"There is no way under the bright Pacific sun that Eleanor Nix and I are going to get engaged."

"Oh?"

"She's been dropping hints all over the place. She thinks she would like to meet my parents." Jerome glared once more at his soup. "Rotsa ruck."

"I thought you two were inseparable."

"Well, I suppose we were. But never till now has she hinted at bloody matrimony. I mean, it's like an ambush. One day, she's this platonic fellow book lover, and the next minute, she's humming the goddamn wedding march."

By this point, I must have been trying to devise an early exit. I had no time for people's entanglements. All I really wanted from Jerome, and life in general, was to pass the Wipeout Course.

"Well, surely *you've* run into these things before. What do I say?"

What exactly did Jerome mean here? Was he assuming that I was worldly-wise?

"Do you think you could tell her something for me?"

He looked so entirely at the end of his rope that I suppressed the obvious response: that he should damn well tell her himself.

"Could you possibly tell Eleanor that I just want to go back to being her friend? Please?"

During Mallow's lecture on Russian formalism, I became

distracted by something in Jerome's doleful revelations. It was the phrase "go back." Go back from where? How far had he gone? Indeed, how exactly does one go back to being just friends? Surely, there are apples in the barrel of love we cannot un-bite. And could that have been what my Adrian wanted? To return to the cozy womb of friendship with a female who made as few demands as possible? But why?

Somewhere during Mallow's lecture, my "why" became a "why not" and then a "why" again.

". . . ago one of my junior professors came into my office and asked me point-blank why Mister so-and-so had received a stronger recommendation for a salary increase than he did, and I said, *'Because he's better than you!'*"

I failed to see what this dictatorial exercise had to do with Russian formalism, but the whole class howled. Adrian Fermin would have howled, too. He would have dined out on Mallow's little story for weeks. I shot an exasperated look in Eleanor's direction.

"Coffee?" she whispered.

I knew what she was going to ask me, and it wouldn't have a lot to do with Russian formalism.

"It's Jerome," said Eleanor once we had our cups. "I mean, he seems to be avoiding me. All of a sudden, I'm this, I don't know, person who wants to devour all his spare time. I've never seen such a change in him." Eleanor leaned forward. "I think he's having a nervous breakdown."

"No."

"I do. He's been acting strange all week. Giving me the silent treatment. I mean, he seems to enjoy other people's company, but all of a sudden, I'm this—and then two days ago, he couldn't have been nicer, and today, he looks right through me. He says 'hi' and just keeps on walking. What am I doing wrong?"

My reaction was anger. In Jerome, I saw the disheartening spectacle of Adrian Fermin frowning around his pipe. And poor Eleanor's innocence was beginning to get annoying.

"What should I do?"

"Beard the monster in his lair," I said. "Confront him."

"Most of the time, I can't even *find* him. Besides, I really need you to ask him a question. What are his intentions?"

"Oh, God, Eleanor. I don't . . . I couldn't."

"Please, I know you can do it. Surely, you've run into this sort of thing before?"

And there it was again. I had somehow been branded as a roving counsellor for star-crossed celibates. Did I walk around with a sadder but wiser look? Could it be that, somehow, my arid months in Hartford with Adrian Fermin were showing on my face?

A wise friend would simply have told her what Jerome had told me. But I knew what Eleanor was feeling. The wrong word from me, and she might have dissolved into a damp mess at my feet. And I had to keep a lid on things any way I could. All of us in Eleanor's circle had just finished our summaries for Mallow's course. We were due to meet for our final exchange of material.

"His lair? That would be the singing place out on the highway." Eleanor was alluding to an "unusual" bar outside of town where Adrian had taken her once. "The clientele are a bit weird, but everyone's kind of nice."

"What do you mean a singing place?"

"Oh," she said sadly, "there's a small jazz band, people pass the microphone around this piano bar, and they sing old pop and jazz tunes. It's kind of fun." Eleanor confessed to me that she used to sing in choirs and that Jerome, whenever he drank, had a fine tenor voice.

"Well," I said, "why don't we all go down there for our big exchange of file cards?"

"Just go there?"

"Of course. All of us in your group. If you two haven't worked things out, then maybe I can help."

"Oh, Jane, would you? I'd be your friend for life."

I must have decided that another talk with Jerome wouldn't kill me. After all, I owed these two something for including me in their scholarly enterprise. And I hadn't forgotten that the real purpose here was to pass Mallow's bloody exam.

Professor Mallow. Much frailer in 1985 at the conference in Chicago. Vile, sneeringly witty, goatish, and a very engaging lecturer. Now, I was sitting beside him. He was squinting through his Coke-bottle glasses at the cleavage of the young woman who probably just wanted a job. *Open wide wide wide.*

"Open what?" she laughed.

"Open your knees, you irresistible wench!"

"Professor Mallow," said the young woman, "would that be before or after the banquet?"

"Open," Mallow intoned. "Open the Gates of Hell."

I turned away briefly out of embarrassment.

A glass shattered on the floor. I looked back. The young graduate student had disappeared. Professor Mallow was sprawled on the rug, massaging his lips. People began milling around, and two or three of the women helped him into a chair, squirming and wailing.

"Look what you've done," said one of the women hovering over him.

"You've bitten your tongue," said another.

"You've cracked your glasses."

It took a while to get Mallow quieted down, but the women managed admirably.

"Would you hold onto these?" one of them asked me.

One thick lens had been shattered. I was squinting the wrong way through the other lens to see if it needed cleaning when I spotted one of the women talking to Mallow. Distorted by the curve of Mallow's lens, peering into Mallow's mouth, she looked like a mother caring for a child. I lowered the spectacles.

"I have no one to go home to," cried Mallow.

"Oh, stop whining and open your mouth. Let's see your tongue."

She was large and capable, and I could see that she had learned, as many of us do, not to suffer fools.

"Oh, my God," I said.

The woman looked up at me. The red hair was darker now,

with sprinkles of white. The same soft weight to her arms and shoulders, but leaner with age. The same blazing complexion, though not so many freckles. She recognized me, and it was clear that she wanted to stand up and greet me, but there was this squinting child and his tantrum, this little Lear, mouth awash with blood and profanity.

"No one to go home to," he wailed.

Eleanor frowned at Mallow's mouth as though she had a truer idea of where the Gates of Hell were located.

After the banquet, I joined Eleanor in the hotel pub, and we did some catching up. She told me that she would soon take over the chair of the English Department at DePaul. This was a nice turn of events, and it served to remind me of how much the wheel had turned.

"No wonder I always deferred to you," I said.

Eleanor laughed. "Of course, my dear. And after all, I did get an A in Mallow's course."

I had forgotten that part. I'd managed to get by on my first attempt with a B, no small feat at that time. I began to prod her on the subject of life. Had she ever married? Did she have a family?

"Remember Martin?" she said. "From our group?"

"Yes!" I said. "He was addicted to puns."

"Yes, well, we stayed in touch after Duckton, and then we tried to make a go of it for a couple of years, but we couldn't find jobs in the same city. I think our marriage just died of long-distance apathy. But I wasn't much good at marriage. I don't like sharing my place."

I sighed. "Likewise."

I am doing my best to summon the spring of 1966. At this time, most of the men in our graduate program were having supper together in the student cafeteria because they needed to confer with each other on their status with the draft board. Jerome was exempt, something to do with heart murmurs.

The singing bar was a world apart from the politics on campus, the debate about the war in Vietnam. It was called Pacifico, an isolated one-story building out on the highway, done up in 1950s art deco, with stainless steel and Formica tables, a bright green neon oasis for all-night drinkers and, yes, quite a few singers and a band. On the night of our last meeting, we all trooped into the bar. We took a table as far from the singing area as we could and began the task of distributing our file cards. I needed more space for my summaries, so I had paid to have mine typed on stencils. I was complimented on my efficiency.

"I simply could not cork my cornucopia," I declared.

Jerome Kopella had been drinking at Pacifico before we arrived. He was in foul humour. He still could not see why we had come to *this place*—as though he had been conspired against. He kept giving me significant looks.

Eleanor, on the other hand, seemed cheerfully apprehensive as though, once and for all, something was about to be resolved. I don't think she had the slightest doubt that I would succeed in clarifying matters between her and Jerome. She ran the meeting with her usual dispatch, and when we were done exchanging our summaries, she suggested that we all go up to the bar and listen to the singing.

We gathered around the circular counter facing a jazz quartet, which bore only the faintest resemblance to what people now call a karaoke bar. The counter was made of polished oak, and the bottles of liquor were kept down below. Someone was singing when we arrived, so we whispered our orders to the bartender. The singer was an odd-looking woman, frail, perhaps in her sixties, a kind of aging Joan Crawford. She held the mic up close to her mouth and sang an utterly sad version of "St. Louis Blues." An old black fellow with the unlikely name of Dink Dangerfield was playing the piano very slowly.

We tried to jolly Jerome throughout the night by urging him to sing something, but Jerome would not be jollied. We tried to get

Eleanor to sing. She said that she would sing something if Jerome went first. Jerome would not budge, so my friends decided that I might be our diva for the night. To encourage me in this, they bought me an enormous concoction with some rum and a greenish liquid and some fruit. They dubbed this concoction Mallow's Magic. I must have taken a couple of decent tugs at it, but I was certainly not about to launch a musical career at Pacifico.

There was a tanned fellow at the bar who reminded me of a basset hound, and I suspect he was a regular there. His eyes, lips, jowls, his whole face slanted downward in a permanent expression of odium. He sang an old favourite, "Where the Blue of the Night Meets the Gold of the Day," and he sounded exactly like Bing Crosby.

I will never forget him.

Jerome Kopella is dead, very likely of AIDS. I read his obit a few days ago in the *Duckton Campus and Alumni News,* which I still get in the mail every year. When Jerome left Duckton, he inherited his parents' hotel, and he ran it for the rest of his life. Nothing, of course, about the man himself. His tenor voice, his solitary ways, whether he ever had someone to come home to.

His obituary precipitated this memoir, and the ghost of Professor Mallow presided over it. Professor Mallow, now no more, RIP. He was my inverse Muse. He was the reason for all our gatherings. If it weren't for Mallow and his infernal Wipeout Course, we would never have gathered around the piano man at Pacifico on a warm spring night in 1966. I've been attempting to summon their sad clientele. The basset-hound fellow with the deep tan. The Joan Crawford woman in black. She had a wonderful low voice.

At some point in the evening, this woman was talking to Jerome. He tried to hush her, but she appeared to be too drunk to listen. I returned my attention to the sad-looking man, and then it hit me: he was wearing makeup. I looked back at the woman in black.

"Eleanor," I whispered, "does that woman seem odd to you?"

"Why?"

"I don't think she's a woman."

Gradually, I realized that Jerome was her friend, or rather his friend, that Jerome was also friends with the Bing Crosby fellow in makeup, and that we had not so much bearded a monster in his lair as encroached, however inadvertently, upon our friend's private identity.

Was it then that Jerome grabbed the microphone, mumbled a word or two to the pianist? Mr. Dangerfield's long fingers rolled into the song. Jerome appeared agitated but terribly determined.

"Eleanor," I whispered, "I believe that we have invaded a club for homosexuals."

"A *what?*" she said.

Jerome looked directly at Eleanor and began to sing "I Enjoy Being a Girl."

We knew the song. It was from a Broadway show. Jerome sang it defiantly, with a strange intensity in his eyes, which were fixed on Eleanor. If ever there was a performance with a message, this was it.

The song ended with an embarrassing silence, and then Eleanor stood up big and proud, smiled at Jerome, and began to applaud. I suppose we all joined in in spite of Jerome's stricken look. It was clear to me that Eleanor just didn't get it. Perhaps she thought the song was a gift for her, and perhaps it was. But since the earliest annals of courtly love, was there ever a more chronic case of denial?

Oh my, that's not fair. Wasn't it just possible that Adrian Fermin had drifted away from me for similar reasons? (I don't know. He disappeared from our old haunts in Hartford, and I never bothered to find out where he went.) I wouldn't rule it out.

Mallow's magic had begun to do its work. Under the spell of the potion, all those years ago, I found myself looking around the circular bar and trying to guess who would pass the Wipeout Course.

Jerome would fail. The race was clearly over for him. But Eleanor, smiling wistfully at the music, I thought had a good chance of passing. There were three women in our group who I think were too easily discouraged, and I thought they had little chance of success.

But Eleanor's man, Martin, had a good attitude. He would quip and pun his way through the final, and the redoubtable Dink Dangerfield, his long fingers like velvet on the keys, he, too, would pass the course if there were an equivalent exam for piano players. Because he seemed to know who he was.

Bing Crosby didn't stand a chance. Joan Crawford, on the other hand, with luck and hard effort, just might manage a B. Joan had a toughness you could count on. When my speculations began to wander toward Hubert Humphrey and Lyndon Johnson, I realized that I was drunk enough to face Eleanor. I turned to her all those years ago, and I made her look at me.

"Jerome does not want to marry you," I said.

"How do you know?" she whispered.

"I don't think he wants to marry anyone."

"But that's not . . ." she began. "That just isn't . . . he *told* you that?"

"Yes," I said to Eleanor, as tenderly as I could, as callously as I dared. "He told me all about it."

That evening in the hotel pub after the banquet, Eleanor talked a bit about Jerome, about a letter he had sent to her after his departure from Duckton, full of excuses, flip humour, and self-loathing.

"The poor man," she said. "He couldn't tell me that he was gay, and I wasn't even nearly ready to hear it. I've sometimes wondered what might have transpired for poor Jerome in a more enlightened era, an LGBTQ era."

"My God, how naïve we were."

"I never want to be young again," Eleanor told me with a far-away smile.

"Hear, hear."

The hotel café was shutting down for the night. Eleanor heaved herself up, and we left together. At the elevator, we hugged goodbye, vowing to keep in touch.

I have never gone back to Duckton, but I will always remember the good old Pacifico like a tableau, a consoling version of Limbo. Bing Crosby and Dink Dangerfield are still there, looking tired, and there we sit, a circle of people with nowhere to go. Bing seems to be saying that where the blue of the night meets the gold of the day, no one waits for me. When you figure that out, you're home-free.

the fuss

THERE WAS nothing wild in Purny's neighbourhood, no wild-looking country, no wild animals, not even wild bushes and trees. The trees had all been planted by the neighbours in their yards. If you crossed the road that ran past the houses, of course, and ventured down to the river, you could see wild trees. But Purny never crossed the busy road. You could get run over by a speeding car, or you could fall into the river and be swept away, or there might be creepy old men down there, or poison ivy, or hungry coyotes. Her mom had a list of nine dangers taped to the fridge, but Purny had forgotten some of them.

The tree in her front yard looked pretty wild to her. It was a tall blue spruce with great downward-sweeping branches and millions of blue needles. Ravens perched there all through the year, croaking like old witches. Their tree was bigger than most others on the crescent, and its bottom branches angled right down to the ground, creating a secret shelter. No one knew who planted it or whether anyone did.

This was Purny's hiding place. It reminded her of a nest, or maybe a cave, because not even the snow could get in there. If her sister Portia was being bossy, or if her mom and dad were fighting, Purny could slip outside, summer or winter, crawl beneath the big branches of her tree, and hunker down on a bed of spruce needles. She and her friend Linda could leave things there, like an old blanket, or a tin of cookies, or a doll, or paper plates, and none of the other kids would find them. You had to look hard to spot anything beneath the branches of the great blue spruce.

A couple of weeks into December, Purny decided that she and Linda should clean out her lair to get rid of the mess: feathers, a dog collar, a mitten, a rabbit's foot, some candy wrappers, some bones, a plastic bag, and tufts of animal hair. This mess was mostly because of people's dogs and cats, and she wanted them to know that this place belonged to her and Linda.

A few days after the girls had done their tidying, Purny discovered a fresh poop beneath her tree. It was way too big for a cat's poop, and it wasn't yucky like a dog's poop. It was just big and long with a little pointy twist on one end, and it didn't smell of anything.

One cold night later in December, she wandered into the pantry next to the kitchen and stole a hazelnut bar from her mom's Christmas bag. Purny would only nibble part of it and return the rest, so it wasn't really stealing. She came into Portia's bedroom, nibbling away.

Portia was on her bed, talking to one of her friends. She smiled at her phone like it was a puppy. "I'm goin' there," she said. "No, no, not tonight, you goof. Sometime when the coast is clear. We should go together."

Now that she was thirteen, Portia talked like a different person. She didn't say *together,* she said *to-gather.* She didn't say *yes,* she said *yass.* She didn't say *but,* she said *buiiite.* This kind of talking made Portia open her mouth bigger and for a longer time. Purny would never talk like that, not even when she was thirteen.

Their dad called Portia *Princess*, and he called Purny *Snuffy*. She asked her dad why Portia got the pretty name. He said Princess was a pretty name for a pretty girl. Snuffy, he said, after thinking for a moment, was a cute name. Purny's actual name was Calpurnia. She didn't like this name because it took too long to say, but she didn't like being called Snuffy because that sounded like a jokey name. Linda had named her Purny, and she was okay with that.

Purny had blonde hair and blue eyes. She liked reading storybooks. She was very short and very sturdy-looking. She could walk with her hands scraping the carpet like a gorilla. She could do other animals, too, including a Komodo dragon and an oyster. She wondered if that was what made her cute.

"Just a minute," said Portia into the phone. Then she made a growly face and waved her little sister away.

Purny climbed up the stairs to Mom and Dad's bedroom door, munching on her hazelnut bar. The door to the bedroom was closed, and her mom and dad were whispering fiercely about something. Purny waited and waited, and finally, she gobbled down the last of her chocolate bar.

As she ambled downstairs, she wondered how cold it was outside. She opened the front door, and the freezing air floated in like a ghost. She heard a raven squawk and closed the door.

I don't care, she said to herself. And then she said out loud, "I'm going to put on my long johns." She stopped to listen. "I'm going to put on my snowsuit too." She listened again. Louder, she said, "I'll just put on my snowsuit all by myself."

She went and changed, but no one came to stop her. All she heard was Portia's squealy voice laughing at something secret.

"I'm goin' there!" cried Purny.

It was snowing again. She trudged down the front walk and looked up and down the street to make sure no one was coming. She checked an outside pocket to make sure she had brought her tiny flashlight. She got down on her hands and knees and squinted hard because of the pointy needles and twigs, and she began to crawl on her belly beneath the lowest branches. She inched her way closer and closer to her dry space by the tree trunk and pulled the flashlight from her pocket. Something growled down deep, like thunder.

She turned on the flashlight.

A wild deer was lying on the ground with its head flopping up and down. Another big old deer with whiskers was lying behind it with the small deer's neck in its mouth. The big deer let go of the little deer's neck, raised its head, and *hisssssssed* at Purny. Hissed like a dragon.

Purny scrambled up the walk like her body got her away from the tree without telling her. She tried to scream. She ran to the front door, and only when she had closed it behind her did she realize that she was scared. Really scared. It had hissed through its fangs exactly like a dragon. She leaned against the door and tried to breathe normally, and after a while, one by one, her thoughts returned.

If you told someone in your family that a dragon had hissed at you, they would just laugh, or they would call the police, and you'd never get to see it again, or they'd scold you for lying, or look at you funny like you were acting *immature*. But if you told a friend, you could say it without getting picked on.

She peeled off her snowsuit, crept into her dad's study and grabbed the phone. "It had a deer's neck in its mouth."

"Holy," said Linda.

"It hissed at me."

"How could it hiss at you if it had a deer in its mouth?"

"It dropped the deer on the ground and hissed at me."

"Holy."

"It didn't hiss like a kitty, it hissed really incredibly loud, like a dragon."

"What did it look like?"

"I couldn't see it very good, but I think it was a Komodo dragon."

"Purny, you should go tell them what you saw."

"Tell my mom and dad?"

"I don't know," said Linda. "Maybe you should tell the zoo."

Purny's mom used to teach English at Mildred Kerr High School, but for the last eighteen months, she had been the vice-principal. She had a Master's degree in something to do with learning. Whenever she had an important thing to say to Purny and Portia, she spoke in a super-serious voice, pronouncing each word perfectly. Tonight, she and Purny's dad had both come home late, and while they ate their supper, her mom apologized to the girls. *We are so sorry,* she kept saying.

"No biggy," Portia said.

Purny's dad was listening to something. "Did you hear that?"

"Just a minute, dear," said Mom. "I want us to tell the girls about our new plan."

"Oh, yes," said Dad. "The new plan."

He smiled at the girls, and his warm brown eyes went back and forth between them. Tonight, he looked old and tired. "Your mother and I have a lot on our plates these days. She has her big conference coming up next month."

"February fifteenth," said Mom, "and I'm on the ground running."

Mom's conference was all about *building clabertive relationships* or whatever *for the facilitation of experientiality* blabberty blab. Their dad was a professor at the vet college. He specialized in big farm animals like sheep and cows. Once he saved a special goat for someone and got a big supply of goat's milk. He had a very soothing voice.

"We're sorry to spring this on you girls," he said, "but we're putting together a plan that will give you a break so we can all move forward."

Purny's dad always said that, as though they had all been walking backward and didn't know it.

There was another noise from outside, a *crack,* and this time, they all heard it. Purny's dad excused himself and went to the front door. Purny crept up behind him and tried to look out. The cold air moved all around them, and her dad closed the door.

"Nothing out there," he said.

Their mother brought in the dessert, a yellow blobby thing with a raspberry on top. She told the girls that she had gone and hired a special young man *to fill in the gaps.*

"Just on school days," she said and gave Portia her special bright smile.

Something came over Purny, the nervous feeling she got whenever her mom put on a bright smile. The smile meant that if you didn't go along with whatever she had in store for you, she would start yelling and walk out of the room.

Portia was not afraid of her mom's bright smile. She just waded right in with her dukes up. "You hired a *man* to check up on us? Okay, you hired him to *babysit* us? Last time I looked, there was only one baby in this house. Why don't you pay me, and I can be the babysitter?"

"This man knows how to cook, Portia. The only food I've ever seen you cook is toast and peanut butter."

"I can cook stuff. Anyone can throw a couple of sandwiches together. So, is he going to *live* with us? What if I want to go out and see my friends? You mean I have to ask his permission?"

"He's not going to live with us, Portia," their dad said. "He'll be there when you get home from school, and he will leave when we get home."

"And," said their mother, "he will be there to enforce the rules."

"Rules!" cried Portia. "What rules?"

"Don't play dumb with me, Portia," said her mother in a soft, low voice, which was almost as scary as her special bright smile.

"Princess, come on," said their father. "You don't have to go all sulky."

Their mom perked up again. "And guess who the special man is who'll take care of you."

The girls sighed together.

"Our old sitter and dear friend, Theodore."

"Who?" the girls cried together.

Still glaring at Portia, her mom said the name again.

Purny brightened up because she had always loved Theodore. He used to bring puppets and tell them stories in funny voices. Sometimes, he wound a scarf over his head and wore a funny green thing he called the Swami smock, and once, he came in his Batman costume.

Portia raised her head, crossed her arms, and glared back at her mother. "He happens to call himself Theo."

They all ate their dessert quietly, and no one looked at each other.

"Dad," said Purny, "did you ever do stuff to the Komodo dragons?"

Portia snickered.

"Did you ever, like, operate on the Komodo dragons?"

"I'm happy to report that I've never had to work with giant lizards."

"Are those dragons still at the zoo?" said Purny. "Because I think we've got one under our tree."

Portia laid her head on the table and closed her eyes. "Purny is always saying stuff," she muttered.

"Afraid not, Snuffy. The zoo officials sent them back to their original zoo down south."

"How far is that?" said Purny, but her dad was gazing at the front door and listening again.

He rose from the table and hauled on his parka.

Purny crept up the stairs and paused by her mom and dad's bedroom door. They were whispering, as they often did, but this time, she could hear some of the words whizzing back and forth. Her mom said she couldn't believe that something *just happened.*

"You say you didn't want it to," she said. "Then why didn't you just walk away?"

The whispering went soft for a moment; then, her dad said that he would sleep in the guest room.

"You'll do no such thing," her mom said.

Her dad said, "You're just getting too emotional about this."

"Emotional? How's this for emotional . . . find yourself an apartment . . . find myself a lawyer."

Her dad said, "You'll never know how sorry I am."

"Sorry enough to end it?" said her mom.

Gritting her teeth, Purny slipped away from the bedroom door and hurried down the stairs.

A week after Christmas, the weather turned warm and stayed that way for several days. It was so sunny the snow began to melt, and Purny could run around without having to wear her snowsuit. Theo was back in their lives once more with his puppets and costumes and magic tricks. Sometimes, he dressed up as a lobster with grabby things coming out of his sleeves. Even Portia laughed at Theo, and Theo was a better cook than their mom. Sometimes, Theo would show the girls how he did his magic. The claws in his lobster costume were just reachers for old people to pick up stuff they couldn't reach. You pulled a trigger at one end, and they grabbed the thing at the other end.

Purny couldn't stop thinking about the monster under the spruce tree, but in the daytime, nothing seemed scary. She had this thought again one Saturday as she and Linda walked from Linda's house to Purny's. Her thought went like this: How could you be afraid of dragons if there weren't any dragons in Saskatoon? There were no animal tracks in the snow around the tree, so what was there to be afraid of? Linda wasn't afraid, so why should Purny be afraid?

Linda always got the best marks in class. She knew things that other kids didn't know, like how to play chess, or what a solar flare was, or what happened when you got divorced. When Linda was in class, she was always listening. She was more fun to be with after school. Purny would never be as smart as Linda, but that didn't seem to matter because she and Linda were best friends anyway.

Anyway. It was sunny out. They walked right up to the blue spruce, checked for nosy neighbours, and peeked around the base of the tree as though it might still be hiding something scary. The branches were covered with layers of beautiful snow from the previous night, and neighbours were out with their shovels and snowblowers, clearing off the sidewalks and driveways. Purny's dad came out to sweep off the front steps. The girls tried to peer through the snow-laden branches to the base of the tree. There was no sign of anything creeping around their hiding place, like dragon tracks or dragon tail marks. The only signs of life near the tree were tiny birds' tracks.

Purny knew she had seen something, but today, it seemed as though it was all just a nightmare, and the thing that caused the nightmare had been swept away by the wind and snow. Everywhere Purny looked, the snow lay bright and clean. The only scary thing in her life was Theo in his lobster costume, telling them stories about sea monsters down deep in the ocean. And Theo was never that scary. He was too funny to be scary.

"You girls going to build a snowman?" said Purny's dad.

"Maybe," said Purny.

"Good day for a snowman," he said.

They waited till he had gone, and then they got down on their bellies, Purny on one side and Linda on the other. In they crawled until they could see the spruce needles on the ground. Purny smelled something strong, and she heard Linda gasp.

She struggled forward, and there it was, lying up against the tree trunk, blinking through glassy eyes at the girls as though they had awakened it from a long sleep. It was big enough to be a dragon, but it wasn't a dragon, and this time it wasn't even hissing. It was just an enormous cat the colour of a deer. Huge. It looked too sleepy to be a threat to anyone, and there was no sign of Purny's unlucky deer.

It curled up its lips and showed Purny its fangs.

Linda reached over and tapped Purny on the leg. Reluctantly, she slid backward, and the two girls stood up once more in the sunlight, puffing hard and staring at each other. Purny's dad was still inside the house, and no one on the street was looking their way.

"It's been hurt," said Linda.

"Huh?"

"Blood," Linda said, pointing to her throat. "All the way down here and on the ground. It was all dried up and ooky."

"I couldn't see that side," said Purny.

Linda stood on the sidewalk, eyes down and mouth open, her breath coming out in plumes. Along came Mrs. Whiteside from next door. From over the fence, she said hi, and they said hi.

"You girls should be making a snowman. You'll never get a better day."

Off she went.

"It looked like a lion," said Purny.

"It's a wild cougar," Linda said.

The girls stood by the tree and put their heads together and whispered like people did on TV shows when something was too important, too secret to share with anyone else.

The lady on *Fear Factor* had made it past the big python. Now, she was trying to sneak past the alligators so she could crawl through the opening. Theo appeared at the door to the TV room. He was wearing one of their mom's aprons, the one with the valentines.

"Portia, your mom said there was some burger patties thawing near the sink, and I can't . . . seem to . . ."

Portia said to try the fridge or the deep freeze.

Theo said he would try Plan B, and he ordered a big pizza. When supper was finished, Portia said she was going over to Franny's place for a while. "To do homework," she said.

"Your mom and dad will be home soon," said Theo, "so you can ask them."

"I can't ask them if they're not here."

Theo leaned forward over the remains of the pizza so that he could glare at Portia up close. He went all stern as though he were speaking in capital letters, and Purny smiled to herself.

"Portia, no. If you try to walk out that door, you will be so busted, you will never recover."

"It's just a couple of blocks from here. I can text you when I arrive."

"Portia, did they tell you about the mountain lion?"

Theo explained that a mountain lion had come up from the river. It was raiding the homes along the crescent. It had already eaten somebody's dog.

"That's what they do," he said. "Eat dogs and cats and bunny rabbits, and when they're really hungry, they *look for bigger prey."*

"We heard a shot last week," said Purny.

"Your dad told me it was conservation officers," said Theo. "They might have winged it, but I guess it got away. Portia, an injured mountain lion. It hunts at night. Just think how desperate it would be to get something nice to eat."

"It couldn't be a mountain lion," said Portia. "There's no mountains around here."

"Then it was . . . I don't know . . . a cougar."

Theo described what a cougar looked like and Purny didn't say anything.

At last, she said, "Do they really eat people?"

"You betcha," said Theo. "And they just love little children."

Theo began to pack up his stuff, singing to himself. He wanted to be ready to leave just as the girls' mom and dad came through the door from their restaurant supper. He told the girls that he was going to see his special friend Jeremy. Purny helped Portia clean up in the kitchen. They hardly spoke a word.

"Oops," said Theo. "I'm missing my lobster claws."

"I sold them to buy drugs," said Portia.

"I swallowed them by mistake," said Purny.

"I threw them in the toilet," said Portia.

"I used them to clean my teeth," said Purny.

The reacher's claw approached the cougar, and the great cat peered at the offering without interest. It couldn't even raise its head, let alone attack somebody. The caked blood around its neck and chest had hardened and turned black. The claw came closer, released its hold and plopped a meat patty on the ground. The cougar sniffed the patty. The other claw was shakier as it moved toward the cougar's head, easing a plastic bowl of goat's milk in front of the cat's great paws.

Linda touched Purny on the leg, and they both crawled backward and away from the tree trunk. Still gripping their metal reachers, they stood shivering together by the tree. Purny wanted to give their sleepy friend more patties, but Linda shook her head. “We should leave it alone.”

“I want to see it eat,” said Purny.

“How would you like it if people sat around waiting for you to eat?”

“They do that to me all the time,” said Purny.

“This is different.”

They took the reachers over to a place nearby where the drifts were piled up and slid them under the snow. They hid the hamburger patties in Purny’s bedroom.

One day later, the girls checked in on their patient. The goat’s milk had disappeared, but the patty lay uneaten among the spruce needles on the ground. The following day, they refilled the bowl with goat’s milk and set it before the cougar, who eyed the girls and curled its lips without quite snarling at them.

The next evening, the patty had disappeared, and the goat’s milk had been lapped up. Purny had to go and fetch the remaining meat patties from her bedroom. She and Linda fed the patties to the cougar one at a time. It looked sulky, anything but grateful. They watched as it snapped them up and gulped them down.

This time, Linda delivered the goat’s milk by hand. As the bowl approached the cougar, it struggled to a sitting position so that its head rose into the branches above. Even in its scrawny state, it was huge. Linda lowered the bowl onto the ground, and again, the cougar curled his upper lip into a silent snarl.

Their dad’s apartment was in an old building midway between the vet college and Purny’s house. She and Portia walked there for the first time in February. He gave them a tour of his new place, which was very tidy and surprisingly large, and then he laid out a lunch of cheese and bakery goodies from the café down the street. Portia wanted to know if he and their mom were going to get a divorce.

"Oh, no," said their dad. "We just need a bit of time off. This happens to lots of couples."

Portia wanted to know about his new girlfriend.

"Nothing much to report," said their dad. "She's pretty busy these days. So am I. End of term coming up. Not much time for girlfriends."

"That's not what Mom says," Portia observed.

"I hear you've had some visitors," their dad said.

He was referring to the conservation officers. They had shown up one night at the front door when Theo was doing a puppet show for the girls. The men said the cougar might be prowling somewhere in the valley. A deer skeleton had been discovered next door in Mr. Whiteside's front yard, buried under the snow. They said the girls should be careful.

"Would they just shoot the cougar?" Purny asked her dad.

"I hope so," said Portia.

"That's not fair," said Purny. "It's just a wild animal."

"They probably won't shoot the cougar," said their dad with his gentle voice and a reassuring smile. "If they find it, they'll just dart it. You know, put it to sleep. Then they'll take it to their truck and release it in the wild."

"Promise you and Mom are not going to get a divorce?" said Portia.

"I promise," her father said.

"Mom gets home from work and cries a lot," said Portia. "She says you don't love her."

"That's silly," her dad said. "Of course I love her."

Purny did a long *blablabla* in her head to stop from hearing anything Portia and her dad were saying. She gazed out her dad's front window, thinking about the turkey that she had left to thaw on the basement floor at home. Theo had found it underneath an inverted laundry basket and had had to do some cleaning up. She told him she'd been playing a game with Linda. Turkey in the Basket, it was called.

Portia said, "You should really talk to her, Dad. You should phone her up. I've never seen Mom like this."

"We're not getting divorced, you can count on that."

Purny said, "Well, then, howcome they shot the cougar? Howcome they didn't just dart it?"

They both gave Purny a look.

Purny prayed that the weather would turn warm, and the weather turned warm. A chinook blew in, and the grey ice by the road, the snow in the shadows between the houses, even the ice on the Whitesides' pond, began to melt. That very evening, Purny prayed that her sister would run off to the party she wasn't supposed to go to and that Theo would arrive too late to spoil Purny's plan. And guess what? Portia disappeared wherever, and Theo was late!

Purny thanked God and Jesus for answering her prayers. She moved quickly, lugging a rib roast down her front walk and up to the great blue spruce. It felt like a ten-pound baby doll, except it was greasy. It would not be long before her mother came home. And this time, her dad would come, too. She wondered what it would feel like to have him back, but she couldn't think about that. Not yet. She had a job to do.

"Lion?" she said in the softest voice. "Lion?"

She looked up at the house. With the approaching dusk, it looked abandoned. She heard Lion moving in his home, a long sound like a big snake would make crawling through the jungle. He came out from beneath his tree. Standing up straight, he was even bigger and longer than she had imagined, big enough for Purny to ride him like a pony. She held out the rib roast, and Lion stared at it as though Purny wasn't even there. She turned and walked slowly to the curb, checked for cars, and began to cross the road. She listened for the sound of Lion's paws following but heard nothing. She reached the far curb and turned around. He was right behind her, eyeing the rib roast.

She glanced up at the house, and just then, the light came on in Portia's bedroom. Portia was at her window, staring in Purny's direction.

"Come on," Purny whispered. "Hurry."

Lion came cautiously as though he was afraid of the dark, and it wasn't even dark yet.

"Come on."

Purny carried her bundle across the boulevard facing the river and descended down a path through the bushes. She turned back and her friend followed her, stopped, glanced around, and resumed plodding. She noticed for the first time the length and strength of its low, curving tail. She marvelled at how noiselessly he came through the bushes, how each paw landed on a quiet place.

At last, she dropped her greasy bundle. He approached, sniffing it, looked up, and coughed out a raspy sound at Purny.

Purny backed up the incline toward the crescent to watch him eat. She waved goodbye for a long time, but he never looked up.

As she crossed the road, she felt as though she were dreaming, and there was Theo, waiting on the sidewalk.

"Nice night for a stroll," he said.

She walked up to him and felt the tiredness, the sadness, coming on.

"What's that thing down there?" Theo said.

"That's Lion. I think he likes his meal."

"And Lion is?"

Purny led the way back to the house. "You forgot your lobster claws," she said.

"Purny, who is Lion?"

"He's our friend," she said. "Linda and me. He was sick from getting shot, but now we've made him better."

"Let me guess. Is he an aardvark? No? Maybe an elephant? No, no. I've got it, his name is Lion, and he likes raw turkeys. He must be a lion!"

Purny turned around and looked up at Theo. "He's a cougar."

"Do your parents know about this friend?"

"It's nice down there," she said. "I like it down there."

"Purny?"

"Does your sister know about your favourite kitty-cat?"

"She saw me with him tonight. Now she'll tell Mom."

Theo stooped down low and lifted Purny's chin with his finger. He looked into her eyes.

"Purny, sweetheart, you need to stop feeding the cougar. You need to back away. You know that, don't you."

"I *know*. But now he's gone."

"You've done a good thing, Purny, and it's all over. Now, don't cry."

"But don't you see? He might come back to his tree for a visit."

The men came the following evening. Purny could hear them talking with Theo.

"O, joy!" said Theo. "Who gets to do the darting tonight?"

One of the men said it was Portia they wanted to talk to. She brought them over to the tree. By parting a branch a few inches, Purny could see Portia's pink runners. She could hear the men approach as they crunched over the melting ice. One of the men told Portia to go back inside and phone her mother and father.

"We'll take it from here," he said.

"Excuse me, but what exactly is your plan?" Theo's voice.

"You'll need to back away, young man," said the officer.

"Back away from what?" said Theo. "How many armed men does it take to summon a little girl?"

She heard some shuffling as the men moved back, and Theo crawled toward the trunk of the spruce tree. Purny had forgotten to wear her mitts, and her hands were cold. Theo crawled under the branches and squeezed in beside her. He took her hands and rubbed them. His hands were bony and warm.

They both crawled out from beneath the lower branches. There were six or seven men in two kinds of uniform. Some of them were police.

"Your sister," said one of the men, pointing to the tree. "She said you were hiding a cougar in there."

Purny let go of Theo's hand and blew warm air into her own hands. She glanced up at the policeman.

"That Portia, she always likes to say stuff."

A week later, Purny woke up to a buzzing, scraping sound outside the house. She got dressed and went outside. Their front yard was a mess, with branches lying around as though scattered by a tornado. A big raven was croaking on the roof of their house. Purny's mom was talking and laughing with some men with yellow hats.

At that moment, Purny realized that the great blue spruce wasn't where it should be. It was lying in sections on the ground, and two of the men were standing over the spruce, what was left of it. They bent down to lift segments of the tree and to walk them over to a dump truck. After a while, all that remained was the stump, and the men gathered around it.

Purny's mother held her phone camera and waved at the men to stand closer together. One of them was holding a chainsaw and had planted his boot on the trunk. The other men were teasing him. Just as her mother snapped the picture, the raven squawked.

Purny began to scream. She shrieked at her mother and shrieked at the men, and they all turned with the very same look on their faces to see what the fuss was all about.

gentle rain

ONE JUNE MORNING IN 1968, while wrestling with a stump in his yard, Luke's father had a heart attack. He was sixty-two. Luke's mother packed him into the car and drove him to the hospital. That night, she phoned Luke and told him to meet her at the cardiac ward the next morning. He saw her standing in the corridor, and when they made eye contact, she shook her head. *No,* she seemed to say, *he might not make it.*

Dr. Flanagan had a different take on his father's condition. "Your dad is very lucky we got to him when we did." A moment later, he added, "But yes, he is a very sick man."

Luke tried to put this very bad, good news together: a not-yet-fatal massive heart attack. The next week would be crucial in determining his father's chances for recovery.

His father wanted to talk but could scarcely whisper. Luke had to kneel down to hear him. "It's amazing," his father said, "in here, how they fix you up."

Luke and his mother consulted with his father's medical team, and Luke phoned his brother in Toronto. He told him not to worry; there was nothing they could do but wait for further developments. The doctors claimed that Luke's father was stable, and there were signs that he might be rallying. Three days after his bypass surgery, he asked to see a newspaper.

After a few days of guarded hopes and worried looks, Luke's mother said, "You may as well go fishing with your friends. Not much is going to happen this weekend."

There is a cabin belonging to friends of Luke's family, the Charlesworths. It sits on the shores of Lac Bonté, which in turn lies not far from the shadow of Pyramid Mountain in the heart of Jasper National Park. At the end of the lake, a feeder stream bubbles up clear and cool from beneath the massive roots of an old Douglas fir and murmurs its way over the gravel, winding through the gloom of a forest of ferns, bush, muskeg, and conifers and into Lac Bonté. The lake is shaped like a pair of sunglasses seen front-on. It would have been two sizable ponds but for the presence of a shallow channel connecting both bodies. The water is absolutely clear. From the shallows to the depths, the lake covers the spectrum from pale green to near purple.

The rainbow trout that spawned in the spring were pampered by a sumptuous array of nymphs, bees, scuds, and minnows. They were known to grow bigger and fatter than any other trout in the park. At twilight, the old lunkers cruised the shallows a few yards from shore. The water was so clear and placid in the evening that you could see them coming a block away.

With the burden of a son's guilt, Luke showed up at the Charlesworth family cabin at Lac Bonté on opening day.

Luke's father was a practical man and a family man. He never crossed the line on such things as drunkenness, womanizing, gambling, or anything of an addictive nature. The lessons he had learned during the Great Depression had much to do with austerity of purse and character, so he disapproved of men who were tempted to stray. He taught Luke how to fish, but he could never have guessed how easily his son would become addicted to fly-fishing. By his twelfth year, Luke was reading *Outdoor Life, Field & Stream,* stocking stats, and angling guides with the devotion of a literary scholar. Writers from Izaak Walton to Roderick Haig-Brown had conversations with Luke in his dreams.

On the subject of politics, his father always said, *Don't get carried away.* On the subject of idealistic quests, his father always said, *Don't get carried away.* On the subject of various girls, he said, *Don't get carried away.* On the subject of anything bohemian, free-spirited, or creative, he said, *Don't get carried away.* Even on the subject of fly-fishing, he said, *Don't get carried away.* On the subject of saving money, however, he would say, *Now you're talkin', son.*

Luke had learned to cast flies with his friend Harry one winter when he was fourteen. Every Wednesday night, they would take a long bus ride to a school in Edmonton's east end. There, they would practice casting under the tutelage of an old Highlander, whipping flies beneath basketball hoops at target patterns on the gym floor. Their guru never tired of telling them, *Laddies, y'kenna catch a fesh if yer line's no' in the water.* By the end of winter, the two boys could cast a straight line forty feet or more and tie a few basic flies. A favourite fly was a streamer known as the Kilburn Killer, named after a man in the club, which imitated a minnow about two inches long.

Luke's father had paid for it all. Luke's first fly rod, his subscription to *Outdoor Life,* his membership in the Edmonton fly-fishing club. *Have fun, but don't get carried away.* By age fifteen, Luke was the monster his father created. Thank God his friend Harry was just as obsessive as he was.

The Charlesworths' cabin was a social, psychological, spiritual, piscatorial, culinary smorgasbord of conviviality. When Luke arrived that night in June, Allison Charlesworth (lean, tall, a hiker, incurably sociable) threw open the door. A scruffy-looking band known as Jesse Colin Young and the Youngbloods was urging all the peoples of the world to smile on their brothers and get together, and everyone in the cabin's largest room was dancing. They were all in their twenties.

Luke and Allison were schoolteachers. She had yet to become a full-time artist. Her genius boyfriend, Armand, had yet to become a lawyer. Luke was almost a decade away from becoming a writer. But anything was possible. That's what the Youngbloods were telling him as he danced. That's what the wine was telling him, what the month of June was telling him, what his father's bout with mortality was telling him: life, love, adventure, and excellent fly-fishing were his for the asking. Born lucky and grown revolutionary enough to be fashionable, Luke was, in all his youthful vanity, getting carried away.

The plan was to party till four or five in the morning and then hit the lake. There would be a prize for the biggest rainbow. Perhaps only a few of them took the contest seriously, but Luke was one of them. His arch-rival in this endeavour was, of course, Harry, his good friend and co-victim of fly-fishing addiction.

Maybe a dozen of them left the party before dawn and went down to the water to cast from shore or troll from the Charlesworths' canoe or fish from some other boat. The water was calm, and so was the fishing, and then the sun rose, the insects in the shallows got going, and Harry got a hit, and Armand got a hit, and one of Allison's brothers got a hit, and Luke got a hit, and all over the small lake, eager voices, mostly male, were calling out, *I got one* or *I lost the (expletive) fish* or *I just saw a monster* or *you just crossed my (expletive) line again.*

By late morning, Allison was barbecuing a rainbow that was just shy of five pounds. It was one of Harry's fish, and the bar for the biggest trout had been set.

One by one, weary anglers returned to their sleeping bags and their cabin bunks, and when at last Luke brought in a five-pounder and claimed the prize, Harry was the only other angler from the party left out on the water. Before long, while Luke was snoring into his sleeping bag, Harry came in with a fat silver rainbow and woke Luke up.

Harry's new fish was clearly bigger than Luke's biggest, and he knew his labours had just begun. He grabbed his waders and set out for the other side of the lake, the shaded end where the feeder stream flowed in, wearing for itself a shallow channel in the lake that dropped steadily off into the deep water where Lac Bonté followed the spectrum from pale green to blue to purple.

This was where the last of the ragged ones patrolled the shoreline. The spring spawn was almost entirely finished, and the old spawners that remained were now legal to catch. Their numbers had dwindled from more than a hundred to one or two dozen. When Luke arrived, these last fish were nosing through the shallows like the last revellers to leave a party. The male rainbows made half-hearted runs at their rivals and continued to circle past the spawning beds as though caught up and exhausted by the perplexing mysteries of desire immortalized by the Youngbloods.

No fish remained in the feeder stream. The rainbows in the shallows were rolling past Luke in about three feet of water. They seemed to prefer the gravel here to that in the shallow stream, where they would have been vulnerable to bears and human predators. They all looked big, but one dark male seemed longer than the others in that exhausted band of spawn-fraught rainbows.

Luke waded in and stripped some line from his reel.

He imagined his father watching this moment of intense concentration from the beach or perhaps hearing about this little adventure from Luke by his bedside. His father would approve. He would say, *That's real living, son.*

Years later, when Luke's books began coming out, his father would be less than enthusiastic. Luke's subjects were embittered and worn-out women, alienated youths, philanderers, drunks, hypocrites, hardened criminals, old people staring at mortality. His books probably left his father wondering where he and Luke's mother had gone wrong. Writing about the sporting life would have been okay with his father, who preferred something he could show his friends without embarrassment. He wanted Luke to have a good job and a good marriage, and if he had to do this writing stuff, let it be a hobby. Let's, for godsakes, not get carried away.

Most of Luke's friends from that summer were either married or otherwise paired off and likely entering their own bouts of intense spawning with their partners, so the month of June at Lac Bonté had, for them even more than Luke, a sweet tumescence with which the rainbow trout, decked out in their deepest greens, reds, pinks and blues, seemed in tune. Or perhaps it was the other way around: his friends, besotted in deepest desire, were in tune with all those pink-sided Cupids sweeping their tails in slow, exhausting circles over the gravel beds and every so often thrusting their bodies into the silted bottom of Lac Bonté.

Luke wondered why he did this. Was winning a challenge for the biggest fish so important that he would disturb this last bout of spawning? Was this done for bragging rights? Or, in the absence of any spawning in his own life, was he simply sublimating into something over which he had some control? At that time, romantically, Luke was a fish out of water.

Enough of that.

He waded as close as he dared to the action before him and sent out a cast that went beyond the school of circling trout.

Once more, he found himself thinking about his grey-faced father at rest in the cardiac ward and how surprised he would be at the sight of a huge trout. Luke would catch it for him. Well, no, he would catch a big one for himself and then *present it* to his father. How would that go? Would he bring it to the hospital to show him? Not bloody likely. But if Luke could catch a big one, his dad would somehow get a kick out of it and maybe stop looking so grey. And his dad would be proud of his son.

Luke was surely getting carried away. When you want your father to be proud of you, you are probably wading through uncertain waters and unlikely to inspire pride in anyone—until you get over the need for approval.

He let his line sink to the sandy bottom and began a slow retrieve. The fly he had chosen was a big, self-tied Kilburn Killer, a streamer fly he'd never seen in any store. It plowed through the sand and gravel like a somnolent minnow or an inebriate who had blundered into a convention for cannibals and become part of the menu.

When the great dark rainbow came back Luke's way, he pulled the streamer up from the gravel and drew it homewards in short, irregular jerks. The big rainbow went right for it. Luke spotted the white interior of the rainbow's lower jaw as it snapped up the fly. He raised the rod, and the battle was on. The rainbow bucked around in slow motion, sending the other trout away from the spawning trenches in a wide explosion of silt. It moved off to Luke's right, changing directions, flopped around, kicked up a mighty spray with its tail, and took off for deep waters.

"Verrrry nice," someone said.

Luke did not recognize the voice, and he didn't dare turn around. Perhaps the voice belonged to a cabin owner or a conservation officer. Luke heard the click of a camera, an authoritative slide of the shutter. It was an expensive sound.

The old rainbow fought stubbornly, but never once did he jump out of the water or do a high-speed run to take Luke's ratchet into the upper registers.

"If I had a cottage on this lake," the voice said, "I would not go swimming out there. Not with guys like *that* in the neighbourhood."

"He's a big one," Luke said to the voice. "I could lose this one. You never know with these guys."

The person standing behind Luke did not sound like a fisherman. His voice was lisping and pedantic, and mildly sarcastic even when opportunities for sarcasm were unavailable.

"Don't let it pull you in, buddy."

This is the point in the story where the angler gazes down on the dark blue back, the wide band of deepest rose on the side that is flecked with tiny dark spots from gills to tail, and he sees his fly protruding from the corner of the kyped jaw. He is struck by the battered beauty of the old trout. He bends down, detaches his fly. He holds the trout by the tail and moves its body forward and back, opening and closing the gill covers, reviving his old adversary, and sending him back to spawn again.

That didn't happen. Luke grabbed a piece of wood, brained the old rainbow, and held him up for inspection.

"Do you think you could kind of clean it up for me?"

Luke beheld the face of a man with a notebook. The mystery voice with the Daffy Duck intonations belonged to a newspaper reporter. Another man, a quiet fellow with a camera, stood beside him.

These two had come all the way from the city to do a feature on opening day for *The Edmonton Journal.* The cameraman shot Luke and his trout from several more angles while the features writer with the notebook asked him questions. And then, with a rush of purest joy and more than a trace of vanity, Luke knew how he could give his father a boost.

Luke's mother was, by her account, sitting in a chair by her husband's bed, reading a section of the newspaper and occasionally looking over in his direction. Luke's father had gone through the front section and the business reports and the editorials and made it at last to the features. He pulled a straight pin from the lapel of his pyjamas and began to slice out an article. He handed the article to Luke's mother with the usual comment.

"Something for the boys."

His mother perused the picture and the article, which she had already read, and handed it back to Luke's father.

"Remind you of someone?"

Perhaps her husband's eyesight had been affected by the heart attack, or perhaps he hadn't been wearing his glasses. More likely, he was still more preoccupied with his own mortality than with the world around him. But at this moment, he might also have heard a note of mischief in his wife's voice. He looked once more at the trout in the photo, and this time, he read the photo caption. "As I live and breathe."

Coming from a man who was so recently on the critical list, these words seemed particularly well chosen. His recovery dates from the day he saw the picture of his youngest son in *The Edmonton Journal.* According to family legend, my father's recovery . . . etc.

Luke had decided on the shores of Lac Bonté that his father needed a homecoming gift. Back in the city, he took his frozen rainbow to a taxidermist. The process took longer than expected, so he presented his trophy to his father on his birthday more than a month after he'd returned from the hospital. It was attached to an oval mount made of stained maple, a twenty-seven-inch stuffed male with the original spawning colours shamelessly enhanced by the taxidermist. His father decided to hang it in the den.

A time came when Luke's parents sold their home in Alberta and retired to the West Coast. They had to downsize drastically, so they gave Luke back his trout trophy. They did this rather easily, as though the value he had attached to the stuffed fish lay in excess of their own sentiments. Luke took it well, but he hid the stuffed rainbow in the basement of his house in Winnipeg. He did not want anyone to think that he made trophies from the fish he caught. Doing this would feel like an ego trip, an act of disrespect toward the fish.

Luke's girlfriend, Peggy, was a visual artist. She, too, abhorred the practice of turning magnificent fish into trophies. But she was drawn to her boyfriend's family saga of Dad and the Mounted Rainbow, and she decided to photograph it. She arranged her shots in the following way: Shot #1, the head of Luke's stuffed fish just up to the gills. Shot #2, the tail of the fish. Both shots in black and white.

Peggy framed the headshot and mounted it on the left side of Luke's study window and did the tail shot in like fashion on the right side of the window. Nowhere in sight, of course, was the body of the fish. An entire window separated the head from the tail.

One winter night, they were snuggling in when Peggy said, "Why not return your fish to that spawning bed?"

At first, this suggestion seemed like a bleeding-heart gesture. But the more Luke thought about her idea, the more it gained an aura of atonement, and it took hold. The following August, they drove west to the Rockies and rented a tent cabin near the Jasper townsite. In the afternoon of the following day, they walked around Lac Bonté, and for the first time, Peggy saw the beloved Charlesworth cabin, the view of Pyramid Mountain, the two sections of the lake, and the feeder stream—blessedly, all unchanged.

There were very few people in evidence around the lake and scarcely any signs of rising trout. The park had stopped stocking its lakes many years earlier. Only a very small population of trout remained, perhaps the progeny of those few that had managed to spawn uninterrupted in or near the feeder stream.

Peggy and Luke had work to do. The light was fading rapidly, as it does that far north in late August. They had brought a hammer and a sturdy five-inch nail. They rolled a large log over to a tree they had selected, a black spruce that perched above the feeder stream. Luke stepped onto the log so that his boots were a good two feet off the ground. He first detached the trout from its maple mount and then drove the spike through the middle of the fish and into the spruce tree. They rolled the log away, and as Peggy photographed the rainbow in its tree, Luke made a final inspection of him. The trout seemed to be drifting above his creek, pointed upstream toward the pure source of his water.

Luke was thinking about his father, the man who had encouraged Luke to fish but who never found the time to learn fly-fishing. His father had taken Luke and his friend Harry fishing on many occasions when he might more happily have lazed around the backyard, resting from his labours. Now, his father was an old man living with Luke's mother, far from the prairies of his youth and unaware of this caper cooked up by Peggy and Luke. Luke was thinking that this was an appropriate ending to the story—the sound of Peggy's camera reminding him of that other camera two decades earlier.

A story that concludes with no one dying or going to hell is hard to appreciate in these anxious times. It can feel morally suspect, as though the writer has decided to look the other way. But once upon a time, like gentle rain on a parched prairie, this story happened. Luke and Peggy got married after six years of living together. Luke had shed that fish-out-of-water feeling of being the odd man out. Oh, yes, and Peggy casts a fine line to the trout. The happy tale can roll on into somnolent territory unless, of course, someone draws a line in the sand.

This one ends in Jasper. It was time for Luke and Peggy's annual drive out to the coast to see Luke's parents in their apartment. To get there, they had to go through Jasper, so once again, they got a motel and went for a drive to Lac Bonté. They parked near the lake and walked down to the feeder stream. A man was fishing nearby, but they let him be.

Peggy and Luke began searching for their old friend the rainbow, nailed to the tree five years earlier. They located the black spruce that had been its resting place by spotting the spike that had impaled it, but the stuffed rainbow was gone. They approached the angler, a man who lived in the town.

"Bet you was lookin' for that Jesus big fish."

Luke sensed a story, so he decided to play dumb. "What fish would that be?"

"Up there, used to be an old trout nailed to the tree. Huge thing." He spread out his hands in that hyperbolic way of biblical scribes and anglers. "No guff, it was three foot long. Musta weighed twenny pounds."

Six pounds would be closer to the mark, several ounces lighter than Harry's biggest rainbow from the summer of 1968. From having recently spawned, Luke's lunker had been a much leaner fish.

The man reeled in his gob of worms and a bobber and checked his bait for signs of predation. Then he stood and launched his wormy delight far out into the lake. "That old rainbow had brothers and sisters, by God. Yessir, they're in here."

Playing dumb to the end, Luke asked him, "How did this monster get up in a tree?"

"They say it was some kind of a . . . like a totem, eh? Some Indian guy nailed it there."

Luke asked him where the fish was now.

"No one knows," the man said, lounging against his beer cooler. "Figure somebody took it." He looked up at Luke. "For better karma, eh? For luck?"

Luke still has Peggy's black and white photographs, the ones of the rainbow's tail and head, separated by the window in his study. It's the big space in between that draws your attention and invites you to imagine just how big that trout was. So, it's no longer a trophy, a vanity, something to make his father proud. But the memory of that rainbow still serves as a reminder of the summer when Luke's father looked over the edge and did not get carried away.

frailing

THE FIRST TIME you really listened to one was when you were seventeen, working in the mountains. It was too early in the decade to be a hippie, probably too late to be a beatnik. You might have become a bohemian, but wasn't that for gypsies or something? *Why work up there?* your father had said. *You won't even earn your tuition.* Your answer to your father was inspired: *I need to learn how to get out and meet the public.*

You were a parking lot attendant on the night shift at the Château Lake Louise. Out in the world, summer was on the way, but up at the Château, it was barely spring. The snow was banked high along the roads and paths, and the big melt had just begun. Avalanches boomed from the high slopes, and on that shift, the snow on the glaciers glimmered beneath a bright moon. The air, the alpine air, was fragrant with all things coniferous. As the bold metallic notes descended from the Hillside Residence, you were struck with a malady that had no name. A few years later, the word turned out to be *enchantment*, but in those half-formed days when you were trying to grow a moustache, such highfalutin words waited in line outside the compound of your bewildered brain.

Brilliant notes tumbled in a minor key down the mountainside.

You knew the song well enough to put words to this bright and mournful clatter. *Bumpa-tiddy bumpa-tiddy* slide and a *bumpa-tiddy bumpa-tiddy* hammer-on-the-string and a *bumpa-tiddy bumpa-tiddy* slide and a-comin' on a-comin' on home. The ballad, better howled than sung, was recounted by a sad fellow from east Virginia. To North Carolina, he did go. There, he met the fairest lady, whose name and age he did not know. Hammer on a slide, *bumpa-tiddy* slide, pullin' off the string down low. Thumb on the drone, finger in the middle, rappin' on the door (rappin' on the door, the big old door) of your love. Lorn. Heart. F.

Call this a cheap epiphany brought on by an overdose of Dylan Thomas and Pete Seeger, but you hurried past your kiosk and out the gate of your parking lot, and you climbed up the path to the Hillside Residence where a young man in kitchen whites sat on a log in a pale slash of moonlight. You thought you recognized him. Yes, it was Beauchemin, the dishwasher from Sept-Illes. Beauchemin, the craggy-faced heartthrob.

The clocks in the Château ground to a halt, your watch stopped ticking, Big Ben took a long coffee break. You wondered how many of the hundreds of waitresses and chambermaids might yearn to be close to Beauchemin just to hear him play. One roll from a nail on his right hand, and how could they help themselves? One pluck of the G-string, and he would be their Elvis.

You shuffled down the path to your parking lot. You checked the licence plates against the ones on your clipboard. The raging moon was deflated now, fading behind the peaks, and the clustering stars burst forth to reaffirm their mythic patterns. Big Dipper. Great Bear. Orion the Hunter. And soon to be discovered, Monsieur Banjeau.

You had to make sure that no one was trying to park for free. You returned to your kiosk, closed the door, turned on the heater, completed your room charges. Leaned back in your chair. This could not possibly be your destiny, you told yourself. To be like Beauchemin, that was your destiny.

There came a rumble from an avalanche adjacent to the Victoria glacier, a validating thunderous roar. You knew then that you were right. Your father, of course, might have disputed this.

A few days later, Beauchemin invited you to hold his banjo in your lap. He made you rest the thumb of your right hand on the drone string, which was attached to a peg at the side of the neck, seven or eight inches down from the four other pegs. He had you rest your index and middle finger on the bottom two strings.

"Hit dose string, one-after heach."

"Hit them?"

"Strike dose string like knockin' honna door."

Beauchemin had been a hockey star in his hometown, which gave him a certain cachet among the university students. His hands looked too big for banjory. You struck the lowest string of his banjo, as instructed, like knockin' honna door, and it responded with a pure, clear note. You made it do that.

"Now keep your fuckin' tumb honna drone string, like I tell you. You knock honna door, den lift your tumb."

Beauchemin took his banjo from your lap and mechanically followed his own instructions. His large frailing hand hardly seemed to move. The middle finger of his left hand went slowly up the neck and back down again. He didn't even look at his hands. Then, in slow motion, he frailed the first few bars of "Old Joe Clark."

"Like so."

In a final flourish, Beauchemin rolled his fingers over the strings, flamenco style, and a G cord burst forth and slowly faded. All the way back to the kiosk, your diaphragm vibrated like the skin on the head of a banjo.

Natasha worked in the camera shop down in Banff, an hour's drive away. Her friend Chrissy, at the Château Lake Louise travel desk, needed someone to drive Natasha from Lake Louise to Banff. Chrissy offered you the keys to her tiny Nash Metropolitan, which necessitated a delicious proximity between you and her friend.

Natasha of the blue-black hair and dark eyes. When she laughed, her eyes disappeared behind the lashes and slowly reappeared to gaze in dismay at the fallen world. Meekly, the tiny Nash puttered downhill from the opulent Château to the cheap and cozy Deer Lodge, a distance of a few hundred yards. In that time, Natasha took on the shape of all your moon-eyed yearning.

"Do you like the Kingston Trio?"

Yes, she said she loved the Kingston Trio.

"They're doing a concert in Calgary."

"Are you kidding me?" she said.

"Nope. You wanna go?"

Natasha sat hunched beside you. Her left arm rested against your right arm. As you gripped the wheel, your elbows were pressed into your ribs to minimize the encroachment and to negate any assumption that you might be enjoying this enforced melding of bodies. Could there be, you wondered, such a thing as romantic osmosis, where unutterable thoughts came and went through the skin of your beloved? Natasha's perfume rivalled the scent of the larches and pines along the road. It drifted into your nostrils like an emissary from a kingdom of merciless delight.

"With me?" you added for clarity.

Natasha said, "Yes, I'd love to go."

Five words, but the first one did the work. It ushered a veritable chinook into the long winter of your boyhood. How could Natasha have known that she was calling you out from the place where Monsieur Banjeau was dreaming his future?

Neighbourhoods have edges, hedges and ledges have edges, even amoebas have edges. You had no edges. In the darkened football stadium, in the midst of a reflection on politics, Natasha peered intently at you as if to locate just one measly edge.

"I'm not sure," she said, "but I might have conservative leanings. And yet, I'd never *vote* Conservative."

"Yeah?"

"I mean, they don't even like labour unions."

"Right."

"They want to cut down on federal programs. You know, support for disadvantaged families, support for international aid. But if people voted Liberal, and I'm not sure if I'm a Liberal either, how could we afford all those good programs?"

"Well, yeah. Exactly."

"They get all their ideas from the CCF. But I wouldn't vote for the CCF because I'm not a socialist, right?"

"You got a point there."

"I don't know," she sighed. "Such acute sadness."

She was being a tad ironic, of course, but you loved how she said that. *Such acute sadness.* Even then, you had a weakness for lofty diction—other people's lofty diction. You had yet to acquire some of your own.

You were rescued from the weight of these speculations when the applause went up for three college boys and an old bass player. They jogged into the spotlight in their short-sleeved, button-down shirts. The short one carried the bongos. The one with the lounge singer smile hoisted a guitar. The tall one with the brush cut carried a banjo with a long neck. They sang "Yonder Stands Little Maggie." The Maggie in question was too wild and dissolute to appreciate the tender feelings of the singers, who affirmed that *flowers were made for bloomin' and the sun was made to shine.* And this was the kicker: *Pretty girls was made for boys to love, surely Maggie was made to be mine.* A mournful song, but the three college boys sang it happy, they sang everything happy, and you were happy, and Natasha was happy because it was the Kingston Trio, and magic was in the air. You wondered which one Natasha would like best. If she liked the short one with the bongos, you might forgive her. But if she favoured the guitar player with the libidinous smile, you might never see her again.

"The short guy," she whispered. "If I had to choose."

You had, of course, given your vote to the tall guy with the brushcut.

"The short guy makes everyone laugh. What do you like about the tall guy?"

He frails the banjo, you ninny. A glittering long-necked Vega five-string resonator-free bright-toned equivalent to the cosmic lyre, the Biblical harp.

You said none of these words. Instead, you said, "Y'know, just the way he plays? The banjo?"

Back to Banff, then to Natasha's front steps. Perhaps out of exasperation or sympathy for your halting conversation, Natasha let you kiss her goodnight. Not exactly a rite of passage, but it felt as though, beyond Natasha's soft lips, the door to that misty world that inspired songs of yearning was open for a glimpse.

You returned Chrissy's keys and said, "You never told me she was brainy."

Chrissy burst out laughing. Not the bright tinkle of girlish laughter you had expected, but a great snot-inducing horselaugh that threatened to dislodge her from the stool.

Chrissy Smith. She was a Brewster transportation agent for the summer, which necessitated the standard-issue blue blazer, knee-length grey skirt, and heels. She had a turned-up nose, freckles, and a great mane of dark-brown hair, and she spoke with a slight lisp. You referred to her as Chrithy Thmith Ethquire, and the name took hold. She liked it because she had never before had a nickname. You had never had a sister, but Chrissy seemed somehow up for the job. If you are enchantment's plaything, you sometimes need a sister to clue you in.

"Read a book," she advised. "Read *Madame Bovary* before you ask her out again."

"That would take too long. What about Dylan Thomas?"

"Natasha isn't the poetry type. Here's a shorter one."

The writer emerging from her handbag had an Irish name, but he was apparently from a rural community in Georgia.

"What's so good about this guy?"

"He's not a guy," said Chrissy. "Just read it."

In the lives of brooding artists there comes a moment of grace in which they are enabled to pursue their vision: the wealthy aunt, the enthusiastic patron, the sharp-eyed editor manning the slush pile. Your moment of grace came early in the summer on the evening shift when the Château courtyard had gone quiet. A call had come to your kiosk from the night bellman, who told you to bring up Mr. Bendickson's car. Blue Plymouth, far end of the lot. You took your time going for the car. You did not want to give the keys to the night bellman because he might claim your tip.

The owner of the Plymouth was a talkative fellow from Fort Wayne. He told you that he liked Canada. "Lotsa friendly people," he said. "Lotsa space for a fella to spread out."

You had been hoping for an American who was conversant with the stories of Flannery O'Connor, but clearly, Mr. Bendickson was not that person.

"Say, I need to hire a fella to do some work for me. After-hours sorta thing. Cash under the table. I'll make it worth your while."

Mr. Bendickson had a red complexion like raw hamburger with a network of tiny varicose veins around his neck and throat. He was gut-hung like a prize bass, perpetually exhausted and sweaty as though life itself was an uphill workout. Regularly, he mopped his face with a wrinkled handkerchief. You liked him from the start. You liked the way he came right to the point (not yet one of your strong suits), and you liked the way he treated you as an adult.

"First off," he said, "I need a fella who can drive my vehicle down to Calvary and meet my old aunty at the airport."

"You mean Calgary?"

"That's the one."

Your heart hiccupped joyfully. Halfway to Calgary was Banff and Natasha's camera shop.

Mr. Bendickson told you to make up a sign with his aunty's name on it and to hold it up for her to see. *Take her anywhere she wants to go in Calvary.* You told him your name, shook hands with the man, and he handed you ten American sawbucks fresh from a bank. They were a dull shade of green on white, and they had an image of Thomas Jefferson on the front. You had heard that the Americans were good tippers, but a tip this extravagant was beyond your greediest fancies.

On the morning of your day off, Mr. Bendickson asked you to drive somewhere and change his plates for him. "Got these Alberta-Canada plates so's I can do business in these parts. All legal and such. Oh, and when you've done the plates for me, could you worsh my Plymouth? Much obliged, son."

As you carried out these chores, Natasha would alight by your side bearing a crescent wrench and screwdriver or materialize next to you with a steaming hot chamois. In such moments, there was a free exchange between you and Natasha on the uplifting work of Flannery O'Connor or the virtues of old mountain songs.

Mr. Bendickson's "old aunty" was probably younger than your mother. She wore a peach-coloured summer suit, high heels, and cat's-eye sunglasses. Her lipstick and nails were reddish purple. She looked Hollywood classy, like Rosalind Russell.

"No need for you to hang around," she said in a remarkably low and worldly voice, a cigarettes-and-whisky voice. "Just drop me off at the Stockman's Hotel, and I'll be fine."

You drove the Plymouth to a cluttered street in a tough part of Calgary. She didn't seem to notice. "Just give this to Mr. Bendickson, would you, honey?" She handed you a nicely wrapped container somewhat larger than a shoebox. "That man is so hopeless. He never thinks to pack enough socks and underwear."

You took Natasha to coffee in Banff for some cautious flirting. Then, with the sad and wistful sound of her voice in your ears, you drove north to Lake Louise. You delivered the package to Mr. Bendickson at the Château Lake Louise, and on your day off the following week, you ran some errands for him down in Banff. You had become his courier, and there was little time to linger with Natasha. There were manila envelopes sealed with scotch tape to deliver, bottles of liquor in ornate boxes, a locked suitcase full of laundry. For these errands, he rewarded you with another stack of tens. By the end of July, you had about six hundred American dollars, which you carried in a wad in your pants pocket. Mr. Bendickson announced that he would soon be pursuing business opportunities in Saskatchewan, and would you run him one more errand in Calvary?

You had been observing things about your American friend. The nicely wrapped container from his aunty had been suspiciously heavy for socks and underwear. The manila envelopes you delivered could easily have been mailed. The Alberta licence plates that you had bolted onto the blue Plymouth had been pebbled and bent. These observations went straight to the back burner, where you stored equally useless things (like how to approach quadratic equations) because you were thinking about Calgary and that burgeoning wad of American money in your pocket. Popeye had his spinach, Mighty Mouse had the cheese. You had a stack of American tens.

This last job in Calgary involved another well-wrapped cardboard container, lighter than the first one. After delivery, you waited down in the car while Mr. Bendickson's aunty freshened up. Then you drove her to see the trotters and pacers at Stampede Park. She claimed to have a soft spot for horses. Drop her there, get lost, then pick her up.

Her name was Desiree Fox.

"I might even place a bet or two," she said.

"I could stick around."

"Oh no," said Desiree, mysteriously. "I might be meeting some people."

She drew from her purse an unruly wad of American currency,

peeled off a couple of tens and handed them to you with a smile. You marvelled once more at the generosity of American tipping.

"Hey, Mrs. Fox, thanks a whole lot."

"Please, call me Desiree. You make me sound like an old bag. Now, buy yourself a nice souvenir of Calgary and pick me up at six. In the meantime, I'm gonna check out those trotters."

You drove the Plymouth straight to a music store downtown. It was dimly lit, and a ceiling fan rotated just enough to stir the soupy air. The owner wore shades and reeked of booze and taciturnity. The morning trade must have been slow, or maybe it was always that way. One of his few customers was hunkered on a footstool with a guitar, trying to pick the notes to "Tom Dooley."

There were two levels to the store and a darkened basement. The main floor featured acoustic guitars, fiddles, drums, ukuleles, mouth organs, and sheet music. The upper story glittered with electric guitars and mandolins. The banjos, you discovered, were all in the basement with a couple of old pianos. In a dark corner, where several banjos dangled from a wooden beam like prisoners from a scaffold, there was a poster of Mark Twain in a white jacket and bowtie, with some words beneath the photograph. *When you want genuine music—music that will come right home to you like a bad quarter, suffuse your system like strychnine whiskey, go right through you like Brandreth's pills, ramify your whole constitution like the measles, and break out on your hide like the pin-feather pimples on a pickled goose—when you want all this, just smash your piano, and invoke the glory-beaming banjo!*

On the other side of the hanging banjos was an old poster for the Christy Minstrels, *circa* 1858, with a man in blackface playing a five-string. *Hoop de doodem doo,* read the poster. Another poster featured a bandy-legged clown in a striped suit flourishing his instrument beneath a banner of lyrics that read *Jenny git yer hoe cakes done.*

On the opposite wall, there were eight or nine more banjos suspended in a row. You had to get close and stoop to distinguish one from the other. Several more leaned upright in the corner by the stairwell, and more banjos lay on the floor on top of their cases. You were so surrounded by banjos that when you stood in the centre of the gloomy basement, you felt the power of a magnetic field that pulled you in several directions. You had come upon the emporium of your dreams, the instruments with their unearthly magic consigned like heretics to the catacombs.

Bowed over and squinting, you drifted from one banjo to the next, agitating over how you might choose. A green rhinestone on one instrument's neck seemed to wink at you. Leaning closer, you began to take in the details: a brassy armrest, totemic patterns along the neck, a resonator with a bewildering design on the back. Up around the pegs was a serpentine image made of multi-coloured rhinestones. In your opinion, the banjo looked garish. Your clothing at that time tended toward the fashion of prairie chickens to blend in with your dusty habitat.

"Which one catches your eye, son?"

"This one."

The owner was still wearing his shades. You had not heard him descend the stairs. He shuffled over to the far wall where you were peering dubiously, with a mixture of fascination and moral disapproval.

"You a college-boy picker?" he said with a note of contempt.

"I just want to play the banjo."

"Pick it up," he said.

It had a beaded strap that seemed to replicate the pattern on the back of a Gila monster. You did not approve of rhinestones or flashy metal, and you had no love for Gila monsters, but with the strap in place over your shoulder and feeling the full weight of the instrument, you felt a subtle transformation coming on. You were toting the Desiree Fox of all banjos.

"What do you mean, a college-boy picker?"

"They don't care about where the songs come from. They try to play eighteen notes per second instead of learning how to play pretty."

"Where did you get all these?"

"Oil guy from Oklahoma. Collected banjos and cars. He said he had to focus on one or the other, so I got the banjos."

Tough luck, you might have quipped at another time, but when you are wearing a gold-plated, ivory-inlaid, mother-of-pearl, ringing monument to extroversion, smart-ass humour sets the wrong tone.

"Give it a strum."

You brushed the strings with your ring finger, and a quintet of bright notes answered you like Vivaldi's harpsichord. Wait till Beauchemin heard this baby ring.

"It's already tuned," you observed.

"They're all tuned."

"What are they doing down in the basement?"

"Someday I'll bring 'em up, when I think the world's ready for these babies. But right now—"

The owner paused to glance up the stairwell, and he started yelling. "Right now, I sell twenty-dollar guitars and plastic picks to college-boy pickers who drool over the Kingston fuckin' Trio." The storeowner said these words with just a trace of pity.

"How much for this one?"

"About the same as a used car. You're wearing a banjo crafted by Kyle Creed and signed on the front by Dock Boggs. Among others. Son, if you want to get a banjo as cool as this one, you're gonna pay through the nose."

"How much?"

"Nine hundred dollars with the case, not a penny less."

"Okay."

The storeowner glared at you. He sported an overgrown black goatee. His shades seemed to magnify his every sardonic gesture. "Okay, what? Can you even play this thing?"

"All I've got is American money."

"This should be a problem?" he said with an incredulous chortle.

You counted out ninety bills from the wad in your pocket. This took some time. You had never imagined handing over this much money to anybody. It made you feel lost and many years older.

The owner placed the instrument into a sturdy case lined with purple velvet, tossed in some reading material, and fastened the brass couplings. You followed him up the stairs and past the young man on the footstool, still earnestly refining his craft.

On your way back to Lake Louise, you turned off the highway into the Banff townsite and parked outside the camera store. You locked your banjo in the trunk and strode inside. Natasha smiled distantly at you, and you were determined not to be discouraged. What did she see at this moment? Perhaps she noticed your moustache, the twin tufts of downy hair too faint to inspire confidence. You were a Joseph in company trousers, a Dedalus of unrequited yearning, and much too close to the sun.

She asked you what you'd been up to, and you told her that you'd been reading a book by Flannery O'Connor.

"Oh, my."

You moved aside for some customers near the cash register, but other people showed up. One or two of the guys looked more like admirers than customers.

"Give Chrissy a hug for me?" she said between customers.

"I'll do that."

Truth be told, you just stood there with your arms hanging out of your elbows. You let the lineup defeat you. You might have managed to get something going on the virtues of Flannery O'Connor. You might have asked her if she'd sorted out her political convictions. You still had a few remaining sawbucks in your pocket, but you did not manage to ask her out for dinner. Making the next move for you was like crossing the Amazon on a swinging bridge.

Weeks later, you saw Natasha, by chance, strolling down Banff Avenue, holding hands with some guy. He had the smile of a lounge lizard.

"Have you actually read it?" said Chrissy.

She was sitting on her bed with her legs curled beneath her skirt. You were leaning against the doorframe.

"I read the one about the guy in the gorilla suit, and I read the long one about Julian and his mum."

"And?"

"Pretty weird."

"Weird and?"

"Both of them. Weird."

Again, Chrissy laughed until she was shaking.

You told Chrissy that you needed a safe place to store your banjo. You could not just leave it by your bunk. The Pit was where the Brewster drivers and carhops lived, a concrete enclosure with twelve double bunks one floor above a grease pit. It smelled of motor oil, stale beer, cigarettes, and man stink. Because she was a travel agent, Chrissy had her own room in the Pink Palace. This garish dive was downhill from the Pit, plopped next to Deer Lodge. As she slid the encased banjo underneath her bed, you found yourself gazing at her rump.

In the absence of Mr. Bendickson and his intriguing ventures, your evenings were free now. Your memories and dreams of Natasha began to fade painfully, hissing out of your system like a slow leak. Mr. Bendickson and his beloved aunty were probably setting up somewhere in Saskatchewan.

One night in August found you in the laundry room, despondent, next to your unopened banjo case. You had good intentions, but you could not manage to open that case. As the wringer washer whined about its monotonous life, you read things to dispel the gloom. You returned to Chrissy's book and read distractedly. You put your clothes through the wringer and tossed them into the dryer. Finally, you took out the magazine from your banjo case, the one the music store guy had given you, and you read it slowly. It wasn't a magazine at all; it was Pete Seeger's *How to Play the Five-*

string Banjo. It was the bible. It beat Flannery O'Connor by a country mile.

Thus began the process in which you learned to frail your banjo, first in slow motion, obedient to the book's tablature. C cord. *Swing . . . your . . . partner . . . skip . . . to my loo.* G cord. *Swing your . . . partner . . . skip to my...* G7th . . . *loo.* Everything came slowly, but it came.

A week or more later, you were trying to frail your banjo in the company of the sad wringer washer when Beauchemin dropped by. You noticed this time that he was relatively toothless. Appallingly toothless. He looked older and weary, but he nodded his head in approval.

"It's good you practice," he said. "Hey, Banjeau, you 'erd of Peggy Seeger?"

"Nope. Is she the sister?"

"You 'erd of Doc Watson?"

"Nope."

"Dese banjo player, hey? You got to ear dese players, get da record. You buy yourself a Cadillac fucking banjo, you got to 'ear what it can do."

Beauchemin must have noticed that your chin was dragging. He sat down beside the wringer washer and leaned forward. "You look like shit, you know dat?"

Magnificent in your self-pity, you dragged your sodden dreams through the usual mud puddle for Beauchemin's benefit. You told him about Natasha. He responded with the usual wisdom about getting good and sozzled, about never showing them that you care, and especially about *talking dem.*

"Talking them? How?"

"Your problem, Monsieur Banjeau, is you talk hanglo to dem. You say *yes,* right? Hit sound like you hissing at dem. You say *oui,* hey? Now dat's a different ting. You say *oui,* you got to kiss dat word right in Natasha's face."

So. It wasn't the banjo that drew the girls to him; it was the magic of his words. Which meant what? That you had to learn French?

Beauchemin reached into his shirt pocket, withdrew a packet of spearmint gum, and handed you a stick.*"Monsieur Banjeau, commence ma gomme?"*

There was an awkward exchange on the finer points of commencing Beauchemin's dry stick of gum. It involved chewing it, softening it, and handing it back to Beauchemin. He inserted the wad into his mouth and smiled a gummy smile. "Doan fall in love like dat, Banjeau. Like a loss pappydog. Dis Natasha, she can buy a pappydog."

Your point, of course, would be that you hadn't even reached the dubious state of being Natasha's pappydog. "You mean, don't fall in love?"

Beauchemin chewed his gum and shrugged his shoulders as though to dislodge an idea of Olympian proportions, and you could sense the onset of his wisdom before he even opened his mouth. "You see, Banjeau . . . you got to love in all of dem, every goddamn one of dem."

And there it was. He stood, stretched, yawned, and said he'd heard there would be a party in the Pink Palace that night. When Beauchemin left, you put your banjo in the case, your clothes in the dryer, and slouched out of the laundry facility and into the dark evening.

The Pink Palace was a hive for dozens of employees. You lugged your banjo up to the third floor and saw that Chrissy's door was ajar. Some guy in her room was holding forth in a soft voice, something about girls with freckles. When you knocked on the door, Chrissy cried, "Come in!"

The guy was tall, lean, non-descript. He had a smooth, insinuating manner. Somehow, he didn't have the look of a Lake Louise employee. Chrissy was on the bed in her bathrobe.

"I was just talking to your girl," he said.

You put down the banjo and sat on the bed next to Chrissy. Some of the partiers walked by, but no one looked in.

"I told her she was pretty cute," the guy said, and Chrissy moaned.

For some reason, you stood up again.

"Well, it was nice talking to you," said Chrissy. "But now we want to go to bed."

You and the tall stranger both stared at Chrissy, waiting for her to elaborate. She was peering up at you with some alarm.

"You're going to bed with this little asshole?" said the stranger. "It isn't even ten o'clock, and he wouldn't know a piece of ass from a toothbrush."

"What did you say to me?" you said.

"I wasn't talkin' to you, asshole."

"He's not an asshole," said Chrissy. "You're the asshole."

"What are you doing here, anyway?" you said.

More revellers went by Chrissy's door. They sounded boisterous because there was a party in the common room.

"Her door wasn't exactly locked," said the stranger.

Someone opened Chrissy's door and looked in: none other than Beauchemin. He had re-installed his dentures. He gazed at the stranger and levered his gum distractedly up to his incisors, which made him look as though he were sneering. With eyelids at half-mast, he was playing with his gum in the manner of movie tough guys. He carried himself with such confidence that you had to wonder if anything got to him. He launched a cold and weary glance at the tall stranger and looked back at you. "Everyting hokay, Banjeau?"

The stranger was observing Beauchemin, sizing him up. "Everything's peachy," the stranger said. "We were all having a fabulous conversation."

The stranger smiled, slowly withdrew, and his boots thundered down the stairs.

Before Beauchemin departed, he said, "You two lovebird, hey, you mebbe lock dis door?"

Perhaps your nickname should have been Lucky. Several people reported the tall stranger. While hitching on the Banff-Jasper Highway, he was picked up for questioning. He was wanted on a rape charge in New Brunswick and an assault and battery charge in Manitoba. There were other charges pending, so when the full range of his exploits came to light, he went away for a goodly spell.

You were not completely surprised at summer's end when you read in the *Calgary Herald* that your friend Mr. Bendickson and his aunty were picked up at a Saskatoon racetrack for passing counterfeit bills. Smitten by guilt, you took the bus to Calgary to look up the music store owner. Someone in the café next door told you that the place had been closed permanently, owing to a charge before the courts of receiving stolen goods.

Luckiest of all, perhaps, was the scene that unfolded between you and Chrissy that night of the unwelcome stranger. Chrissy was clearly upset, so you offered to stay with her. She unrolled a sleeping bag on the floor. Just before nodding off, you glimpsed her smiling down at you fondly. When you left in the morning to pick up your laundry, she was sound asleep.

Often, you needed to get your banjo from under her bed. By early September, the visits to Chrissy's bedroom had taken on a greater importance to you than virtuoso frailing. The banjo remained under her bed while you found yourself happily occupied above. As the bedsprings fiddled their monotonous jig, you and Chrissy became each other's greatest gift. At summer's end, you felt as though you had stridden into the world.

You and Chrissy returned to your respective cities. She was hoping to finish up a degree in history, and you were hoping to lurch through second year without embarrassing yourself. The two of you planned to resume things the following spring.

Lake Louise was a place where young people fell in love. It was the summer school of romance rather than the degree-granting institution. Young people tasted first love, and, more often than not, they moved on from the slippery blisses of youth to what people called adulthood. Chrissy got a job with Trade and Commerce, met a man with a good head on his shoulders, married him, and settled in Tokyo.

A few years later, you met Wendy, a bookstore employee with a great smile and a weakness for banjo music. You were frailing unobserved in the boiler room of an old B & B in the Cypress Hills. You were down in the basement so that no one would be bothered by the sound of your banjo. For some reason, however, you left open the door to the boiler room. Was this an attempt to minimize the murkiness of the basement? Was this mere vanity?

Your banjo tune tripped up the old wooden stairs to the kitchen above, where Wendy was making tea. As she stirred in the milk and sugar, she found herself listening to a frenzied voice followed by a banjo solo. The voice cried, *Run here Sally with a snigger and a grin/Run here Sally with a snigger and a grin/Groundhog gravy all over her chin/Pore groundhog.* The banjo rippled along as though the groundhog's demise was little more than an excuse to do some picking. She found herself stirring her tea in time with your frailing. You had heard recordings of many a banjoist in concert with a spoons player, but this tinkling sound was special. In the ensuing silence, you trudged up the stairs, and there she was, long hair drying in the sunlight, drinking her tea.

"Could you please do that again?" you said.

She did it again, and she married you as well.

No one calls me Monsieur Banjeau anymore. But I've been calling you up quite often this winter. Some people pray when they're in a fix, but I've settled on getting reconnected with you, the boy who tried to emulate Beauchemin in Lake Louise. A good many of those old banjo tunes were about lost love, poverty, endless yearning, and mortality. I have at last become familiar with some of those old sorrows. It's your luck I need, if there's any more available.

Mr. Tumult came knocking last year in the guise of a brand-new white Dodge Ram. The driver was an angry kid out for a spin, the truck a graduation gift from daddy. The kid ran a red light and whacked us at a quiet intersection. He wasn't even drunk. Wendy was gone before she reached emergency, and I got away with a broken body, numb from the waist down. Some have told me I was lucky to survive. They mean well, I suppose.

How could you have foreseen, in your Lake Louise days, that this was how it ended?

I am at Glad Tidings Care Centre, where I reside in a small room, mostly reminiscing like a good septuagenarian. My TV set is out of commission. I don't even have a telephone. No one to talk to when I fall into that stupor, that feeling you get when you've run out of luck.

I suppose I could call an attendant. One of them is quite nice. Good sense of humour and a boisterous whinny of a laugh. Her name is Melody Driedger. The minute she walked into my room, we seemed to connect. She teases me about flirting with all the ladies in Wing C. (Beauchemin's advice: *You got to love in all of dem. Every goddam one of dem.*) Melody has reminded me more than once that my spinal cord injury is incomplete, that rehab and physio might bring about some improvement. My visiting daughter has been speaking with Melody about ways to get me back in the game. That's Melody now, lugging something up the hallway.

All this looking back has me roaming over the trajectory of my life: Lake Louise. Graduation with a degree in journalism. Poet *manqué* and occasional studio musician. Bookaholic. Wendy's new boyfriend. Husband and father. Features writer for the local paper. Widower as of last year. Paraplegic in a care home. Shit out of luck.

I need to snap out of this. I didn't die in childhood. I never felt the crush of poverty. My father despaired over the dreamer I had become, but he paid for much of my education. And I'm a middle-class white guy. I wasn't kidnapped from a reserve and sent to a residential school full of predatory priests and heartless nuns. I was lucky to be alive in good times rather than wartime or depression. I was lucky to work at Lake Louise. And when I married Wendy, my life changed in a wonderful way. Unlike the girls of Lake Louise, who now seem like fantasies to me, Wendy was always utterly real. She loved to tell jokes, but she had problems remembering the punch lines. She seemed to make everything better: motel rooms, birthdays, long road trips, tenting in the rain, even visits to my parents. She had a wide repertoire of brilliant smiles from wistful to sardonic to pure delight to sated with pleasure. Men noticed her, loved to banter with her, but she had no patience with the ones who tried to charm her. She was the great abiding love of my life. Forty-one years of sleeping and waking next to her. I miss the wondrous, nightly flesh-on-flesh of her.

At this moment, on the blank screen of my useless TV set, Wendy has become my screensaver. She is leading a chorus of voices: my long-dead parents, my daughter, Mr. Bendickson, Desiree Fox, Chrissy Smith, Beauchemin loudest of all. They are chanting to me in monotone like monks at Vespers: *Quit your bellyaching, bellyaching, bellyaching.*

The room is dark.

Melody Driedger butts in on my reverie. “Where can I put this?”

“My God!”

“Don’t have a conniption. It’s just your old banjo.”

“Can you put it somewhere safe?”

“In this tiny room?” says Melody. “Lotsa luck.”

I shrug, and she gazes around.

“How about under the bed?” she says.

“Fine idea, Melody. It worked once, why not again?”

Melody gives me her perplexed look. “Wait a sec,” she whispers from the side of her mouth. “Let’s raise some hell tonight. Come on, Mr. Banjo, play me a tune on this thing.”

acknowledgments

Sections of “The Carl Quartet” were published in Nicole Haloupis and Geoff Pevlin’s collection of flash fiction, *release any words stuck inside of you.* The story was inspired by a brief play by Harold Pinter entitled “Last to Go,” and further enhanced with stories told by John Newlove and (especially) Bruce Rice. “Marty Opens the Door” was published in *Grain.* “Mallow's Course" was originally published as a chapbook by Happy Leopard Press. An early version of “Gentle Rain” was published in *Numéro Cinq* and re-issued in Jake MacDonald’s *Casting Quiet Waters.* The more recently finished stories are published here for the first time. Many thanks to all of the above editors, writers and raconteurs. I am deeply indebted to Dave Margoshes for his editorial work on this manuscript, his championing of it, and his early critiques of it. Many thanks as well to Dwayne Brenna, a member of the storied Titans literary collective.

about david carpenter

David Carpenter began his writing vocation as a critic and translator in Winnipeg and Toronto. Inspired by a reading by the Moose Jaw Movement (Gary Hyland, Robert Currie, Lorna Crozier and others) in Saskatoon, he switched to writing his own work, which began to emerge in 1985. He is the author of fifteen books of fiction and nonfiction and one book of poetry. His literary awards and honours include the Saskatchewan Book Awards 2010 Book of the Year for *A Hunter's Confession*, the Kloppenburg Prize for Literary Excellence (2015), the Code's Burt Award (Toronto) for *The Education of Augie Merasty* (2016), and most recently, the High Plains Creative Nonfiction Award (Billings, Montana) for *I Never Met a Rattlesnake I Didn't Like* (2023). As well, as a recognition for his writing, he was awarded an Honorary Doctorate from the University of Saskatchewan (2018). He lives and writes in Saskatoon.

available or coming soon

Literary Fiction

Theories of Everything by Dwayne Brenna

Elephant in the Room by Betty Jane Hegerat

Thickwood by Gayle M. Smith

Let us be True by Erna Buffie

The Lavender Child by Harriet Richards

Waiting for the Piano Tuner to Die by Harriet Richards

Dollybird by Anne Lazurko

Small Reckonings by Karin Melberg Schwier

Poetry

First Light, Last Light by Glen Sorestad

The Door at the End of Everything by Lynda Monahan

The Glass Lodge by John Brady McDonald

Phases by Belinda Betker

Stay by Katherine Lawrence

Literary Nonfiction

Tales This Side of the Elysian Fields by Trevor W. Harrison

Cupboard Love: A Dictionary of Culinary Curiosities by Mark Morton

The Crow Who Tampered With Time by Lloyd Ratzlaff

Backwater Mystic Blues by Lloyd Ratzlaff

www.ingramcontent.com/pod-product-compliance
Lightning Source LLC
Chambersburg PA
CBHW020249030826
48979CB00030B/2751/J

* 9 7 8 1 9 9 8 2 7 3 2 7 0 *